RESCUING the SHERIFF'S Heart

Other Books By Lorin Grace

American Homespun Series
Waking Lucy
Remembering Anna
Reforming Elizabeth
Healing Sarah

Artists & Billionaires
Mending Fences
Mending Christmas
Mending Walls
Mending Images
Mending Words
Mending Hearts

Hastings Security
Not the Bodyguard's Baby
Not the Bodyguard's Widow
Not the Bodyguard's Boss
Not the Bodyguard's Princess
Not the Bodyguard's Bride

Misadventures in Love
Miss Guided
Miss Oriented

Spellbound in Hawthorne
(with Maria Hoagland)
Taste of Memory
Sprinkle of Snow
Hint of Charm
Dash of Destiny
Stir of Wind
Essence of Gravity

Bradford Brides
Rescuing the Sheriff's Heart
Bending the Blacksmith's Heart
Converting the Preacher's Heart
Healing the Doctor's Heart

Stand Alone Titles
A Little Clean Fun
Love in the Valley

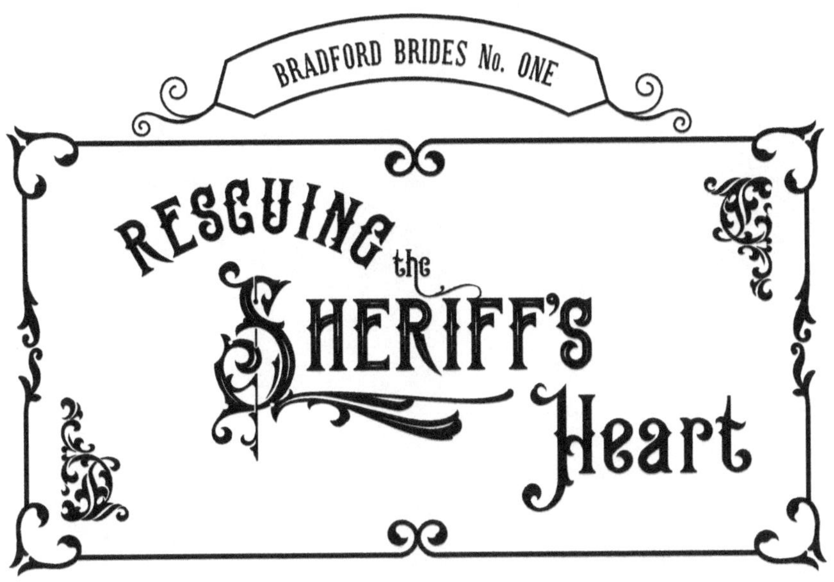

Lorin Grace

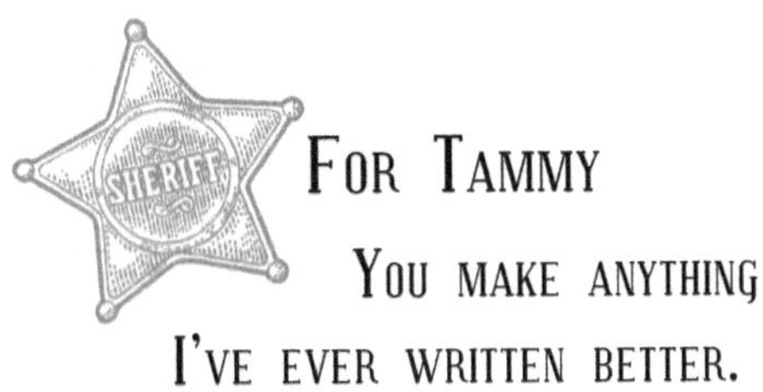

FOR TAMMY

YOU MAKE ANYTHING
I'VE EVER WRITTEN BETTER.

A train whistled a warning as the engineer released the steam brakes, obscuring the last of the well-wishers waving to loved ones. Emily's heart sped in time with the clicking of the wheels on the tracks as the departing train gained speed toward far-off places and new beginnings. Were any of the passengers bound for a fresh start, too? She clutched her chatelaine bag to still her hands. As a recent graduate of Bradford College, she must always act with utmost decorum in public. Only a half hour more and she would board one of those trains, the first step of her one-way trip to a new life and freedom.

"Emily? Emily Anne? Emily Anne Wilson?" Uncle Carl's voice brought her back from her musings.

"Sorry, Uncle, I was daydreaming."

"No need to leave before your train does." A hint of mirth tinged her uncle's voice. At least he didn't dismiss her dreams. The Civil War veteran leaned heavily on his son Percy's arm. "You have the money we gave you?"

"Yes. It is safe." Emily smiled, not wanting to tell her uncle she'd hidden the majority of her funds inside of her corset.

She'd gained a healthy fear of train robbers from reading the dime novels her cousin Barbara left around the house. Thus she spent an hour sewing the five gold double eagles into the lining of her undergarment. If the coins were meant for cousin Percy's future, she didn't want them. "Your gift was so generous. Are you sure it is not too much?"

"I've been waiting years to give you something that your Aunt Melba couldn't get her hands on. Speaking of…I thought they'd be here to see you off." Her uncle shifted his cane. According to Percy, the injury his father received at Gettysburg had been giving him more trouble than usual the past few weeks. Which was why Uncle Carl missed her graduation.

"I'm sure they went to the wrong station." Percy laughed. With four railway stations in Boston, it would have been an easy mistake. However, they all assumed that wherever Uncle Harlan, Aunt Melba, and Barbara were, it would be nowhere near any of the stations.

A portly man rushed up to them, his face red from the June heat. "I made it." He puffed between each word. "Where are Melba and Barbara?"

"I thought they'd be with you, Uncle Harlan." It was the politest answer Emily could give.

"No, I've been at the bank this morning, working on the expansion of the warehouse. I told her to meet me here. After the way she—" Uncle Harlan's voice faded as he looked around.

That was probably as much of an apology as Emily would get for the snub she received from Aunt Melba at graduation last week.

"Did our girl tell you about the honors she won?" Harlan asked his brother Carl.

"Our Emily isn't one for bragging, but Percy did enough for both of them. He said Emily out shown them all in her beautiful dress and her Valedictorian speech was better than the one at his own graduation at Harvard." Uncle Carl's warm gaze was worth a dozen fatherly hugs.

She'd tried to explain the dress was nothing more than a dress left at the school nearly two decades ago and made over by a dozen charity students like her. In Texas, she'd never have to take charity again.

Percy nodded. For a moment, Emily was afraid he'd launch into his nonsense about how every man there was jealous, because Percy was Emily's escort in the absence of a father and Uncle Carl. Uncle Harlan had escorted his own daughter for the final promenade across campus.

"A fine speech it was." Uncle Harlan pulled a watch from his vest pocket and craned his neck to look around. "Something in Latin about service, I believe."

"*Surgo Ut Prosim.* I rise to serve. It is Bradford College's motto. I delivered the entire speech to Uncle Carl after dinner on Sunday. He endured it well."

Percy's mouth quirked at the inside joke. His father had cheered so loudly that a policeman walking down the street hushed him through an open window. Emily's cheeks warmed at the memory.

Uncle Carl eyed his brother. "Percy made her put on her graduation dress. Our girl is a fine seamstress. If she didn't want to be a teacher out west so badly, she could start a shop here in Boston. I wouldn't have believed it was made over if she hadn't told me."

Uncle Harlan swallowed and looked away. If they were not in a public place, Uncle Carl would likely point out other deficiencies in the care she received in the decade since her parents' passing. Although her uncle's arguments had won her some freedoms and privileges over the years, it wouldn't matter anymore.

"I'm not that good." Emily had only planned on keeping the lace she'd added to the bodice, which was all she could afford on the allowance her aunt sent to supplement her scholarship money. However, the school matron felt that after fifteen years the white dress could not handle being made over again. With white wedding dresses being all the rage, many of the graduates were planning to use their graduation gowns as a base for their wedding. Others, like Emily, were always destined to be teachers and would eventually dye the dresses a more serviceable color.

Uncle Harlan wiped his brow with his rumpled handkerchief. "I have something for you. Probably too little too late, but..." Uncle Harlan pulled four gold coins from his pocket. "Hopefully, this will help you on your journey. There isn't much of your father's money left. I'll guard the remainder for you as a kind of dowry. I thought I should give it to you now, but Melba warned me that any extra money is likely to be stolen by one of those outlaws."

With effort, Emily kept her jaw clamped shut. There was still money? Aunt Melba told her the inheritance had run out years ago. Emily slid the coins into her reticule. "Thank you, Uncle, that is extremely generous of you."

To the surprise of everyone, Aunt Melba and Barbara joined them. "There you are. I thought we would have missed the train."

Uncle Carl pulled Emily into a one-armed hug. "We were just discussing how honored Emily's parents would have been—their little girl making a speech and finishing first in Bradford's class of 1879."

Aunt Melba cleared her throat. "It's a shame Barbara didn't speak. Why, with her thespian medal, she would have charmed us all, not read scripture and discussed the future."

Bradford College had deep religious traditions. Scripture wasn't optional. A full third of the women in her graduating class were either marrying ministers or heading out as missionaries to foreign lands.

"And my dress would have looked ever so much better up on the stage, Mother." Barbara smoothed the front of a green day dress Emily had never seen before, drawing attention to the flounces. "Do you like my newest gown? I am to have luncheon with Mrs. Gray. Her son is in line to inherit the family business, you know. He paid particular attention to me after church on Sunday."

"Young Mr. Gray told my darling Barbara he hoped to see her again. All of Boston recognizes what the college regents missed when they passed over Barbara as a choice for the graduation speech." Aunt Melba fluttered her fan to bring attention to her, as the feather fan wasn't necessary yet in the morning's cool.

Dramatic didn't cover her cousin's acting skills, both on and off the stage. Emily held her tongue one last time. She'd learned years ago that contradicting her aunt always ended up unpleasantly for all. Even at school, she had to be careful about what she said lest Aunt Melba find a way to cut off the few dollars left from her inheritance after her parents died. Pointing out that Barbra's less than stellar grades were the reason she was never even considered as a representative for the graduation class may bring a momentary satisfaction. But she was her mother's daughter, not her aunt's.

A tight-lipped smile was all Emily could manage. For nine years she'd worn Barbara's cast-offs, and endured Aunt Melba's explanations about how her father had squandered his share of the business. She'd been dependent on others for too long. Emily would not be beholden to anyone for her care again.

"Oh dear, look at the time. We can't be late to your luncheon, dear. We have calls to make first." Aunt Melba rushed out of the station with Barbara in tow as the uniformed man announced the ten-minute call for Emily's train.

"Be sure to write." Uncle Harlan kissed Emily's cheek and disappeared out of the same door as Aunt Melba.

Uncle Carl wobbled on his cane.

"Father, why don't you sit down, and I'll walk Emily to her car. I am sure her friend's family is nearby." Percy led his father to a wood bench.

Emily followed and kissed her favorite uncle on the cheek. "I love you and I'll write."

Uncle Carl pressed three silver dollars into her palm. "They might help get an extra meal and a room if the train gets stuck."

"Thank you." Emily choked back the tears. She was leaving the only two people in the world who cared for her. Moving as far as Texas meant she would probably never see Uncle Carl again. "Goodbye."

Percy tugged on her elbow. "Come Emily, I believe I see your friend's family waiting near the last Pullman car."

"Of course." Emily took Percy's offered arm.

"Is our aunt always so short on praise?"

Emily carefully considered her words. She'd rarely been in both of her uncle's family's presence at the same time. An estrangement with unexplained nuances only allowed her a few days each summer with Uncle Carl and Percy. Emily never told them about life at Uncle Harlan's home. "Aunt Melba would rather I not outshine our cousin. But she has been kind enough since I am nothing but a poor orphan."

"Not poor, surely. Your father owned a third of the business."

Emily shrugged. "That was then; times are difficult now. But I had enough for my schooling." Uncle Carl would feel badly if he knew most of the funds had come from the scholarship alluded to in her speech. "Now I shall go out on my own. I dare say Aunt Melba will be relieved as she intends Barbara to wed by next spring and I would only be in the way of her prospects. I am not entirely sure she believes Texas is far enough."

Percy paused and studied her. "I'm afraid I don't comprehend your meaning. The fellow who would wish to win Barbara's hand could never interest you. Perhaps because I don't have sisters, the intricacies of your situation baffles me. Must you go so far from home for a job?"

"I found a job at a private school in Hiramsville, Texas. They teach year-round, so I can start as soon as I get there. They even sent an advance for my train tickets. I'll be teaching English and history and earn sixty dollars a month. Very few jobs offer even half as much."

"Are you sure the offer is legitimate? Texas is full of villains. Some cowboy could be trying to get you down there under false pretenses." Percy looked down at her, eyes full of concern. An older brother couldn't be more protective than her cousin. Life would have been so different had she been permitted to live with him and Uncle Carl after her parents' deaths.

"I've been exchanging letters with Mrs. B. Leblanc for almost three months now, working out the particulars. Her handwriting is too fine to be anything but a lady's. And her letters are on official letterhead."

"I worry about you." Percy's words were foreign to her ears.

A hundred "if only's" raced through her head. Before any tears could escape her eyes, Emily changed the subject. "See, there's Amanda and her family. Her fiancé is a minister near Austin. I'll be traveling with her and her old governess almost all the way. Safety in numbers."

Percy nodded. "Take care. Write often. We will worry about you." He hugged her tight. Ignoring the shocked looks of Amanda's family who likely didn't know of her relationship.

Emily hugged her cousin back. "It will all work out. I know my purpose is to teach and help others. Remember my speech, *surgo ut prosim,* I rise to serve."

———◆———

The moments before sunrise hailed in the peaceful hour of the morning after the bars and bordellos closed and before the stores and respectable establishments opened. Over the past three years, mornings had become TJ's favorite time of day. That hour before the sun could attempt to do what Santa Anna hadn't done over forty years ago at the Alamo and chase the men out of Texas became his refuge from the day. TJ gathered his papers, intent on reading as he sat on the porch behind the two-and-a-half story stone jail overlooking the Brazos River. There he'd watch the eastern sky change from grays to golds to blue to remind himself that in the chaos of the day to come, God existed.

Pounding on the boardwalk chased away the silence. A dust-covered boy burst into TJ's office. "Sheriff! Sheriff! Doc Palmer says come quick!"

TJ tossed his papers back onto the desk, toppling the nameplate proclaiming him Sheriff Thomas Jefferson Morgan. So much for the quiet morning. Dr. Palmer wouldn't have sent Donny for anything other than an emergency. "Office or house?"

"His house. Ya gotta hurry. Doc says she's dying!" Donny didn't stick around to see if the sheriff followed him into the deserted street.

TJ closed the door behind him and ran the short distance to Dr. Palmer's home, cutting through backyards and alleys as Donny had. A dog barked as he sprinted past the minister's house. The doctor's chickens squawked when TJ burst through the back gate.

A lamp burned in Dr. Aidan Palmer's kitchen window. TJ hopped up on the porch and entered through the partially open door.

"Doc?

"In here, TJ."

TJ followed his friend's voice into a small room off the kitchen. A woman, unrecognizable under the bruises and swelling to her face, lay on a narrow cot. The torn silk gown exposed a lace covered corset.

"Rose wants to talk to you." Aidan stood and whispered the next words. "She doesn't have long."

Rose? One of Belle's girls? Most of her scalp was missing. What remained of her blonde hair lay bloodied and matted. None of Mrs. Belle's girls would have been far enough out of town last night to meet up with the occasional Indian who'd escaped removal to Oklahoma. Someone had meant to throw suspicion in another direction. TJ knelt next to the cot. "Who did this to you, Rose?"

"You came. My name is Cecilia Pru...it...Belle changed... drugged..." Rose closed her eyes and dragged in a ragged breath, "deceived me. I was to teach—" She clutched TJ's hand as if holding on to a lifeline in a rushing river and gasped for breath. "Stop...tea...from Bost...on...save..." The words rattled in Rose's throat. She fell silent, her gaze fixed on the ceiling. The secret Rose tried to tell died with her.

Aidan held his stethoscope to her chest for a minute. "Sheriff, I'm sorry to say you have a murder on your hands. The only animal that would do this is a man."

The doctor's conclusion matched TJs. "She didn't say who beat her by name, did she?"

Aidan closed Rose's eyes and pulled the sheet over her head. He paused a moment before looking at TJ. "No, but we can both guess. Belle doesn't let her customers do this much damage."

It wouldn't be the first time Belle instructed her henchmen to make sure one of the doves knew her place. Not that he'd ever been able to prove it. "How did Rose get here?"

"Your guess is as good as mine. She woke all the chickens less than a half hour ago. Got to my back porch before she collapsed. I'm not sure how she found my place, she's never been here before." Doc didn't need to explain. He wasn't the kind of man that stepped foot in Belle's for non-medical reasons. "She's been repeating herself and asking for you every minute or so. I'm surprised she held on as long as she did."

"What am I supposed to prevent? Tea in Boston? I'm a hundred years too late for the Boston Tea party." TJ ran his hand through his hair. "She must have thought it very important. More important than her life." A different name? Drugged? TJ's mind whirled as he tried to put the pieces together.

"Rose kept talking about teaching and being tricked and asking for you. I think there might be someone else she wants you to save." Surely Belle had more than enough working girls she didn't need to trick more of them into the trade.

"Information that someone didn't want her to pass on. Tea could be a teacher. But Boston is so far away, it must be another town."

Aidan washed his hands in the basin on a corner washstand. "It's my fault she's dead."

TJ looked at the covered body. In his unprofessional opinion, no doctor could have saved Rose. "What do you mean?"

"In March, when Dr. Jones was out of town, they called me to Belle's for the health check on her employees. Belle wasn't happy it was me instead of Jones since I'm against legalizing the brothels. She's afraid I'll convince her ladies to leave. But to be licensed, the girls need their health checks, so she let me in. Rose had bruises on her ribs. I'd asked her about them, but her only response was to look at the ruffian Belle assigned to witness the examinations and shake her head. I asked her the normal questions about being a willing worker. Rose's answer was so carefully worded I only realized a few days ago what she'd meant when she told me, 'As willing as Briseis.' I was going to see if I could talk with her again this week."

TJ never heard of the name. "Who is Briseis?"

"A captive slave in Homer's *Iliad*, forced to become a concubine. I was rereading it last Sunday night." Aidan dried his hands, shaking his head. "I've forgotten some of my old school lessons. Two months! She asked for help two months ago and I couldn't figure it out."

"I didn't think any of Belle's girls were educated enough to have read Homer." TJ turned away to avoid looking at the body, not admitting that he never finished his reading assignments that term.

"Neither did I, but what little she told us paints a grim picture. It isn't uncommon for Belle's or Harold's girls to use opium or cocaine to dull their pain. What if Rose didn't enter the profession willingly? I only heard a bit more than you did. If I understood her, Rose—or Cecilia—found herself trapped in a world she didn't want to be in. If Belle did trick and drug her, I think you also have kidnapping on your list of charges."

"Why didn't she leave in March? She could have when you talked to her then."

Aidan paced across the room and back. "The message she gave me was so cryptic. I should have done more to figure it out. Other girls have been more direct in asking to leave. Maybe she had no place to go. What friends or family would take her back after working in a brothel? You know people's attitudes. And if she had no family, who would even come looking for her? Why didn't I try to piece it together?" He walked to the doorway and back.

"For her to use such a cryptic message, she may have been threatened. So why run now and risk death? And who am I supposed to save?"

Aidan shook his head. "I'm a doctor, not a detective. Why don't I tell you what I can from an examination? Then I'll send Donny for the undertaker."

"Better hurry. I don't want the whole town gawking."

"No great mystery about how she died." Aidan uncovered one limb at a time, cataloging the injuries. "Some of these bruises are older than tonight. Look at their color. It's a wonder she made it to my backyard on this ankle. It's been twisted for a while. Oh…what do we have here?" He extracted a bit of crumpled paper from the dead woman's fist and handed it to TJ.

"Looks like part of a telegram." The paper had more blood than ink on it.

THE WESTERN UN—
    Received advan—
    Arrive Jun—
    Teac—

TJ turned the paper over. "The cable originated in 'Massa—' so the 'Bost' Rose mentioned could be Boston after all. Not much to go on, is it? Could Belle be offering women teaching jobs and tricking or drugging them into her service? Belle claims that the best come begging to work for her and she turns them away. How am I supposed to find a teacher when I don't know what she looks like or when she is coming?"

"A woman from Massachusetts in Hiramsville will stand out like a hot-house flower in a field of bluebonnets."

"I'll have Donny watch the Fort Worth and Rio Grande trains for the next few weeks. Someone from that far away would change lines in Dallas. Belle will send someone to meet whoever is coming."

"Pay Donny well if he is watching the station as he won't be doing as many errands." A grin lit the doctor's face.

"It's my privilege to keep the kid employed." Not a hardship. They'd been seeing to Donny's family's welfare by keeping him honestly employed.

Aidan covered the body again. "I'm sure he will still find work with me. If I hadn't delivered him myself, I would think he was twins or even triplets. He is always around when I need him, but then I see him working for Henry's store, delivering things or running for you just as often."

"He is a hard worker. I gave him a dime last week, and he told me I overpaid him. Swept off the walk for free the next day. There are only two trains a day from Fort Worth. It won't take all his time."

TJ walked home the long way on streets filled with men going about their business and children anxious to play before their mothers called them in from the heat. Trouble was coming. He felt it in his bones, sure as Old Man Whitaker knew when a tornado was brewing.

The novelty of watching out of the windows grew old after the first day. Emily pulled out her writing paper. Mrs. Smyth, their chaperone, snored softly in her sleep, leaving Amanda and Emily to their own entertainment.

"Who are you writing so soon after leaving?" asked Amanda.

"Widow Manning. You know how much she enjoys receiving letters from the graduates and the summers are so long for her alone in that big dorm." The lead of her pencil was already rounded with use, but the moving train would not be a safe place to sharpen it.

"I thought she would relish the silence as much as she used to try to get us to quiet down."

"Only if we woke her up. I thought she might enjoy some notes about our journey." Like how plush their Pullman car was compared to the third-class car she had seen during their last stop. If it were not for Amanda's family, Emily would be sitting on one of those wooden benches now, not in the upholstered comfort of the luxurious car. The constant movement of the train and the changing scenery were worth a few paragraphs.

"Write a salutation from me. I promise I'll write after my wedding." Amanda pulled her tatting shuttle out and the lace she had been working on for the last year. She was determined that her wedding dress would have five lace flounces down the back, as well as the sleeve cuffs. Since she was to be a pastor's wife, she felt that she should make it rather than purchase the lace. Several of the other woman at the college had helped. Like some of the engaged students, Amanda had used her white dress, without the lace, for her graduation dress.

"Your dress will be the talk of the town. Your daughters will want to wear it someday."

"It will probably be out of fashion, like Mother's hooped skirt. I don't know how she walked through the door. I wish I had your talent for sewing. I can't believe what you did to that old dress. Even your cousin Barbara was green with envy when she saw it."

"I was fortunate enough to have excess material to work with and a good pattern. Widow Manning let me keep it, since the poor dress had been made over so many times. I'm trying to decide what color to dye it as white is so impractical."

"Don't you dare. With white dresses all the rage for weddings, you will need the dress when you marry."

"I don't believe I shall ever enter into matrimony." Most of the men of Emily's acquaintance offered little encouragement after the obligatory greeting or signing their name to her half-empty dance card. Not that she returned any of their flirtations, preferring to avoid Aunt Melba's lectures. Most of the kind men had entered into the ministry, like Amanda's fiancé. Emily didn't possess the temperament to be a reverend's wife, foreign missions didn't entice her, and most society men desired a wife who looked comfortable on his arm and entertained his friends. That was Barbara's world, not hers.

"Why ever not?"

"Who would have me? Besides, love isn't something I seemed destined to have in my life." When her parents died, all that was good died with them. Only her Uncle Carl and Percy welcomed her. If Bradford College's matron hadn't importuned Amanda's family, Emily would be alone on her journey west.

Mrs. Smyth raised her head. "To love even for a little while, like I did, is better than to not love at all."

"You should listen to Mrs. Smythe. She is very wise. And just because one of those dandies that showed up at the dances didn't choose you doesn't mean you'll never find love. My fiancé never attended one of those frivolous events. You could meet someone. Promise me to not dye the gown for at least one year?"

"I will not dye it until next spring, when I shall color the dress a robin's-egg blue. Or a delicious green." Unlike her classmates, Emily had no intention of waiting for some man to come take care of her. Thank goodness she didn't have to endure Aunt Melba's prepping Barbara to catch the most eligible man society could offer. From what she'd seen, society marriages were seldom happy. After watching friend after friend suffer broken hearts, consoled by the creative chocolate confections they'd made over their gas lamps in the dorm room, Emily wanted nothing of pretended love. If she did marry, it would be a solid man like her father, Uncle Carl, or cousin Percy. Emily would choose with her mind, not her heart. Being practical didn't cause pain.

"How inane. One can't put a time clock on love." Mrs. Smyth shook her head. "If love comes, don't run from it."

Love was the stuff and nonsense of novels. Only a lucky few like Amanda even imagined themselves in such a state.

The thought gave some comfort to the pain from the demise of childhood dreams of ever having a home and family.

Last fall, when the town council had approved the licensing of brothels, claiming the revenue would help raise money for the new courthouse, they hadn't expected the local business to multiply; stretching TJ and his deputy to the limit to keep the ruckus under control. Each Friday dragged longer than the last. TJ finished signing in the three drunken brawlers who sat in the cells a floor above him and returned to the street. The noise crescendoed as a second out-of-tune piano joined the racket. Half the Hiramsville citizens complained about the noise; the other half yelled louder. Every lonely cowpuncher for twenty miles flocked to the town every payday, filling the city coffers with money and the air with their whoops and yells until midnight Saturday, when working, gambling, and the consumption of alcohol were prohibited until Monday. Sunday was the only day TJ could breathe for a few hours. The minister was trying to get the ordinance changed to make the brothels illegal again. If he did, TJ could avoid asking the town council for a second deputy. Both he and his current deputy spent half the week exhausted after working forty out of forty-eight hours keeping the peace. Fortunately, the rest of the week was manageable due to only regulars frequenting the bars and brothels.

Gunshots rang out from across the town square. TJ checked his gun before leaving to discover who was shooting up Belle's sign now. Had there been a gunfight, the shots would be accompanied by shouts or silence. By the time he arrived at the Bull's-Eye Saloon, Belle's henchman had two cowboys trussed up and waiting for delivery to the jail.

"About time you got here, Sheriff. Did your job for you again. Perhaps one of us should be elected." Bart, the larger of the two, repeated his weekly taunt.

"If you'd paint over the bull's-eye on the sign, the customers who've had too much to drink wouldn't use it for target practice." TJ took charge of the bound men.

"What's the point of naming her establishment 'Bull's-Eye' if there isn't a target on the sign?" asked Cline.

TJ shook his head. Belle wanted them to shoot the sign, if only to cause him grief. He prodded his two prisoners along the street and through the town square. As soon as the men sobered up and paid the fine, plus Belle's standard five-dollar fee for damaging her sign, he'd send them on their way. Judge Granger didn't even bother seeing the yokels who took aim at the red and black sign. In any given week, TJ collected enough money for the sign to be repainted and rehung, sometimes twice over. But Belle only replaced the sign once in the past year. Pity—the local sign painter could use the work.

Donny sat on the front stoop of the jailhouse as TJ walked up with the drunks. "Howdy, Sheriff. They've been at the sign? I don't know who is more stupid—the men who shoot at the sign or Belle."

"I reckon Belle is pretty smart. She makes a fair bit off the drunks." TJ herded the men into the building.

One of the men grunted.

"You should get on home, Donny."

"Not until I talk to you."

"I'll meet you in my office as soon as I get these men upstairs." TJ marched the men up the narrow stone steps to the floor for holding prisoners. Hiramsville's unique jail design put the sheriff's office and residence on the ground floor with the cells above. So far, there hadn't been a single successful jailbreak. He opened the vacant one of the two large, barred cells. So far, he only had five men in the two cells. Tonight might be one of the nights he'd have to use the isolated women's cell. Unlike the two large, barred cells, it had walls and a solid steel door with only a small window. He had never used it for a woman, but one day he intended to find a way to lock Belle in there. "You two'll share this one."

The men went in peaceably. An inmate in the other cell rattled the bars. "Sheriff, it's as hot as the devil's own fireplace up here. You gotta let me out before I die."

"Haven't lost a prisoner yet. Maybe next time you think about breaking the law, you'll remember our stone jail isn't the most comfortable of places to spend the night." TJ locked the door to the cell and went back downstairs. He locked the barred door at the bottom of the stairs to keep unwanted visitors from going up.

Donny sat in his swivel chair, paging through the wanted posters that had come in this morning's mail. "There is a whole stack of these this week."

"Have you memorized their faces?"

"Sure, but that isn't why I am here. Nellie…ya know, Belle's kitchen girl…gave me somethin' for you. Belle ordered her to get rid of Miss Rose's things and clean up the room 'cause they's expecting a new girl soon. Nellie said I could have anything I want out of the trunk. There were some dresses that looked real proper, so I'll take those to my ma. There were these books—*Iliad, Great Expectations*—and two by Mark Twain. I kept them for learning. I really will go back to school this fall. There were these girl books I told Nellie to keep and some children's books I gave to my sisters. They'll like *Alice's Adventures in Wonderland*. But this book is all handwritten and isn't proper English. I thought it might be a clue." Donny handed TJ a brown leather-bound book.

TJ turned over the tome and flipped through the pages. Donny was correct. The book was unreadable. He'd learned basics of Latin at the college in Thorp Spring, but this wasn't Latin or English. "Thanks. I'll take a look. Did you hear anything about the new girl?"

"Only that she's expected in about a week. Nellie thinks Rose ran away and was attacked by Injuns and is real scared. I told her not to worry. Nellie's too ugly for Injuns to want."

TJ put a hand on Donny's shoulder. "That wasn't a very nice thing to say to her. There haven't been hostile Indians in the area for eleven years. And they only ever took horses. I don't think they had anything to do with Rose, nor would they bother Nellie. You don't need to scare her with falsehoods."

"But she's so ugly." Donny twisted his face into a grimace.

"When Nellie was a little younger than you, someone threw lye in her face. The burns caused those scars. She hurt for a very long time. You don't need to tell her how she looks. She knows. What a person looks like on the outside doesn't matter as much as who they are on the inside. Nellie is a nice girl. What happened to her became a blessing. She can work at Mrs. Belle's and not worry about—" TJ realized he talked himself into a corner.

"I know, Sheriff. The men leave her alone, and she doesn't want a customer anyhows. And she is nice. Always saves me some of her food and watches out for Belle's doves better than Belle does."

TJ dug in his pockets for the two quarters he knew were there. "Your clue is worth at least this. Now skedaddle on home. Your ma will worry I'm keeping you out late."

"Thanks, Sheriff. Ma will be happy to see this."

"Make sure she gets all of it."

"I will." Donny lit out the door faster than a coyote running from a skunk.

TJ turned up his lamp, opened the journal, and tried to make sense of the letters on the page. He took a piece of paper from his desk and copied a few sentences. Maybe Aidan would have better luck.

Kvohioxaer aw o duuo oaoc. A lozu o nef ejjuv ar Lavo-qwzappu

Emily and Amanda stepped off the train in Dallas with the help of a conductor, followed by Amanda's old governess, Mrs. Smyth. The heat of the station platform wasn't tempered with any breeze and was only mildly cooler than the sweltering train. Once again, they were late to their destination. Amanda sent Mrs. Smyth to find their trunks while they went to check with the ticket agent. "What will John think? I am days late. What if he thinks I'm not coming?"

Emily listened to Amanda's worries over her fiancé again. Four days late. The day they lost to a track repair and the delay at St. Louis had been most frustrating in addition to the two nights they'd needed to spend in hotels. Emily checked the station clock. Today's delay due to a herd of long-horned cows would cost her a third unplanned expense. Her coffers were dwindling at an alarming rate. The money from her uncles' gifts had been put to use, as the Hiramsville Ladies Academy's advance didn't cover the costs. Though, if not for Amanda's parents' kindness of allowing Emily to travel with Amanda and her chaperone, the situation could be far worse. The Pullman train allowed them to travel with some comfort throughout the nights. The money Mrs. Leblanc sent wouldn't cover such a luxury. If Uncle Carl was right about her inheritance, it might have paid for it, but according to her aunt, the money was gone.

When Mrs. Smyth returned, the three women inquired about Amanda's train to Austin and Emily's to Hiramsville. The last train of the day for Austin had left an hour before they arrived. The ticket master named several hotels, then consulted Emily about her train.

"The train to Fort Worth and on to Hiramsville leaves in fifteen minutes on track two. I'll send a porter to help move your trunks, miss." The ticket master yelled at a dark man dressed in uniform and pointed to Emily.

Emily turned to Amanda. "I won't say goodbye. Write to me as soon as you are able at general delivery. I want to know how your wedding goes."

"Tomorrow by this time I'll be Mrs. Goddard, wife of Reverend John Goddard. I can hardly believe it. Write about your school. I hope you meet the man of your dreams."

Emily dismissed Amanda's comment. There was no reasoning with a woman in love. They exchanged hugs, and Emily hurried off to find her trunk.

The old trunk had once been her father's. His initials, EAW for Emory Alan Wilson, graced either end. Emily believed it fortuitous her initials were the same as even Aunt Melba couldn't claim the trunk belonged to anyone else. She pointed the old steamer out to the porter and followed him to the waiting train, carrying her carpetbag and hatbox. At the train, she gave the porter a three-cent piece and an apologetic smile. The only other coin in her purse was a silver dollar, which was far too much to pay him. Thinking she wouldn't need much money today, she'd added most of her money to the gold double eagles sewn into the lining of her corset. Not the most comfortable place to keep it, but also not a likely place for a robber to try to search in the case of a train robbery.

The rear-facing wood bench on the Fort Worth and Rio Grande wasn't as comfortable as the plush ones in the Pullman cars she'd traveled in for the last three days. But she could survive this one for the next hour and a half if no one near her smoked one of those vile cigars. The mother and two children across from her were unlikely to smoke. Emily hadn't factored in the way the young boy's swinging legs were connecting with her shins.

Only after they had pulled away from the station did Emily remember she was supposed to send a wire to Mrs. B. Leblanc stating the time of her arrival. Hopefully the stop at the Fort Worth station would be long enough to send the message. Emily needed this job too much to make a bad first impression.

The clack-clack of the tracks tugged at her insides, alternately convincing her she was prepared for her new adventure, then warning her she was doomed to fail.

⟻◆⟼

The front door slammed against the wall. Donny gulped, catching his breath. "Nellie says she's a comin'. Didn't give enough warning. Cline is heading to the station now!"

TJ glanced at the clock. The 3:50 p.m. train was due in ten minutes. "Thanks, Donny. Go make yourself scarce. Stay away from the station." TJ checked his gun before heading out to meet the train. His horse waited at the livery across the street.

Belle's henchman Cline leaned against the east wall of the station, waiting for the train to come. TJ dismounted, leaving his horse near the station door, and circled the small wood building. Mr. Long waited in his buggy for his wife, and a delivery wagon from the mercantile sat off to one side near a rented livery wagon. That one must be Cline's transportation. TJ rubbed his jaw. He'd only have a few moments to find the woman and convince her of possible duplicity. The station master exited the station, looking at his gold fob watch. TJ approached him. "Train running late?"

"Not yet. Waiting for someone, Sheriff?"

"Not too sure."

"Not expecting trouble on a Thursday, are you? That usually comes Friday, on the east-bound train." The station master referred to the cowboys that came in from the ranches west of Hiramsville.

The whistle of the train sounded. Mr. Long left his buggy and limped across the platform. "Afternoon, Sheriff."

TJ tipped his hat. The brakes of the engine screeched as the train slowed its approach. Only three cars. Miss Whoever-She-Was should be easy to find. A cowboy exited, followed by Mrs. Long, the church organist. A young woman exited next, carrying a carpetbag and an old hatbox. TJ sauntered closer as he watched Cline close in from the corner.

As the young woman looked back at the baggage car and around the platform, TJ stepped forward before Cline could reach her. "May I help you, miss?"

The woman looked at his badge. "Sheriff, I—"

Cline stepped between them. "Miss Wilson? I'm Cline Brown. Mrs. Leblanc sent me to get you and your things. Is that your trunk?"

"Yes, Mr. Brown. Thank you." She turned to TJ as Cline headed for the baggage. "I guess I don't need any help. I am so excited about my new job."

"What job brings you to Hiramsville this time of year?" He couldn't interfere if she wanted to work at Belle's.

She looked around the platform and backed up a step before answering. "I'm a teacher. This is my first position.

I'll be teaching English and history. Tell me—" She stopped talking when Cline approached.

"I'm ready to go, ma'am. We shouldn't keep Belle—I mean Mrs. Leblanc—waiting." Cline grabbed Miss Wilson's elbow and propelled her toward the wagon.

Miss Wilson couldn't be more than twenty. Her wide eyes spoke of an innocence rare in the West. TJ would eat his sister's rattle-snake stew if this was one of Belle's regular girls. Probably had never even been kissed, which under normal circumstances would be a shame. Had Rose been like this when she arrived? Sweet, innocent, and full of wonder? "Wait!" TJ hurried after them, stopping where Cline stood with the teacher at the front of the wagon. "Miss Wilson, please don't go with this man. Cline is the bouncer for the Bull's-Eye Saloon and Belle's Beauties—the town's most infamous brothel."

Her cheeks flamed. "That's preposterous! I have several letters in my purse—" Miss Wilson pulled a fistful of papers from the small bag hanging at her wrist. "These are on official letterhead regarding a teaching job at the Hiramsville Ladies Academy."

She yelped as Cline lifted her onto the seat and hurried around the wagon. "Mr. Brown, I was talking to the sheriff. You did not have leave to hoist me up like a sack of flour."

"Sorry, ma'am. We must hurry. Mrs. Leblanc hates it when people are late."

A cloud of uncertainty masked her eyes. Miss Wilson looked from Cline to TJ and back again.

With only a few more seconds to plead his case, TJ grabbed the side of the wagon. "You are making a huge mistake. There is no—"

Cline flicked the reins, and the wagon lurched forward as TJ leaped back to keep his toes from being smashed under the wheels. Miss Wilson watched him for a moment before turning to face forward. TJ ran for his horse. He had to keep her from Belle's clutches. As long as Miss Wilson didn't step foot inside Belle's establishment, he could protect her. Once the madame slammed the door in his face, only a miracle could get her out, as a judge needed evidence for a warrant. And stingy Judge Granger rarely gave them where the brothels were concerned. TJ raced after the wagon, praying Miss Wilson would listen to him.

Emily gasped as the sheriff jumped back. He didn't seem to be hurt. "Mr. Brown, the sheriff was talking to me, and you practically ran over his toes. That is very rude."

Mr. Brown flicked the reins, not acknowledging Emily's words. Perhaps he hadn't heard her over the rattle of the wagon. Emily spoke louder. "What did the sheriff mean when he said you worked for a saloon and a house of ill repute?" Emily held onto the seat as the wagon bounced down the road.

"I do many odd jobs. Sometimes I help keep the peace on Friday and Saturday nights." Mr. Brown turned down a narrow, rutted street.

"Oh." Wasn't keeping the peace law enforcement's job? Percy's words about a cowboy wanting a wife came back to her. If anyone other than Mrs. Leblanc met her at the next stop, Emily would run. Even if she couldn't outrun Mr. Brown, someone might notice.

She was surprised when the sheriff rode up to the side of the wagon. He nodded but didn't speak—or couldn't, with the dust the wagon stirred up. If she needed to run, it might be from the tall sheriff, who looked unusually dangerous.

They stopped next to a yellow two-story wood building. To the left of the door, a clean white sign announced the building was indeed the Hiramsville Ladies Academy. Emily took a deep breath, glad to find a bona fide school and not a brothel. The door opened, and a woman in a dark-blue silk dress with a high collar and long sleeves descended the steps to the street. No rouge, obviously not a madame. The sheriff dismounted and situated himself between Emily and the school.

Mr. Brown helped her down from the wagon. Maybe he only lacked manners where the sheriff was concerned. The two men were roughly the same height and build, but where the sheriff's gray eyes glowered, Mr. Cline's blue eyes danced. The sheriff frowned, a deep scar on his cheek warned of danger. If there were houses of ill repute in Hiramsville, one glare from the sheriff should close them. Mr. Brown's open smile invited her to smile back. He had a face Barbara would swoon over. Between his manners and his mustache, Emily would save her swoons for someone else.

The older woman nodded at the sheriff and circled around him, extending both hands to Emily, who couldn't return the gesture because of the carpetbag and the hatbox. The woman dropped her hands. "Miss Wilson. I am so glad you arrived safely, even if you are late. Do come in. I have afternoon tea waiting." The woman wrapped her arm protectively around Emily's shoulders. Mr. Brown hefted her trunk and mounted the steps to the school.

The sheriff again blocked her way. "Please, Miss Wilson. Listen to me. This isn't what it seems. Belle is one of the best-known madams this side of Dallas."

Mrs. Leblanc blinked several times. "Why, Sheriff, you do tell tales. No one would believe that about little old me."

Emily shifted her carpet bag and hatbox to her other hand. "If this woman is running an illegal establishment, why don't you arrest her?"

"In Hiramsville, prostitution is licensed and legal." The sheriff spat out the words, obviously displeased.

Mrs. Leblanc patted Emily's arm as she explained. "Several towns in Texas that see the vice as a way to earn money for the city's needs. Nothing for you to worry your pretty head over."

Emily opened her mouth, then closed it. She had no response. What kind of town had she come to?

"Sheriff, let me pass." Mrs. Leblanc propelled Emily toward the stairs.

The sheriff took Emily's other arm. "Don't go in there, miss."

Emily nodded at the sign. Maybe the sheriff was the villain here. "Why should I not go into the school?"

"It isn't a school, ma'am. You won't be doing any teaching here," answered the sheriff.

"Nonsense. Miss Wilson will give an education to many." Mrs. Leblanc pulled Emily up the first stair. Emily felt as if she were a rope in a human game of tug-of-war. One of the two parties was dangerous. But which one? Even if prostitution were legal here, she had shared so many letters with Mrs. Leblanc. And who painted a brothel bright sunflower yellow? The sheriff matched the description of the villain out of every dime novel she'd ever read. The long dangerous scar pulsed menacingly.

"At least walk around the entire building before going in." The sheriff's eyes changed from glowering to pleading.

Mrs. Leblanc pulled Emily up another step. Mr. Brown held the door open, and the delicious smell of fresh biscuits spilled out. The carpetbag weighed heavily on her arm. Emily didn't need to be propelled to take the next step. If she could set down her burden and eat something, they could sort this out.

The sheriff firmly held her arm. "Stop! This woman is under arrest for bank robbery!"

W hat?" shouted Cline, Belle, and Miss Wilson in unison.
Miss Wilson spun around, her hatbox dropping to the ground. The lid popped off, and a ball of snow-white yarn rolled under the wagon. Her crochet needles, book, and bonnet tumbled out. "I am no thief!" She shook herself free of Mrs. LeBlanc and the sheriff, then rushed down the stairs to collect the box and scattered items. Belle and Cline tried to follow, but TJ moved to the base of the stairs, blocking them.

Dusting her yarn off, Miss Wilson muttered, "Ruined. Just ruined," before standing to face him. "Sir, you are mistaken. I have never robbed a bank in my life."

"The Texas Rangers sent out a wanted poster last week. I need to take you in. You can come peacefully, or you can be the first woman I use my new Tower Double Lock handcuffs on." This part wasn't a lie. There had been a poster sent out last week for a female bank robber. The chances Miss Wilson and Pretty Polly Paulson were the same person was infinitesimally small, but lying to get Miss Wilson away from Belle was his only chance. Then he could prove to her the danger she was in.

"Sheriff, do I look like a bank robber? You saw the contents of my hatbox. Did you see anything of value? A hat made over twice, my crochet, a tattered book of Wordsworth poems, and a copy of Austen's *Sense and Sensibility*. Hardly what a robber would carry."

Belle crossed her arms. "She is as much of a bank robber as I am." The madam didn't need to rob the bank. The saloon and brothel took in most of the money that came into town.

"Come along nicely, miss, and we can get this sorted out. Maybe I'm wrong, and maybe I'm right." TJ pulled out the pair of handcuffs and reached for the teacher. "Do I need to use these?"

"I am not a thief!" Miss Wilson swung her carpetbag, hitting him in the leg.

TJ grabbed her wrist and clamped one of the cuffs on it. She dropped the bag on his foot. Pain shot up his leg, and he let out a yell as he captured her other hand. Did the lady carry an anvil in her bag? The hatbox fell to the ground again. This time, the lid remained closed. Miss Wilson tried to kick him. TJ scooped her up and plopped her into the wagon bed. Fool woman. Couldn't she work with him a little? He was trying to spare her from a fate she seemed ill prepared for.

"Cline, I'll return this wagon to the livery for you. Bring her trunk out, please."

Belle stopped her henchman with a look. "If she's the thief you claim she is, she stole a hundred dollars from me, and I am keeping her trunk until I receive my money back."

"A hundred dollars? I never stole anything in my life. Not even a sweet from the kitchen. You only sent me a fifty-dollar advance for my train ticket. How can I owe you twice your advance?" Miss Wilson's hat sat askew on her head, her eyes flashed with anger. TJ's gut curled. He shouldn't be treating a lady this way, even to prevent a worse fate.

"I also rented the wagon, sent Cline after you, and now I have to start a new search for a teacher, which means lost wages. One hundred." Belle didn't move from the top step.

"The trunk could be evidence. I'll need it." TJ put the carpetbag and hatbox in the wagon bed beside Miss Wilson and started up the stairs.

Belle blocked the door. "Send the Texas Ranger for the trunk when he comes to collect your robber. It stays here until I get my money. Call it collateral. I deserve at least half the reward money for finding her. Either way, I'll need a hundred dollars to release the trunk."

"I need your word that no one will touch the trunk." Not that he trusted Belle's word, but if he spun this right, she might keep out of it.

"You have my word."

"Belle, if the trunk is evidence, it won't be the local judge who tries the case. The bank-robbery case will go to Dallas or Austin. If you or anyone in your employ is caught tampering with the trunk, you will lose your license. And you may be charged for damaging evidence. You are better off letting me take it."

Belle gave him a half smile. "I will keep her trunk until I get paid." Cline flexed his arm and stepped forward. If the bouncer knocked him out, they'd drag Miss Wilson inside over his prone body. This woman was more precious than any knickknack she had tucked away in the trunk. To leave safely with her was the better choice.

TJ backed off, then tied his horse to the back of the wagon. Miss Wilson glared at him, her face red from either heat, anger, humiliation, or a combination of the three. TJ didn't care how mad she was if she was safe. Wordsworth and Austen. Miss Wilson wasn't one of Belle's typical girls. His gut said she wasn't one of Belle's kind of women at all. Now to convince Miss Wilson of that.

Emily tried to keep her head high as the wagon bumped along the streets. The people they passed wouldn't be able to see her cuffed hands. Aunt Melba would screech threats to cut Emily off for good the second she learned of her arrest. Granted, swinging her bag at the infuriating man had been less than wise, but the handcuffs were unnecessary. Whoever had voted for this man must have assumed the intimidating scar equated with being a good sheriff. They had voted for the sheriff, hadn't they?

The wagon turned a corner sharply, and Emily slid to the side. The sheriff could learn a thing or two about driving as well. He stopped the wagon in front of a narrow two-story limestone building topped with a tower on the southwest corner. A boy of ten or so emerged from the shadows. "Did ya save her, Sheriff?"

The sheriff jumped down from the seat and reached over the side of the wagon for Emily's hatbox and carpetbag, handing them to the boy. "Go put these by my desk. Donny, take the wagon and horse over to the livery, please."

The boy ran off with her belongings.

The sheriff came around to the back, untied his horse, and let down the tailgate. He waited while Emily scooted forward, then placed his hands on either side of her waist and lifted her to the ground.

Emily bit the side of her cheek to refrain from speaking. The comments running through her head wouldn't help her now. The sheriff looked south to the town square and frowned. "Hurry in."

His grip on her elbow was light and supportive, unlike Mr. Cline's. Once inside the door, the sheriff pulled out a set of keys and unlocked an iron-barred door. "Up here, please."

Emily mounted the stairs. With her hands behind her back, she couldn't hold up her skirt, and her toe caught in the hem, propelling her forward, but before her knees hit the stone steps, the sheriff's arm wrapped around her waist and pulled her back against his broad chest. Never had a man not related to her held her so close. He smelled of dust and horse, along with something not unpleasant mixed in. Before she could place the scent, he steadied her and let go.

"Sorry about that." The rumble of his deep voice vibrated through her. "Let me take these off." He used a little key on the handcuffs. A lock clicked, and her right wrist came free. Her arm tingled as she brought it to her front. Another click and her left arm was freed. "Upstairs please, miss."

Emily looked over her shoulder. His large frame filled the narrow stairway, blocking any plan of escape. With no other choice, she continued up the stairs. At the top, she stood on a small wooden landing. This second-story jail challenged any previous notions of prisoners in dark dungeons. Above her rose the tower, a single beam crossing the space near the top, which was illuminated by a small window. "A jail is an odd place for a bell tower." She covered her mouth, embarrassed the thought had escaped.

"It was built for a hangman's noose. Only used it once. All capital punishment must take place at a state facility."

Emily shuddered. If all this confusion wasn't cleared up, did she face such a fate? "Why did you arrest me?"

The sheriff opened one of the two barred doors. "This cell will give you more privacy until I can figure out what to do with you. The other cells are only separated by bars."

Emily crossed the threshold into the stone-walled room. The only ventilation was a barred window six feet off the floor. She returned to the hall. "It's hot as the third circle of Dante's inferno in here!"

"I've heard from others that it is only the second, but I have no experience myself." He held the door open like a gentleman would to a shop in town. "Please, Miss Wilson,

I need to get back downstairs. Belle sent someone to watch you. I'll bring up some cool water and supper in a few minutes, and we can talk."

Talk? Emily narrowed her eyes. He knew she wasn't who he claimed, and still he insisted on jailing her like a common criminal. She lifted her chin.

"Please get in. I'm trying to protect you." The sheriff stepped closer. Emily craned her neck to try to see into his eyes. But so little sunlight penetrated the two-foot thick walls, it failed to illuminate his face.

Plots from the dime novels she'd read in the barn loft when she should have been searching for eggs filled her mind. Was the sheriff corrupt, or was Mrs. Leblanc? In a book, a man with a scar would be the evil one, but life rarely ended up as neat as a book. Attempting to escape now would leave her with no answers and with nothing but the money sewn into her corset. Which would get her only halfway back to Boston even if the train wasn't forced to wait for repairs. Emily compliantly entered the stone room. A warm breeze from the slot window high in the wall threatened to push the temperature in the room to another level of the inferno. The key scraped in the lock behind her. The sheriff stood still for a moment before his footfalls echoed across the wood plank floor.

Emily sat down on the lumpy cot. Dust motes danced in the shaft of light. Emily studied her wrist, the manacles having left no mark proving the sheriff hadn't tightened them as much as he could have. Her purse still hung from her wrist. She pulled out one of the crumpled letters from Mrs. Leblanc and reread the words, looking for hidden meaning. The letter failed to address how many pupils she would have or the level of English she would be teaching. The "progressive selection of books" might not mean a full collection of uncensored Greek classics. Last year, a visiting minister had alluded to the evils of the printed word and indicated there existed books containing scandalous content. If a brothel had books, they would be of that type, wouldn't they?

In frustration, Emily stuffed the letters back into her bag, then pulled one out again to use as a fan. How did Texas women survive this heat?

⋘◆⋙

Donny spun slow circles in TJ's swivel chair. "You arrested that lady?"

"In a manner of speaking." TJ set his hat on the corner of the desk.

"Never seen a lady in jail before. She doesn't look like someone who done wrong."

Explaining things to the ten-year-old would only lead to more questions. "Anyone come by?"

"Bart came into the office, looked around, and left. I asked him what he wanted, but he only grunted." Donny stood and dusted off the chair. "Do you know what I read today? Thomas Jefferson, the president, not you, invented the swivel chair and wrote the Declaration of Independence in it. I think it's only fitting you have a chair like his since you share his name and all."

TJ's mother would agree. She'd named him after the third president in the hope that TJ might in some way live up to the legacy of the brilliant man. "Did Bart do anything else?"

"Naw, he only looked around. I told him you were upstairs locking a woman in jail. He grunted again."

"Did he look at the wanted posters?" TJ moved to the wall, where he had them pinned in neat rows. He couldn't let Miss Wilson go with Bart nosing around. She'd find herself back in the brothel before the night was over.

"Not for very long."

TJ pulled down Pretty Polly's poster and tucked it into the top drawer of his desk. Anyone who read the description closely would know Polly had brown eyes, where Miss Wilson's were blue. The height and hair matched, though, and the sketch could have been any number of women.

"Is that the woman you have locked up?"

Not wanting to lie, TJ didn't answer. "Have you seen my ma?"

"She left right after you went to the depot, said she was going to Widow Reese's. Your supper is in the warmer, and there is extra if you get a prisoner."

"Have you had your supper yet?"

"Nope, Ma was making corn mush and pork again. Wasn't enough pork for all four of us, so I told her I'd eat while I was working."

"Let's get you fed and make a plate for my prisoner." They exited the main building and entered the kitchen, which was attached to the back of the jail next to a dog run. On the counter sat cornbread, neatly cut into four equal pieces. In the warmer, TJ found sliced, fried ham, with cubed potatoes, and carrots. He divided the meal into thirds and sent Donny to fill a fresh bucket of water from the water pump. "After you eat, go see if you can find out where Bart and Cline are."

"Yes, sir." Donny sat at the table. Half his meal was gone before TJ finished preparing Miss Wilson's food and filling the tin pitcher with water. On the way out the door, he grabbed a clean towel. In the office, he set the tray down on the desk and retrieved the coded journal and scrap of telegram from the locked bottom drawer of his desk. Getting upstairs with the trays was always difficult. He set the pitcher and tray on the steps and locked the iron-bar door behind him before ascending to the jail level. Taking the steps one at a time, he balanced the tray so as to not spill the water.

He set everything down on a stone shelf jutting out from the wall across from the cells and took the water and a cup with him when he opened the isolation cell. Miss Wilson was resting her head against the north wall and fanning herself with a piece of paper, evidence TJ had not even bothered to search her person for weapons. She'd removed her hat and set it on the cot. Escaped wisps of blonde hair curled in damp ringlets around her face. There must be a hatpin concealed some place out of sight. As long as she didn't attempt to use the six- or eight-inch mini spear on him, he'd allow her to keep it.

"I brought food and water." TJ filled the tin cup and handed it to Miss Wilson. He left the door open while he retrieved the tray with their dinners.

"Why did you bring two meals? I was under the impression I am the sole occupant of your jail." Miss Wilson took a plate from the tray he held.

"This is my supper. We have much to discuss, and, unfortunately, we have to talk up here." TJ leaned against the opposite wall and slid to the floor as the only other place to sit was on the cot.

She eyed the open door, then him, then the door again. Even if she tried to run, the lower door was likely locked. Instead of bolting, her shoulders relaxed a fraction of an inch. TJ hoped by sitting folded up on the floor, he looked no more threatening than his dog, Bones—a sad-looking mutt too old to move from his spot outside the kitchen door unless he sought shade.

"And what do we need to discuss?" Miss Wilson straightened and looked at him the way Widow Reese had when she'd caught him stealing peaches from the tree in her backyard when he was twelve.

"Why I falsely arrested you."

ater spewed across the small cell. Emily covered her mouth in embarrassment. "You did this deliberately?"

The sheriff nodded and took a bite of his ham. He wasn't fooling her, all folded up on the floor like Barbara's cat, Beelzebub, ready to pounce.

"Why? Why would you do that to me? Mrs. Leblanc will never hire me now." She set the plate beside her on the cot. There were few teaching jobs that paid as well, and most of those were open only to men.

"Miss Wilson, is it? We were not properly introduced. I'm Sheriff Thomas Jefferson Morgan, although most folks around here call me Sheriff or TJ." He didn't stand like a proper gentleman would. "As I tried to explain to you, Belle doesn't run a school. She runs the largest brothel in Hiramsville."

"But the sign…my letters…I earned a degree from Bradford College. I am supposed to be a teacher." He had to be wrong. Aunt Melba's predictions of ruination couldn't be coming to pass so quickly. Emily pulled the letters out and thrust them at him. "Read them!"

"Please drink the water while it's still cool." He pointed to her cup and waited for her to drink before opening the letters. "Most Northerners find they need twice as much water down here."

The water was tepid at best but felt good in her dry mouth. Emily filled the small tin cup a second time.

He didn't speak until she put her cup down. "Cline, or Mr. Brown, brought you to the back door of the Bull's-Eye. I'm not sure where the sign for the 'school' came from. I've never seen it there before. Belle Leblanc is the proprietor of the establishment, which is a saloon and a brothel. These letters are for a school that doesn't exist. There is a college here, but it's a coeducational institution."

Emily finished the second cup of water and poured a third, emptying the pitcher. If the sheriff wanted more, he could go and fetch it. "Preposterous! How can I believe such a thing? Everything about her was respectable." Mrs. Leblanc's state of dress and lack of rouge ran contrary to every imaginative narrative of a soiled dove Emily had ever read.

"I debated about driving the wagon around to the front of the building on our way here, but I figured the fewer people who saw you in cuffs, the better. I do apologize for using them on you. But after you hit me with your bag, I had little choice. Belle and her men need to believe my ploy so I can get you safely out of town."

Emily took another drink and studied him over the rim of her cup. He hadn't combed his hair after removing his hat. His mud-colored, wavy hair was dented where the rim sat. The lack of care countered the rakish look of the scar. "So you arrested me and put me in jail to get me out of town, but let the brothel owner go free?"

The sheriff set his empty plate on the tray. He must have inhaled his food to have finished so fast. "I needed to get you out of there before you took one step into her establishment. Since the town legalized the brothels last year as a way to raise money for the city hall, I am powerless to interfere inside those walls. Belle pays a hundred-dollar annual licensing fee, five dollars a week in taxes, and an additional dollar-per-week tax on her working women. As long as she has her girls seen by a doctor every three months, I can't interfere. Your insistence that she hired you to be a teacher affirms what I thought at the depot. You are not one of Belle's normal girls."

Emily set the cup by her feet and picked up the plate. Legal brothels? Belle's girls? Her mind spun. There must be another explanation. "Well, I am not one of those types of women. Once I realized my mistake, I would have left."

Sheriff Morgan ran his hand through his hair and looked at the ceiling. His tone softened. "I doubt they would've let you walk out. Two weeks ago, one of Belle's girls, Rose, died from a beating." He paused and swallowed. "Before she passed, she asked to speak with me. She claimed she had been drugged and tricked into working for Belle."

Emily gasped, her plate wobbling on her lap. She grabbed her dinner before it fell. "You mean they—" The words to ask what she wanted eluded her. This was worse than any penny dreadful or nickel mystery she'd ever read.

"She was the one who warned me you were coming. My guess is her realization that there was another woman destined to meet the same fate gave her the courage to try to run." The sheriff handed her a piece of torn paper. The cell was so small he only had to move a foot to reach the place she sat.

Emily turned the paper over, the words familiar. She'd counted each letter twice when she'd composed the wire so as to not pay a penny more than necessary. "This is the confirmation telegram I sent two weeks ago." Emily read the scrap over again, the words on the paper blurring as the room rotated.

"Miss Wilson!"

⬥◆⬥

Heat sickness. TJ yanked the handkerchief out of his pocket and grabbed the pitcher to dampen it.

Empty. His hand hovered over the buttons of her jacket. Best not undress her unless she didn't revive. He ran downstairs to his office.

Cline stood in front of the wall of wanted posters. "Where is Miss Wilson's I mean Pretty Polly's poster? Belle wants to know what her reward will be."

A half-empty water jug sat on the side table. TJ grabbed it. "I pulled the poster off the wall. I don't recall the reward."

"Funny. I thought Polly had brown eyes. Miss Wilson's are a shade of blue that reminds me of those blue glass bottles of Belle's elixir."

No, they are lighter than blue glass. "Is that so? Well, I'll check the poster later. If you'll excuse me, a prisoner needs water."

"Overheated? Must be all them clothes she's wearing. We don't have that problem over at the Bull's-Eye."

TJ grabbed a half empty jug off the side table. Warm water was better than none. He opened the iron-bar door.

"Up there alone with her, Sheriff? Tsk, tsk."

TJ locked the gate behind him and hurried upstairs to the sound of Bart's lecherous laughter.

⬥◆⬥

Emily blinked up at the plastered ceiling. The sheriff applied a cool cloth to her forehead. "You fainted. Drink some more water."

She sipped from the cup he held to her lips, then tried to sit up.

He assisted her, keeping one hand on her shoulder. "You need to drink more water. Our Texas heat can melt a Yankee in a few minutes."

"This room doesn't help."

"It's as cool in here as on the street. The jacket you are wearing is more suited to winter." The sheriff dropped his hand and stepped away from the cot.

The deep-blue woolen jacket and matching skirt were one of Emily's finest ensembles, one intended to make a good impression on her employer. "This is a summer suit." She dusted crumbs from the front.

"Maybe up north, but not down here. My ma can help you pick something more suitable until you can go back."

"Go back?" To what? To whom? There had to be a teaching job. There had to be.

"Before you fainted, we were discussing the job you thought you had." The sheriff sat back on his knees.

"There is a college here. I know it. The dean of education looked up Hiramsville College in one of her books before I agreed to come here."

The sheriff nodded his head. "As I said before, there is a Hiramsville College, a coeducational school. I've not heard of any open positions since they filled the two vacated spots last spring. The college doesn't start up again until September."

"Oh, there must be something. A primary school?" Any job was better than going back to Aunt Melba's. Well, not quite. A brothel was much worse.

"I can ask around, but you are better off going back to your family." He handed her another cup of water.

Emily sipped the rapidly warming water. "There is no place to go back to."

The sheriff scowled. "Did you tell Belle that?"

He must be very familiar with the woman for him to keep calling her by her Christian name. "Mrs. Leblanc asked what my family thought of me coming all the way to Texas. I wrote that my aunt would be thrilled to have me out from under her roof. Both my uncles like me well enough. But I have always been somewhat of a problem, as orphaned nieces tend to be. Not that it matters. I don't have enough money to get even halfway back to Boston, and I am not leaving without my trunk. I can't."

"I don't believe Rose had any family either. I wish I—" He paused. "After she died, there was a journal found among her things, written in code. I wish I could understand it. Rose may have written enough information to arrest Belle and her men if she was forced into employment. As far as your trunk, you are lucky that is all you lost."

"Lucky?" Emily jumped up, hands on hips. "My trunk has almost everything I own in it!"

"Clothes and doodads can be replaced." The sheriff stood but stayed near the wall.

"Doodads? I suppose you mean dresses and clothing and the like. Which I need, and which, as you say, can be replaced. But my mother's hairbrush and my father's Bible can't! Neither can my grandmother's sugar bowl—made by Paul Revere himself." And my books! Emily didn't add the last item. He was probably of the mind that books could be replaced too. She glared at him.

"Are they more valuable than your life?" His gray eyes— honest, serious—bored into hers.

Unable to speak, Emily shook her head and plopped back onto the cot. She closed her eyes against her imagination. Even living with her belongings wouldn't be worth having them if she were to be ruined and forced to live a life of shame.

"I will work hard to get your trunk back. I promise you, Miss Wilson, I will get it back, but not at the cost of you. I have a plan—if I can get one of the Rangers to help. We can get you and your trunk to someplace safe."

"How? A Texas Ranger isn't going to go along with your crazy scheme to jail me, and I don't have a hundred dollars."

"My brother is a ranger." The sheriff stood with the tray.

A warm gust of air blew through the window—raising the heat level to the fourth or even fifth circle of the inferno. Crawling back to her aunt and uncle could not be much worse. Amanda's new husband might know of a position. Austin was much closer. Emily placed her hat on her head. The town had a hotel, didn't it?

The sheriff moved between Emily and the doorway. "Where are you going?"

"You can't keep me here. You know I am innocent. I refuse to spend the night here. I'll die of the heat!"

"I can't let you leave, ma'am. One of Belle's men was snooping around my office. If I let you go, he'll snatch you up before you cross the street to the hotel. Sadly, this cell is the best I can offer to keep you safe. You'll have your privacy. I'll leave your door open, but the gate at the bottom of the stairs stays closed. If I come up, I'll make as much noise as possible, especially if I am bringing in a new prisoner. If I do, close the door to your cell. The way this door is set back when closed, you can't see in from the main cells. This room was built for women or for isolation. I'll bring up your belongings. There is a closet with a bucket across the hall to take care of your personal needs. Do you own something lighter to wear?"

The hat and hatpin bounced to the floor as she plopped back onto the cot. "My aunt always said I'd come to no good." Jail? House of ill repute? Even Aunt Melba's direst predictions were not as bad. She closed her eyes and willed away the tears that threatened. Not in front of him.

"No good? Things aren't that dire. So far you are only in an unpleasant hold place between here and a better future." The sheriff took her empty plate away and returned with a thin leather book. "This is Rose's journal. Maybe you can make more sense of her writing than I can. I'll come back up soon."

"May I have a lamp?" The light from the north window had faded as they ate.

The sheriff nodded and left her alone.

Emily waited until she heard the clang of the iron-bar door below before removing her jacket, pulling the least soiled of her handkerchiefs from her purse, and letting the tears flow.

Ma sat at his desk. "Donny says you have a female prisoner." She consulted the clock. "You've been up there for quite a while. Is there something you need to tell me?"

"Yes, but not here. Have you seen my deputy?" TJ set the tray and dishes on the table next to the door leading into the living quarters.

His mother raised a brow. "Just Donny. If he was older, he'd make a good one. I haven't seen Jerome."

"He must not be back. I sent him down to Glen Crossing this morning. Where is Donny?" TJ took his hat off his desk.

"I sent him home, where he belongs. He isn't old enough to be working for you all day long." Ma stood and gathered the tray.

"Not that you'll believe me, but I sent him home too, but I'd rather he work here than in one of the bars on Second Street. I'm going to go walk around the square and make sure everything is quiet. Then we can talk." Ma didn't need to know the jail was being watched by Belle's men.

The town square was quiet. The play at the opera house was already in session, and the bars and brothels on Second Street were less active than normal on a Thursday night. Bart leaned against the post in front of the Bull's-Eye. Cline wasn't visible, but that wasn't unusual. Belle kept him inside most nights to deal with customers as he was the more conversational of the two henchmen.

According to Aidan, both men kept the girls in line and were the source of more than one broken arm suffered by a wayward cowhand.

TJ tipped his hat at Bart as he continued down the street and back up the other side. Completing his circuit, TJ returned to the jail. For good measure, he walked around the jail and checked the outhouse. No one openly surveilled the jail, but the tingling at the back of his neck had TJ checking the area twice.

The sheriff's office was empty. The carpetbag and hatbox sat at the side of his desk. TJ added a pencil and paper and a lit lantern to the collection of things to take up. He'd have to return for another pitcher of water or risk dropping everything. After locking the gated door behind him, he whistled "Early in de Mornin'" as he walked up the stairs. Miss Wilson stood in the patch of fading light from the high window in the tower, arms crossed.

"Sorry, it took me longer than I thought." TJ set the lantern on the stone shelf.

Miss Wilson relieved him of his parcels. "Thank you for bringing these up so quickly."

Well-deserved sarcasm. TJ suppressed a grin. She'd need every ounce of the pluck she showed earlier to survive. "I'd like to say all my plans go as I want them to, but with only one deputy, I find my time is rarely my own."

"I understand. Thanks for the lamp. Would you mind bringing me more water?"

Miss Wilson handed him the empty pitcher.

"I'll bring your water back as fast as I can." TJ ran back down the stairs, careful to lock the door behind him to keep any unwanted visitors out of the jail level.

Ma was in the kitchen finishing up the dishes. "Ready to tell me?"

"As soon as I get some more water up there. She's from Boston, and this Texas heat is melting her faster than one of those half penny candles." TJ filled the pitcher and dashed out of the room. He stayed only long enough to make sure Miss Wilson didn't feel faint. She'd only nodded at him from the edge of the cot, where she sat studying the indecipherable pages of Rose's journal by lamplight. At least she had something to do. Most prisoners were left with nothing but to count the blue lines of the ticking or the bricks in the wall.

Ma sat in her favorite chair in the dog run where the breeze off the Brazos cooled the air. Bones lay at her feet, licking a ham bone.

TJ scratched the dog behind his ears. "Lazy Bones."

"When you found him a dozen years ago, you called him Skin and Bones." Ma gestured to the seat beside her.

"This is official business, Ma. I can't talk out here." TJ offered his arm and escorted his mother into the parlor, where he closed the windows before sitting down. "Miss Wilson is the woman Rose warned me about."

Ma blinked twice. "What is she doing up there?"

"She wouldn't believe me, so I arrested her, claiming she was a bank robber before she could enter Belle's."

"Thomas Jefferson Morgan! What would your father say?"

"I hope he would compliment me on my fast thinking and for saving a woman from a life full of pain." He didn't mention the handcuffs. Pa would have given him one of those silent stares that made him squirm.

Ma looked at the ceiling. "Why is she still up there?"

"Belle's men have been snooping around. I don't dare let Miss Wilson walk out of here, not after the way Rose died. Belle has Miss Wilson's trunk and wants a hundred dollars for its return unless a Ranger comes for both it and Miss Wilson. Keeping Belle thinking Miss Wilson is Pretty Polly gives me time. I was hoping this would be a simple case of getting the trunk and sending her back north, but she doesn't have a place to go." His plan sounded sane, didn't it? He couldn't tell from Ma's expression.

"Well, she can't spend the night up there. What if you or Jerome need to put someone in the other cell?"

His deputy would be a problem. Jerome gossiped too much for TJ to tell him the truth about Miss Wilson. "Where else can I put her? Not like I can take her to the hotel. I know our jail isn't the best accommodation, but she has the private cell."

"You mean the one that is hotter than a frying pan? Give her your room, and you sleep up there. I'd offer to share, but you know how loud I snore." Ma stood. "I'll go change your bedding."

TJ left the windows shut and headed back upstairs.

⟴

The bedroom the sheriff showed Emily was several degrees cooler than the cell upstairs, but still hot enough to qualify for a level of the inferno. A woman Emily assumed to be the sheriff's mother fluffed a pillow. The sheriff set her bag and hatbox just inside the door.

"Miss Wilson, I persuaded TJ to switch you rooms for the night. I'm Harriett Morgan, Widow Morgan, the sheriff's ma, or Harriett." Mrs. Morgan pulled Emily into a hug.

Arms pinned to her side, Emily's throat constricted. No way would she cry in front of the sheriff, who stood in the doorway. Emily stepped back before her emotions got the better of her. Until encircled in Mrs. Morgan's arms, she hadn't realized how desperate she was to feel loved. "I can sleep on the sofa in the parlor. You need not put the sheriff out."

"Nonsense. There is no point in you sweltering all night so TJ can keep you safe with his fool idea. Even if arresting you worked to get you away from Belle's clutches." Mrs. Morgan crossed her arms and looked pointedly at her son.

"You agree with him—I was in danger?" Even though his sincerity had convinced her that her job offer wasn't for a teaching job, she longed for confirmation, since such evil couldn't exist. Could it?

"Knowing Belle, you may still be. I don't agree with the way my son rescued you. Arresting a lady." Mrs. Morgan rolled her eyes. "But he is right. Better you be here than where Belle's men can find you."

The room tilted, and Emily sat on the end of the bed. A lightweight lace curtain fluttered in the screened window. "Will I be safe here?"

The sheriff reached out and pulled the curtain back. "We have bars on the windows, even down here. No one will come in. If you hear someone, come and get me. Bones will bark if he doesn't recognize someone. Problem is, he knows everyone in town, especially those who have been in the jail."

"Not a very good guard dog, then?" Emily took a deep breath. Sleeping in a strange man's bed was better than a jail cell. The bed looked much more inviting than the lumpy cot. "Where will you sleep?"

"Ma suggested I sleep upstairs, but I have a cot in my office. My deputy, Jerome, sometimes uses it. I'll sleep there. If someone needs me, I won't have to explain why I am in jail." One corner of his mouth raised in a half smile. The scar looked less sinister. "In the morning we can decide what else there is to do." He nodded and left the room.

Mrs. Morgan sat next to Emily on the bed. "TJ says you're from Boston."

Emily only nodded.

"You must be exhausted. All those days on the train. Do you have something to sleep in? I understand your trunk is at Belle's."

"I have a nightgown. I fear my traveling clothes are too heavy for summer in Texas." Not that light clothing mattered. The sheriff planned on her leaving soon.

Mrs. Morgan patted Emily's knee. "We'll worry about your clothes in the morning. Get what sleep you can. Don't worry. Everything will work out. The good Lord rose from the tomb in three days and changed the world. In three days, your world can change too."

Three days ago, she had been on a train and had a job to look forward to. Three days from now would be Sunday. Emily couldn't see how things could change for the better that fast. She nodded out of politeness.

"There is cool water in the pitcher. Drink what you can. If you are too hot, use the cloth to dampen your skin, just not too much. If the night is humid, too much water makes a body more miserable." Mrs. Morgan closed the door behind her.

Emily turned down the lamp, aware that if someone was watching through the lace curtain, they might be able to observe her bedtime preparations. Sitting on the bed, she waited for her eyes to adjust to the filtered moonlight in the room. The sounds of night insects filled the air. At least the windows had some screening on them, so the bugs couldn't join her in the room. Emily removed her traveling suit. The coins hidden in her corset had left circles of dampness in her chemise. With the heat, she was tempted not to put on her nightgown, as she only had the heavier one she'd packed for traveling. But in a strange room—a man's room—she didn't dare sleep in only her underthings.

Unpinning her hair, Emily realized how tangled it had become. She should have worn a hairnet. *Disheveled, bedraggled, unkempt.* Worse than all three… If she had a mirror…Never mind. Seeing her reflection might be worse than her imagination. After counting the precious pins, Emily ran her fingers through her hair to loosen the knots before brushing it out. The silence pressed upon her. Usually she had chatted with her roommates at this time of night. Other than the few nights she'd spent at her uncle's home over the Christmas holiday, she hadn't slept alone for years. The past week, she'd rarely been out of Amanda's or Mrs. Smyth's company.

Alone and lonely. How had that happened? Emily pulled her hair over her left shoulder and plaited the strands as various conversations floated through her head. Not real conversations, as no one's opinion countered her own. Would Mr. Brown's handsome face have deceived her school friends? Was the sheriff's smile intriguing? Why had she ignored the sheriff's first warning? And how was she going to get out of this predicament? Perhaps she could take up journal writing, like the woman whose journal the sheriff asked her to transcribe.

Whoever wrote the journal had used codes or ciphers. One entire section contained numbers and letters that appeared to be entirely random. Emily pictured the pages in her mind, but the letters floated around as sleep claimed her.

Until a woman screamed.

Emily sat up and joined her.

⚊⚊◆⚊⚊

Stupid cougar! TJ rolled over and hit the floor as the woman in his bedroom screamed in unison with the cat. Across the river, the cougar answered her. TJ grabbed his shirt off the hook and yanked it on as he crossed the office and hurried through the parlor. He knocked on the bedroom door. "Miss Wilson? Miss Wilson, it's a cougar."

The scream inside the room stopped. Good. Bursting into the bedroom probably wouldn't help matters.

"Miss Wilson? Don't worry. The cougar is on the other side of the river."

Something rustled on the other side of the door. Miss Wilson's frightened voice floated through the crack. "It sounded like a woman—a woman being hurt."

"Trust me. It's one of the cougars."

The door opened a half inch. "How can you be positive? How do you know the scream wasn't—" The question hung between them.

The cougar screamed again. The door opened another inch. On the other side, a wide eye stared out.

"Don't worry. She is a mile or so away, and she's never come into town."

"She?"

"A couple of the farmers have seen her. She's never come into the town." TJ repeated himself, not knowing how to reassure her.

"But it sounds like a woman."

"Uncanny, isn't it? But have you heard any words? People tend to shout 'Help!' when they are in danger."

The cat scream came again, fainter this time. Miss Wilson turned her face from the door in the direction of the window.

"I shouldn't have screamed." Miss Wilson's voice wobbled, as did the door.

"I've known grown men to panic the first time they hear a cougar scream. Being woken in the middle of the night by the she-cat is bound to upset anyone." Dogs barked across the river now, and the cougar answered them. "Will you be able to go back to sleep?"

Miss Wilson took a deep breath. "I'm still keyed up. My brain understands I am safe, but my heart doesn't want to believe it."

"We can talk, or I can see if Ma has left tea to cool overnight."

"Iced tea?"

"With lemon and sugar, but no ice."

The eye closed. "That does sound calming, but my dressing gown is in my trunk. I need a few minutes to dress."

"On the peg behind the door is a robe of mine. You could use it."

"But it's—"

"Miss Wilson, you won't sleep until you are calm. I won't sleep for worrying. My robe is large enough that you can wrap it around yourself twice. You'll be more than modest."

"Very well. Tea does sound good." She nodded and closed the door.

Before going to the kitchen, TJ lit one of the lamps. Light tended to calm people. Bones opened one eye. The dog only guarded the kitchen door in his imagination. The tea steeped in a large glass jar. TJ poured two tumblers full, adding the sugar as his mother had for years, then he added cool water to weaken the drink. No use staying up half the night due to strong tea.

Miss Wilson sat on the edge of one of the wingback chairs, back straight. If not for his robe pooled on the floor around her feet and the turned-up sleeves, she could have been in any society woman's parlor at midafternoon. TJ handed her one of the glasses before taking a seat in the nearest chair.

Miss Wilson took a sip. "Thank you very much. I appreciate your trying to calm me."

"No problem, ma'am. Gave me an excuse to have some of Ma's sweet tea. Usually by the time I get it, it's warm."

Miss Wilson tipped her head to the left and studied him. "Why is that?"

"Trouble never happens at convenient times, but I can usually count on it before sunrise, right after I've gone to bed, or when I sit down to a decent meal."

"My train arrived in time for supper, didn't it?" The corners of her mouth turned up in the smallest of smiles.

"There. You prove my point." He smiled, trying to assure her he felt no malice for his late meal. Quite the opposite feeling filled him. If he'd met her under better circumstances, and if she could stay—She tugged the collar of his robe tight under her chin. "I didn't mean to be trouble. But I suppose I always am."

TJ set his empty glass on the lamp table. "What do you mean?"

Miss Wilson shrugged. "Nothing. I think I should go back to bed now so you can sleep." She set her empty glass next to his and stood.

Following the manners Ma taught, TJ scrambled to his feet. "You don't need to rush on my account."

"I do. I've already commandeered your room. I shouldn't deny you what little sleep you have the chance to get."

TJ reached out to touch her arm, but she stepped back, and he dropped his. "Tell me, honestly, will you be able to sleep?"

"I think so. Sorry I woke you."

"You didn't. The cougar did. Good night, Miss Wilson. If you need me again…"

"Good night." The bedroom door clicked shut.

TJ leaned against the wall until the irrational desire to hold her until she wasn't scared faded. The squeak of the ropes of his bed indicated she had at least laid down. "Sleep well," TJ whispered before returning to the office cot and removing his shirt. He hung it on the hook and then plucked the shirt back off. For propriety's sake, it was better he keep the shirt on. Miss Wilson was not the kind of woman who would have seen many shirtless men. He'd already exposed her to a jail. TJ slid the shirt back on and buttoned the middle two buttons.

Apparently, protecting Miss Wilson included protecting her from him too. TJ lay on the cot, gazing up at the ceiling. He'd met the woman less than twelve hours ago. In twelve more she'd be gone. That was the proper course of action. Too bad Miss Wilson couldn't stay.

unshine filled the room. Emily sat up in the strange bed, surprised she'd fallen asleep. The last thing she remembered was a rooster crowing. Bits of dreams floated back to her. A screaming woman—no, a cougar. A conversation through a partially open door. Gasping, Emily covered her mouth. She checked her nightgown. The sheriff couldn't have seen anything, could he? No, his robe had hidden everything—but smelled too much of him for comfort. Mortification upon mortification. Bradford graduates did not have midnight conversations with men, even with a closed door between them. He must think she was every bit what he'd tried to rescue her from.

Having little choice, Emily dressed in the skirt and the cleaner of the two blouses she'd worn during her train journey. She rebraided her hair and rolled the plait into her hairnet, pinning the net tightly in place. The tiny shaving mirror hung too high on the wall for Emily to see much of her face, even standing on her toes. She tried hopping up and down and caught a glimpse of the dark circles under her eyes. Not surprising. Sleep hadn't come easily after her encounter with the sheriff last night. He almost touched her, and she'd nearly allowed him to. A man she had met only hours before. She'd slept in his bed, which smelled like him. There were scents she didn't recognize individually, nothing like the colognes the men at the Christmas ball wore. What on earth was she thinking? Heat flooded her face. Emily put her palms to her cheeks, willing the blush to end before she exited the room.

Enough of her silly thoughts. She straightened her skirt and lifted her chin. Today she had problems to solve, and thinking about a man wouldn't help. More than likely, the sheriff would only complicate them. Unsure of what to do with her carpetbag and hatbox, Emily stacked them by the door and surveyed the room to make sure nothing of her presence remained. She took a deep breath and opened the door to face the day.

Mrs. Morgan sat in the parlor reading a Bible. "Good morning. Did you sleep well? TJ says the cougar was screaming last night. Did you hear her?"

"Yes, didn't you hear me screaming back?"

"Can't say I did. At my age, nothing wakes me up. My daughter, Abigail, says it is because I can't hear anything over the sound of my own snoring. That's why I live with TJ. He doesn't mind the noise so much. Claims he can hardly hear me through the stone walls. Abigail's husband is much more truthful. Your breakfast is over on the side table. I put the last of my iced tea with it. Usually I have more, but TJ got thirsty in the middle of the night."

Hadn't he told his mother about their late-night talk? Emily lifted the tea towel on the tray to find a boiled egg and two biscuits with raisins in them.

"Come, sit and eat. I am sorry to say I am under strict instructions not to let you out of the house. If you need to use the necessary, I have a chamber pot under my bed."

Emily crossed the room to the chair she'd sat in last night. "Thank you for breakfast."

"Don't thank me. I get paid five cents for every meal I make for the prisoners." Mrs. Morgan fanned herself. "Not that you are really a prisoner…I mean, not a criminal or um—"

By morning light, her situation did have humor to it. "I need to confess I was a party to the theft of the tea last night."

A smile filled Mrs. Morgan's face. "The most honest prisoner to grace these walls. Confessed without me asking. Not that you needed to. I wrangled the truth out of TJ. Like I wouldn't notice two freshly washed glasses."

"Nothing happened. We just talked." *Unchaperoned in the wee hours of the morning, me in his robe.* If she were in Massachusetts, the wedding would already be planned.

"Of course, nothing happened. I wouldn't think otherwise. I remember the first time I heard one of those cougars scream. I near jumped out of my skin. My poor husband couldn't calm me down for hours. I was sure there was a murder happening right outside the door. That was back in the day when the Comanche still gathered on the peak. Although we never had any serious problems with the Indians, one did hear stories. If my tea helped calm you, I say it went to good use."

"I'll know better next time."

"Are you staying long enough for there to be a next time?" Mrs. Morgan set aside her Bible.

Emily took another sip of her tea to give her time to compose an answer. "I don't know. I need to stay long enough to get my trunk back, and I need someplace to go and money to get there." She spread the last of the creamy butter on the biscuit.

"TJ went to send a cable to my oldest son, GW, for George Washington, of course, who is with the Rangers. If all goes well, you'll have your trunk back in a day or two."

Emily set her empty plate on the side table. "Then I need to find a new teaching position. I'm apprehensive to do so. What if my next employer is as unscrupulous?"

"I would suggest you write the local pastor or sheriff. They'd know if the offer was valid." Mrs. Morgan gathered the tray from the sideboard. "I'll go put these in the kitchen. I left my chamber pot in the corner of my room. Please don't leave these three rooms."

"I understand, and thank you."

Alone in the empty parlor, Emily was assaulted by dozens of worries. She picked up the worn Bible and opened it to a random verse, hoping to find some comfort.

"Then I turned, and lifted up mine eyes, and looked, and behold a flying roll." The first verse of Zechariah chapter 5 wasn't very comforting.

Mrs. Manning claimed they always found the verse they needed by the third try. Emily closed her eyes, opened the book, and pointed to another verse. The word at the top of the page jumped out at her. *Psalms*. This would be the one. The Psalms always bolstered her soul. Emily focused on the verse her index finger had landed on. "Kiss the Son…"

Her finger got caught in the book as she slammed it shut. Emily checked to make sure she was still alone. She'd gotten verses like the roll one or some of the begats, which made no sense. Reading a verse about kissing in the Morgan home in their Bible brought to mind imaginings of last night. Emily was just as curious as any other woman about the process, but this verse could not be her answer! Mrs. Manning had always said to give finding an answer three tries. The last time Emily peeked through her eyelashes to make sure she didn't choose Song of Solomon.

Psalms again. If chapter 37 had one word about kissing…

"Trust in the Lord, and do good; so shalt thou dwell in the land, and verily thou shalt be fed."

Should I stay in Texas? Emily set the Bible back on the table, more confused than when she began.

⬦

The westbound train whistled in the distance as TJ approached the station. The door to the telegraph office stood ajar to circulate the early morning air. "Morning, Saunders. I need to send a wire."

"Official sheriffing business or personal?" Mr. Saunders adjusted his glasses and handed TJ the form.

He couldn't send a cable to just any Texas Ranger. "A bit of both. Put the charge on my personal account."

> **GW,**
> **Have prisoner. Please come. Ma sends love.**
> **TJ**

He didn't dare write more. Mr. Saunders might not talk to everyone, but there was no telling if Belle and her men would find out about the telegram's contents. On the surface, it would look like he'd contacted the Rangers about Miss Wilson. 'Ma sends love' was a signal they had used a couple of times to tell the other the situation was dire.

Mr. Saunders read the paper. "Is this all? I heard you caught some female bank robber last night. Sure you don't want me putting more in?"

TJ shook his head. "You never know who is listening to the wires. I think it is best handled this way."

"Seems if you took the part off about your ma sending her love, you could charge the telegram to the sheriff's account. It's going to Waco, correct?"

"Yes, to the Rangers in Waco. But I'll pay for the wire and not risk angering Ma. Mr. Saunders, you have never had

65

Ma's iced tea or honey cake, have you? It is worth the money to not anger her. Keep the charge personal."

Mr. Saunders grinned. "I would do the same for my own ma's cooking. That will be $1.75."

TJ laid down his money as the train from Fort Worth pulled into the station. "Thank you, Saunders."

Only one passenger disembarked. Judge Granger. TJ tipped his hat but didn't approach. Workers off-loaded stacks of crates. The stock boy from the general store and Bart waited with wagons nearby. Bart sneered. TJ tapped the brim of his hat, turned, and walked to the engine. The engineer and boiler man were busy checking the boiler. Reaching the end of the platform, TJ turned to walk back.

Bart strode purposely toward him, a newspaper in hand.

"Sheriff, look at the *Daily Herald*'s headline. Looks like you didn't catch Pretty Polly, after all. Some Ranger up in Denison caught her coming out of a saloon. Guess you have to let that pretty filly go." Bart held up the paper.

PRETTY POLLY NABBED

Of all the rotten timing. It was hard to argue with the daily Dallas newspaper. Couldn't Polly have waited until next week to be caught? TJ took the offered paper, hoping there was some shred of doubt to the story. According to the reporter, the Rangers had positively identified Pretty Polly using an eyewitness from a recent robbery in Dallas. TJ folded the newspaper and handed it back to Bart. "Looks like I made a mistake. I'd better get back to the jail and free my suspect."

"Hope she has the hundred dollars for her trunk. Belle won't hold the trunk for too long without opening it and removing any valuables Miss Wilson may have packed. She was hopping mad you took her new girl from her. Special order, she was. Not very often we can get a dove with a genuine college education. Belle's got customers with discerning tastes. Business has been hurting since Rose ran off with a drifter."

TJ ignored the blatant lie. "Remind Belle the trunk doesn't belong to her, even if she is holding it as collateral. If the trunk is damaged or tampered with, I can arrest her."

Bart took a step forward, the air filling with stale cigar smoke as he spoke. "You are getting really good at making false arrests. Wonder what Judge Granger will think of that."

TJ held his face steady, refusing to even blink.

Bart held his stance another minute before stepping back. "I'll let Belle know you'll be wandering by to apologize."

The train whistle blew. TJ walked around the station to the telegraph office. "Saunders, did you get the wire sent?"

"Of course, Sheriff Morgan."

"I have another one to send." TJ's pencil hovered above the form.

> GW,
> Mistaken. Abby misses you.
> TJ

Hopefully that would keep GW wherever he was. The line about their sister was a gamble, but she was forever blowing little things, like a spider in her room, out of proportion. All TJ could do was to send the wire to the Ranger office in Waco. With any luck, his brother would get both wires at the same time. When GW learned the truth about his arresting Miss Wilson, there would be no living it down as GW, would like the president he'd been named for to have a better solution. GW possessed the rare quality of finding humor in everything. It might even be worse than when he had to tell Miss Wilson she was free to leave when he knew she was in danger.

The sheriff stormed into the parlor. "We've got a problem."

Emily set aside the encoded journal and waited for news of the latest calamity.

"The real Pretty Polly was arrested the day before yesterday." TJ handed her a newspaper.

Emily stared at the sketch on the front page. Pretty Polly didn't look a bit like her, at least not in this artist's rendition. "I don't see that my problem is any different from an hour ago. I am still not a felon. Belle still has my trunk, and I am without a job. The only difference is Belle now knows I am not a bank robber." Only everything *was* different. An hour ago she had hope that there was a plan that would work to get the trunk back and she'd have enough money to travel to another job. The black-and-white newspaper had destroyed all hues of hope, as there was no color left.

The sheriff took the seat opposite her. "And my plan to get your trunk back has failed."

"There is that. How long do you think she will give me to come up with one hundred dollars?" Time. All she needed was time. There must be a job for a shopkeeper or a seam-stress.

"You? I'm the one who lost your trunk for you. I'll find a way to get the money." Belatedly, he took off his hat.

"Sheriff, I don't rely on others to deal with my problems." Even without her belongings, she need not be a beggar.

"And I suppose you happen to have one hundred dollars sitting around?" He leaned back in his chair.

"Just like you have a fund set aside to rescue women who accidentally accept jobs to work in houses of ill repute when they meant to teach school." Emily crossed her arms. All she had left were a few shreds of dignity. She would get her trunk back without his help.

"Out of curiosity, how much money do you have?"

"Fifty-seven dollars and thirty-three cents. Both my uncles gave me a graduation present. I spent a few dollars to subsidize what Mrs. Leblanc sent for the trip." All but a dollar of her funds remained hidden in the secret pockets of her corset.

"How much of your own money did you spend to get here?"

Emily kept meticulous records, so she didn't need to stop to calculate. "Including food, $13.67. I was fortunate I could share lodging with my friend and her chaperone, but a train derailment, not ours, closed the tracks for two days. In all, we arrived four days late."

Sheriff Morgan tapped his chin. "Belle is charging you double for her expenses, which didn't cover all of yours. If you charged her double for your expenditures, that would be—"

"$27.34."

The sheriff raised his brows.

"Sorry, I didn't mean to interrupt. Math comes quickly for me." Emily ducked her head. She knew better than to bother a person while they were thinking.

"Working numbers in my head is not as easy as on paper. So, what is one hundred dollars less that amount?"

"$73.66 less the money I have. I need $15.32 to buy back my trunk. Which means I would still be penniless, with no foreseeable way to earn the money to leave town or pay for room and board." Emily struggled to keep her tone even. If she had her trunk, she would have nearly enough money to get back to Boston but would be in the same predicament of having no place to go. Next job, she wouldn't rely on the newspaper ad and the atlas. She wouldn't apply for another teaching position without some knowledge of the school. The worst thing about returning to Boston would be her aunt's censure. Admitting failure would be nearly as bad as if the sheriff had truly arrested her.

"I'm very sorry I didn't manage to get your trunk when I arrested you." The sheriff leaned forward, his scar looking almost like a tear path.

"As you pointed out last night, better that you got me out of there than my belongings. There are other ways I could have lost my possessions—fire or theft. Perhaps it is better that I…" Emily swallowed, unable to finish the sentence. The more she thought about things, the worse they appeared. As much as she wanted her father's trunk or her mother's hairbrush, having them wouldn't mean a thing had she woken up in a different place this morning.

"Better that you what, dear?" Mrs. Morgan swept into the room. An older woman dressed in black followed her.

The sheriff relinquished his seat to the newcomer. "Miss Wilson and I were discussing how to get her trunk back, as my original plan won't work. I was going to have GW come and demand the trunk. Belle said she would release it to the Rangers if they came to get my prisoner."

The woman in black fanned herself with the newspaper. "And since your prisoner isn't a prisoner but one of

Belle's girls, whom you wrongfully incarcerated, that won't happen."

Emily jumped up. "I am not one of her girls!"

"Of course you aren't, dear." Mrs. Morgan put an arm around her. "Mrs. Reese was repeating the gossip."

"Gossip? Are people saying I'm a…a…um—" Emily fell back into her seat.

"A soiled dove, a woman of the evening, a prostitute? Not everyone repeats what they hear. But so far, Belle has been the source of all information about the pretty woman who got off the train yesterday and willingly left with one of her men. She has been spreading tales faster than a skunk can spray a nosey dog. With no story to counter the tale, the gossip is all there is to tell. I came to see for myself what manner of woman you are. From your blush, you aren't one of her girls and never will be. I best take you under my wing now." The older woman leaned on her silver-handled black cane as she stood.

Emily blinked at the woman. Who was this Mrs. Reese?

"Didn't you hear me, child? We need to get on fixing this. Don't sit there. Put your best foot forward."

Emily stood.

"Is that your best dress?" Though Mrs. Reese stood four inches shorter than Emily, there was nothing small about her presence.

Emily smoothed the skirt. "I have the dress I wore yesterday and this. Everything else I own is in my trunk."

"Well, hurry and get something out of your trunk."

Emily opened her mouth to explain, but the sheriff beat her to it. "She can't. Belle has the trunk and will only return it after Miss Wilson pays her back for the train ticket from Boston and an additional fifty dollars for Belle's other losses."

Mrs. Reese pointed her cane at the sheriff. "You mean to tell me you let Belle do that? I'll have to change my opinion as to your intelligent idea to keep Miss Wilson out of Belle's clutches. Oh, don't look at me that way. You know your ma can't keep a secret from me. But she didn't tell until after we saw the paper. Why else do you think I came over here? To fix what you can't."

Emily looked from the sheriff to the widow. "Pardon me, but how can you fix things?" *My reputation, trunk, and future seem rather unfixable.*

Mrs. Morgan removed her arm from around Emily. "My apologies. I should have introduced my friend. Mrs. Roberta Reese is among the youngest of the Alamo widows, which understandably gives her a certain amount of influence. Since Elizabeth Crockett's passing twenty years ago, Roberta has been our town's sole link to those brave men and our claim to fame."

"All fuss and nonsense, if you ask me. However, if I can use my fame to help someone, I'll do it. Do you have a hat? Best get it."

Emily looked at the sheriff and pointed at his bedroom door. He nodded once. Emily crossed the room and opened the door.

"Why ever are you going into a man's room?"

Mrs. Morgan took responsibility for explaining while Emily ducked inside to get her hat and gloves. The mirror was no help at all as only the top of her hat was visible. She closed the door behind her as she reentered the parlor.

"I suggest you not divulge your sleeping accommodations when you tell people the real story." Mrs. Reese swept out of the room, Emily racing to keep up. Obviously, the cane was naught but a foil.

⟭◆⟬

TJ shook his head. If Miss Wilson had left with any other person in town, he would worry about her well-being. But there wasn't a soul for one hundred miles who would cross Mrs. Reese. According to some folks, she'd even convinced the Comanche chief to see things her way and leave her and her child alone in exchange for a loaf of bread and a jar full of ginger cookies. Some claimed it was chicken and dumplings and corn pone.

"You should have your room back tonight. If Mrs. Reese likes Miss Wilson, she'll ask her to take a position as—how do the English put it—a lady's companion? She claims to be lonely in the house, with only her maid and her cook." Lonely? Mrs. Reese took in more strays than Widow Wells took in animals. At last count, Mrs. Wells owned fifteen dogs and twenty-three cats. Mrs. Reese collected all kinds of lost souls, but mostly women down on their luck.

Ma folded the newspaper left on the table and handed it to TJ. "You can go put this in your office. Knowing Mrs. Reese, I'd go check on them in an hour. Belle may need rescuing after Mrs. Reese is done getting Miss Wilson's belongings."

TJ kissed his mother on the cheek and went into his office. He put the newspaper in the drawer with the old wanted posters, as well as Pretty Polly's now outdated one.

Donny sauntered into the office. "Folks are saying all sorts of things today. Some say you deliberately arrested a woman knowing she was not an outlaw. Mr. Carter says Belle's all stirred up about it. One of her customers wanted a woman of intelligence. Miss Rose was plenty smart. That is why she hated working for Belle. I don't think any smart woman would. But it's hard to tell when someone is smart, ain't it? I mean, I think you are plenty smart, but lots of folk are saying you were plum loco to arrest any woman." Donny pulled a stool up to the side of the desk and sat down.

"So, why am I crazy?"

"Mostly because you got Belle really angry. And nobody tangles with Miss Belle and wins. A man would have a better chance in a pit of copperheads. Oh, and I'm supposed to give you this." Donny slapped a telegram on the desk.

TJ turned the paper over. "Next time you deliver a telegram, hand it over before the gossip."

"What's the fun in that? I'm going back out to follow Mrs. Reese and the lady you arrested. I like hearing what people say when they walk away."

"Her name is Miss Wilson, and it is rude to eavesdrop."

Donny stuck out his lower lip. "Aw, but that is the only way to learn things."

"There is also asking questions." TJ unfolded the telegram. GW wasn't coming. A small feeling of relief filled his mind. The teasing that was sure to come the next time he saw his brother would be slightly delayed now.

"Ma says I ask too many questions."

"Will you let me know if Mrs. Reese and Miss Wilson get in any trouble?"

Donny hopped off the stool and saluted. "Yes, sir!"

Fifteen minutes later, TJ tucked the last of the paperwork he had been catching up on into his desk, checked his gun, and left on his morning rounds.

Jerome dismounted his horse in front of the jail. "Morning, Sheriff. I heard a funny story over at the mercantile."

"I bet you did. Give me a half hour to do a round of the square, and I'll tell you the truth of it."

"So, you did arrest one of Belle's new girls?"

"Nope." TJ crossed the street to the hotel side of the street. Miss Wilson would never be one of Belle's girls.

Mr. Davis swept the boardwalk in front of the proud three-story establishment. He paused when he saw TJ. "Morning, Sheriff. You did a good thing yesterday. Peculiar, but a good thing saving that sweet girl from Belle's clutches. Will you tell Mrs. Reese I don't have a job for the girl, but if she is willing to take in laundry, I'll pay her a fair price?"

"I'll let her know." Even a generous wage for doing the hotel's laundry would not be enough for Miss Wilson to live on.

As TJ reached Hiramsville Mercantile, the women chatting on the boardwalk dispersed, ignoring him. TJ ducked into the store, and all talk ceased. In the far corner, Old Mr. Conway narrowed his eyes. Philip Tarr stood behind the counter but didn't greet him.

"Morning, Phil."

Mr. Tarr turned away.

"Problem?"

Mr. Conway pushed his chair back from the checkerboard he sat in front of. "We don't have any use for a sheriff who breaks laws for a soiled dove. Even if she is as pretty as a new spring day. Ya had her all night without even paying."

"That is not what happened. I arrested the schoolteacher before she made the biggest mistake of her life. Never once did I act in a way to shame my pa."

"That's not what Cline said. According to him, she even spent the night in your bedroom. Saw her through your window this morning."

"Ma had me give her my room last night and banished me to the cot in my office. You've known me my whole life. Do you believe I would dishonor any woman?"

"Your ma was there? The whole night?"

"She got home around seven thirty, around the time Donny left."

Mr. Conway crossed the room and peered up into TJ's face. "So you never touched the woman?"

"Not in the way you are implying. I handcuffed her, so, of course, I touched her to get her out of the back of the wagon and such, but nothing inappropriate." There had been the moment on the stairs before he'd removed her cuffs and last night when he wanted to pull her into his arms, but neither incident was anything near what they accused him of doing.

Mr. Conway stared at TJ. The silence in the room weighed heavy. The old man didn't blink. "Like I told ya, Phil. This boy ain't the kind to take advantage of a girl. His pa would figure out a way to get back on this side of them pearly gates and whoop him if he did. Don't know why you'd take Cline's word over his."

Mr. Tarr grunted. "You got to admit, the whole thing is mighty strange. Arresting one of Belle's girls and all."

TJ leaned over the counter. "I've seen the letters Belle sent her 'new girl,' as you call her. Not once did Belle even hint at the true nature of her establishment. They lured Miss Wilson here under false pretenses, with the promise of a teaching job. As a recent graduate of Bradford College in Massachusetts, Miss Wilson is qualified to teach at any school. The only thing peculiar is why good folks like you are painting dispersions on Miss Wilson's character."

"Maybe, maybe not, but I am not giving that woman a job here." Mr. Tarr pointed to the sign in his window. "My wife and I run a proper establishment."

Only through the front door, that was. Both Belle and Harold, the other bar and brothel owner, regularly purchased supplies at the door in the alley, the same way he'd witnessed Phil entering Belle's. Not trusting himself to keep a civil tongue, TJ tipped his hat and left. How many people believed Phil's version over Mrs. Reese and Miss Wilson's? The sooner he could get Miss Wilson to leave town, the better life would be for her.

The front entry to the Bull's-Eye left little doubt as to the purpose of the building. If she had seen this last night, there would have been no need for Sheriff Morgan to handcuff her. The reflection in the mirror over the bar confirmed that her face was red with embarrassment. The color intensified as she realized the significance of the scandalous carvings on the gilded mirror frame. Emily turned her gaze to the only safe thing in the room—Mrs. Reese's back.

Cline came out of a back room. "We are not open."

How had she thought the burly man's face somewhat handsome yesterday? His sneer reeked of evil intent.

"Tell Belle that Mrs. Reese is here to see her and if she doesn't come out, I'll park myself at the front door until she does."

"I said we are not open."

"And if I am sitting in front of the door, you won't open later. As I understand it, Friday is your busiest day or night. And no man on this side of Dallas is going to cross one of the last widows of the Alamo even to get to Belle's beauties. Go get Belle."

Cline wavered for a moment before disappearing into the back. A girl with a mottled face scrubbed a table in the far corner.

"Nellie?" Mrs. Reese crossed the room. "I thought you said you were going to find a better job."

"There ain't no one gonna hire the likes of me. Belle pays me decent, and the men stay away from me. My ma done see to that. 'Sides, who else gonna take care of the girls and make sure they eat right? Gotta have food with all the opium and whiskey." On closer inspection, Emily could see the girl was probably fifteen or sixteen. The brown, shapeless dress she wore was of fine cotton, the loose fit practical for the heat as well as for hiding any bit of femininity.

"Nellie, I've offered to hire you a half dozen times."

"And I'll keep turning ya down. I got my reasons. People respects you, Miz Reese, your husband having died at the Alamo and all. People see my face and look away, or learn my ma worked in the cribs and walk on the other side of the street. You don't need someone like me causing people to look down on you."

"Nevertheless, my offer still stands. If you ever need a better place to go, you come to my place."

Nellie shook her head and pointed at Emily. "You shouldn't have brought her. Belle had herself a conniption last night. I had to sweep up two vases and three broken liquor bottles. Told Daisy she had to read a book or lose this week's wages. She wanted an educated girl, and now that Rose done gone, Belle got no one."

Mrs. Reese narrowed her eyes. "She will find someone else."

"Hush, no one needs to know I got me some education. But you changed the subject. Belle's determined to have the Boston woman upstairs working. That be why she is spreading gossip. Give her no choice. And if that don't work—"

Nellie stopped mid-sentence as her employer swept into the room dressed head to toe in fuchsia silk.

"Mrs. Reese, Cline tells me you have some business. And, Miss Wilson, what a delightful surprise. Are you ready to work after your night in jail?"

Emily looked Belle in the eye. She couldn't think of her as Mrs. LeBlanc anymore. "No, I am here to claim my property."

"As I explained last night, you cost me a great deal of money. I want you to pay me for my trouble."

"You sent me fifty dollars to travel here, an amount that, due to a line closure, was inadequate to cover the expense. I will only reimburse what you spent on me."

Belle pulled a small book and a short pencil from her pocket. "I sent you fifty for travel expenses. Then the buckboard and horse rental were four bits. And I commissioned three dresses for you."

Emboldened after an hour at Mrs. Reese's side, Emily stepped forward. "We never discussed any clothing commissioned for me or otherwise. And since you had no idea of my height or measurements, I fail to see how you could have had them made before I arrived."

Belle walked in a circle around Emily. "The dresses are mostly done. You told me you were, and I quote, 'three inches over five feet, of average build.' In another letter, you indicated you had dark-blonde hair and blue eyes, so I would recognize you at the train station. For the type of dresses you'd wear working for me, that was enough information."

Anger surged through Emily's veins. Each beat of her heart echoed in her ears. "Still, they were never discussed or agreed upon, nor do I believe they are the type of garment I am likely to wear anyplace. They are entirely your own folly."

"Then there were the fees for the advertisements."

"You mean your lies? Teaching position at Hiramsville Female Academy. There is no such thing." Emily crossed her arms.

Belle stepped forward, leaving only inches between them. "I did not lie. You will be able to teach a great many things to many people. You may have to take lessons from Daisy first. She is by far our best teacher here, and she never even finished a year of schooling."

Heat filled Emily's face as she lifted her chin. "I agreed to teach English and history, not, not—"

"Read your letter's carefully, dear. I only asked you to teach. Assumptions as to the subject matter are entirely your fault."

"You knew I wouldn't agree to working on your terms and deliberately misled me."

Belle's smile didn't reach her dark eyes. "And you accepted my money."

"I want my trunk back."

"I still say you owe me one hundred dollars." Belle flicked her fan.

"Clarabelle White, I know for a fact you can do sums better than that." Mrs. Reese used her cane to insert herself into the small space between Emily and the madame. "You may have spent fifty dollars on her train ticket, but she had to supplement your money with her own when her train was delayed. Whatever she spent cancels out what you spent on the so-called dresses. As for renting a buckboard, you could have used your own."

"How dare you call me that?" Belle spat the words through clenched teeth.

"You mean the name your mother and father gave you? Clarabelle White is a perfectly respectable name. But then, you aren't respectable people anymore, are you? Best you not drag your father's name through the mud."

Belle raised her hand as if to slap Mrs. Reese, but the older woman caught her by the wrist. "Think twice before you assault an old woman. I believe there are laws against it."

"The judge won't convict me." Belle sneered, the paints and powders she wore wrinkling and cracking.

"I wouldn't be too sure of that. Judge Granger is up for reelection. He might find the votes Mrs. Reese can sway mean more to him than one of your employees' devoted time." The sheriff's deep voice came from the doorway behind Emily. All three women turned to face him.

Belle yanked her hand out of Mrs. Reese's grasp. "Are you going to arrest me, Sheriff? I didn't slap her."

"I don't arrest people unless they give me reason to."

"Like last night? Isn't it a crime to falsely arrest a lady?" Belle pointed her fan at the sheriff.

"If Miss Wilson wants to file charges, she can. I will maintain there was a case of mistaken identity."

Belle raised a painted brow and turned her attention back to Emily.

"I have no intention of filing charges. The arrest was a fortuitous mistake. Now, about the trunk. I believe I owe you fifty dollars."

"Fifty dollars it is, but only if you can pay the full amount right here, right now." Belle smiled slowly as silence filled the room.

Emily swallowed before answering. "May I return in five minutes with the money?"

Belle shook her head and patted the tabletop. "Here. Now."

⟨◆⟩

TJ felt in his pocket, wishing he had stuck the twenty-dollar gold piece in there. Mrs. Reese opened her bag.

Miss Wilson looked wildly around the room and out the window, then leaned over and whispered to Mrs. Reese. Mrs. Reese nodded.

"I have the money on my person, but not easily accessible. Do you have a place I can extract the money in private?"

Belle waved her hand in the direction of the stairs. "You are welcome to use a room up there."

"No." Mrs. Reese objected in unison with TJ. He didn't trust Miss Wilson would be allowed to come back downstairs. What had Mrs. Reese been thinking to allow Miss Wilson to come here in the first place?

Miss Wilson fumbled with the broach pinned at her collar. "Sheriff, if you would be so good as to turn your back on me and deter anyone from entering the room. Mrs. Reese, I may need your aid."

TJ turned to face the door. She must have the money in her clothing. He'd heard of women sewing money into the seams of their petticoats and whatnot. He turned his attention to the door into the back rooms. It was far more likely that Bart or Cline would enter the room than an early customer. He ignored the sounds coming from the direction of the women. Miss Wilson groaned, and Belle laughed. Coins clinked on the table.

"Ooh la la. You could make so much money with—"

Mrs. Reese cut her off. "Clarabelle! Miss Wilson has made it perfectly clear that she doesn't want to work here."

"You could work at the bar serving drinks. Not a foot upstairs. You'd make a bundle in tips, especially if you wear the dresses I commissioned."

"Never." Miss Wilson's voice sent a chill down TJ's spine.

"Why not? You have what you need." Cline's voice came from the landing at the top of the stairs. "A man would pay just to look at you."

There was a gasp, presumably from Miss Wilson, as Mrs. Reese thumped her cane on the floor.

TJ turned to stare down the blackguard.

"Oh, Sheriff, you missed a good show." Cline leaned over the railing, a lecherous grin on his face.

TJ pushed a table aside, trying to reach the stairs.

"TJ!" Mrs. Reese's yell stopped him in his tracks. "Will you be so good as to help Cline with Miss Wilson's trunk? Deliver it to my house. She'll be staying with me."

TJ turned to acknowledge the order with a nod.

Miss Wilson's cameo rested somewhat lopsided at her collar, her face red, her chin still held high. "If you will get my trunk now, please? I want to ascertain that my belongings haven't been damaged."

Belle scooped the money off the table. "Cline will show you where it is."

Cline descended the stairs and crossed to the doorway to the back rooms.

"Not you, Sheriff. Miss Wilson." Belle counted the money in her hand.

Miss Wilson took a step forward, but Mrs. Reese stopped her. "Clarabelle, Miss Wilson is under my protection. She stays with me."

"How is she going to get her trunk?"

"I'll go," said TJ.

"I'm afraid you can't do that. Remember, you can only go into the public rooms unless you have my permission or a warrant." Belle grinned in triumph.

TJ crossed his arms. No way was Miss Wilson going back into who knows what room with Cline. They'd be back to where they were last evening.

"I've never seen your back rooms, Clarabelle." Mrs. Reese hooked her arm through Miss Wilson's. "I wonder if they are as clean as Harold's old place. We used his bar and hotel for a hospital during the Indian skirmishes in '51. Place burned down before the last war." Mrs. Reese often marked time by wars, battles, or skirmishes. "Cline, open the door for a woman. Didn't your mother teach you any manners?"

Cline obliged and held the door open as Mrs. Reese and Miss Wilson passed through.

"Do leave the door open. I have my reputation to think of." Mrs. Reese tapped her cane loudly.

Cline exchanged looks with Belle, who gave the slightest of nods. TJ stood outside the doorway but lost sight of the women when they followed Cline around a corner.

"Not one step, Sheriff." Belle placed herself at the entrance to the hallway, blocking his view.

TJ nodded. Anything he wanted to say would make the situation worse. The ticking of the clock on the shelf behind the bar filled the room. Every other sound came from the street. What was taking so long?

Belle tapped her right foot in time with every other tick-tock of the clock.

A scraping sound came from the hallway. Belle spun around. "My floor! Miss Wilson, stop scraping that across my floor!"

Belle was blocking his view. "Cline, what were you think-ing! Pick up the trunk and take it out to the boardwalk. Don't you dare scrape another inch out of my Linoleum. I ordered it clear from England! Nellie, what are you doing helping her? See if you can polish those scrapes!"

Cline came through the doorway, hefting the chest on his shoulder. TJ followed him to the saloon entrance, where the bouncer dropped the old steamer trunk. "It's your problem now, Sheriff. Cline bumped TJ's shoulder as he turned back into the building.

Mrs. Reese and Emily joined him. TJ refrained from scold-ing them both.

Miss Wilson ran her hand over the trunk and glanced back into the bar. "It doesn't look damaged. I'll wait to open it in private."

The wily widow had won. Miss Wilson was safe. For the moment.

⟨⬦⟩

Seven dollars and thirty-three cents. No matter how many times Emily counted it, the coins added up to the same amount as yesterday when she'd paid Belle to get the trunk back. The money would be gone in a week if she had to stay at the hotel. The only item in the open trunk that might fetch some money was the silver sugar bowl, a wedding gift to her great-grandmother, made by Paul Revere. Her mother's silver-handled hairbrush might fetch a little. She was not desperate enough to sell either heirloom, even if she was temporarily living off Mrs. Reese's thinly disguised charity.

Mrs. Reese had offered Emily the position of lady's companion after they'd found the boardinghouse curiously full despite the *Room for Let* sign in the window. Emily doubted Mrs. Reese needed a companion. She hadn't yesterday after they'd retrieved her trunk and Mrs. Reese left Emily to unpack in the pink-papered room while she went to visit a neighbor. Nor was Emily needed this morning after breakfast when Mrs. Reese announced she had calls to make. Mrs. Reese employed a maid of all work, as well as a cook, leaving Emily with little to do to pay the widow back for the room and board—unless reading a chapter from *Great Expectations* after dinner counted as work.

Work—another problem.

Becky, the maid, tapped at the door. "Mrs. Reese has returned and asks if you will come read to us again."

Last night's reading had been a singular experience as Mrs. Reese invited the maid and cook to come sit and listen too. From the conversation flowing between the women, Emily gathered they often sat and talked. Emily tried to picture Aunt Melba or any family she knew in Massachusetts doing the same with their domestics. From Becky's use of the word *us,* it was to be a nightly event.

Emily returned the coins to her purse and followed Becky out to the porch, where Mrs. Reese and the cook, Thelma, sat talking. Emily picked up the book in her chair before sitting. Becky poured them some lemonade.

"Emily, dear, tell me about your day. Was your search for employment successful?" Mrs. Reese sipped from her glass.

"No. It was much like yesterday when I inquired about the job advertised in the dressmaker's window. Either they forgot to take the sign down or I am unsuitable for the job. I fear the only position open is that of a laundress."

Mrs. Reese tapped her cane on the wooden floorboard. "Pompous pack of pretentious pretenders."

Emily smiled at the creative alliteration, as did Thelma. Becky giggled.

"Well, it is true. Perhaps things will look up after church tomorrow," said Mrs. Reese.

"What would church have to do with it?"

"When you sit in Mrs. Reese's pew with us and lightning doesn't strike the building, a few people will have to revise their opinion of you." Becky almost made it through her sentence without giggling. "The first time Mrs. Reese dragged me into church, three women fainted."

"I didn't drag you in, I pushed." Mrs. Reese gave Becky a motherly smile. "I trust I will not need to coerce you to attend, Emily?"

"Er, no, of course not." Emily hadn't given any thought to not going to church any more than going. After all, it was what one did on Sundays.

"Tomorrow is a picnic day. I made three pies and two cakes today as the Q to Z families are in charge of the deserts," said Thelma. "If we put you at the serving table, the pompous pack will have to speak with you."

"Either that or go without the best desserts in town. I don't care how much Mrs. Younger brags about her cook, her pies are simply no comparison. Mrs. Carter's cake, though delicious, is unlikely to be servable after her boys are done with it," said Mrs. Reese.

"Her boys?" Emily asked.

"Poor Mrs. Carter has seven boys who are always hungry. Last time we had desserts, she brought a cake, but when she cut into it, the entire thing was hollow. The boys had eaten it from the bottom up, like a mole in the cabbage garden." Becky laughed again. Emily liked the girl's laugh and joined in.

Mrs. Reese finished her drink and checked her pin watch. "Emily, will you read for us before the sun sets? I hate to light a lantern outside at night. They attract so many moths." The screened-in porch kept them away, but there was something disconcerting about them crawling on the screen.

Emily opened the book and began to read. If she had to accept charity, at least it was from people who accepted her.

The razor had nicked his chin again. TJ took a deep breath. This always happened when he rushed his shaving.

"Hurry up, son. I don't want to be late to church." Ma called from the parlor.

"I'm hurrying as fast as I can." Ten arrests last night and all from the Bull's-Eye. After the fifth, TJ asked Jerome to stay at Belle's to watch things. Thank heavens the law required all saloons to be closed on Sunday. Although it would probably give Belle time to come up with a more creative retaliation than paying a bunch of drunk cowboys to shoot up her sign—a fact he'd learned from the tenth, who protested his arrest because "the lady promised a gold double eagle if he could hit dead center." TJ had been tempted to shoot the sign himself, but instead he marched into Belle's and announced that the only space left in the jail was the isolation cell, and that it was hotter than high noon in August in there, and that anyone who shot the sign from then on would stay in the cell until Monday morning with whatever other idiots chose to break the law.

They hadn't had any problems after that. Perhaps he should make it the permanent policy for shooting the stupid sign.

"TJ? We are going to be late!"

"Coming." TJ toweled off his face and grabbed his Bible. They were in no danger of missing the opening of the meeting, only of Ma being able to observe the other congregants coming in.

Whispers filled the chapel. No one played at the harmonium to drown them out. Mrs. Reese stood near the pulpit, talking to Reverend Green. She beckoned Miss Wilson to join her. The whispering paused, then increased as everyone present regarded the exchange at the front. TJ took his customary seat near the door as his mother joined his sister Abigail's family in the third pew. Most Sunday's Abigail traveled over the river to attend the Hiramsville church rather than the one in Acton.

Mrs. Reese returned to her pew, tapping her cane on the floor louder than necessary, but Miss Wilson continued across the room to the Mason and Hamlin harmonium purchased last year. The whispering came to an abrupt halt as the first notes of a hymn filled the room. In the pew in front of TJ, Mrs. Brant's fan picked up speed, as did those of others in the room.

After one verse, Reverend Green stood at the podium. "We are truly blessed today to have Miss Emily Wilson join us and fill in on such short notice for Mrs. Long, who is ill this morning. Miss Wilson is a recent graduate of Bradford College for Women in Massachusetts. I hope you will greet her with open arms."

Mrs. Brant dropped her fan, the clatter echoing in the silent room.

Reverend Green cleared his throat and continued. "Our opening hymn will be 'Safe in the Arms of Jesus.'"

Half the congregation sang. The other half looked around nervously or whispered to their neighbors. From Miss Wilson's pale face, it was evident she knew the whispering centered around her. If he hadn't been in a church, TJ would have stood and applauded her for her bravery. Not to mention her skill. Unlike Mrs. Long, she hadn't missed a single note. The rest of the meeting continued normally.

TJ remained in his seat as the congregation filed out to the music of the pump organ. Mr. Adams, a widower of many years, remained in his seat, eyes closed, his hand keeping time. When the final notes faded, he stood and met Miss Wilson in the aisle. "Young lady, I thank you. That was the best playing these old ears have heard this side of the Mississippi, since my wife passed."

TJ couldn't hear her reply. Ma tapped on his arm. "We need your help to set up the tables for the food." TJ followed his mother outside.

A few of the gossipers paused as he passed. Miss Wilson was by far the most popular topic.

"I heard she was arrested—"

"—one of Belle's—"

"Colossal mistake—"

TJ stopped to correct one story and received a sharp poke in the back.

"It is best you don't respond." Ma pushed him past the clusters of people to where two other men moved sawhorses to support the makeshift tables.

TJ kept his voice low so only his ma could hear. "But they are lies."

"And most of them will dissipate in a week or so as soon as something more interesting comes along. If you get involved, it will only spur things on and make the stories about her spending the night in your room more credible."

"You've heard those?" Of course she had, even if she knew the truth of it.

Ma patted his arm and pointed to the tables. "Go help. Leave the gossips to Roberta."

The men swiftly set up the tables, and just as quickly, platters of food appeared, some pulled from the backs of wagons, others from the storm cellar under the church, where they'd been stored before services.

"I've never seen a cellar under a church before. In Boston, some of them, like Old North Church, have crypts, but that is extremely different. We would never put food down there." Emily stood at his elbow, holding a pie. "Did they build it for picnics?"

"No. Tornadoes. Safest place is below ground. We get two or three each year, but fortunately, Hiramsville hasn't taken a direct hit. Most of them hit farmland, but some are close enough to blow out windows. Mr. Adams claims he once had one drop a cow on his barn."

"Oh, goodness."

Mrs. Reese joined them. "Emily, put that pie over there." As soon as Emily was out of earshot, Mrs. Reese turned to TJ. "Stay away from her today. She doesn't need any more gossip starting."

"We were only talking."

"And that is all it will take to get the town talking."

TJ nodded but failed to see the point. Miss Wilson had started the conversation. If it was that bad for her reputation, she wouldn't have spoken first. Widow Wells signaled him to come help carry her trays of baked chicken from the church cellar. After he finished helping her, he found other women who needed his help. A handful of bachelors did the same, mostly because it guaranteed first pickings of the best food.

Dennis Graff set his mother's rolls next to the platter of

bread TJ carried. "Is it true the woman who played the organ was Belle's girl you arrested?"

"No, she isn't Belle's girl, but, yes, there was a misunderstanding and I arrested her. Miss Wilson is a fine, upstanding citizen."

"Rumor has it she spent the night in your room, not the jail cell."

"Miss Wilson was provided private sleeping accommodations, as are all female prisoners."

"Uh-huh."

TJ changed the topic to Dennis's longtime girlfriend rather than using his fist to wipe the lecherous grin off Dennis's face. "I understood Mary Beth's mother ordered a bolt of white satin the other day. Have you officially proposed?"

Dennis's face turned red. "Got her father's blessing last Sunday night. We are planning on a September wedding."

"My heartiest congratulations." That was one man he didn't have to worry about chasing Miss Wilson. But from the crowd of males gathered around her area at the dessert tables, one would hardly make a difference.

——◇——

Emily cut another slice of Thelma's cake for yet another male. It hadn't escaped her notice that the majority of women, children, and fathers chose other desserts. The second man she sliced cake for may have proposed. His pronounced stutter was difficult to decipher. She cut him an extra slice of peach pie and sent him on his way, making sure not to comment lest she inadvertently accept an invitation to matrimony. A cowboy asked her if she wanted to get hitched. As if she were a horse.

Next in line was a middle-aged man wearing a black mourning armband. A child not more than three and so covered in grime as to make guessing its gender impossible clung to the man's leg. Behind him, two more children, a boy and a girl both dressed in black, waited their turn. Widower. He tipped his hat. "Afternoon. The name is Collins. Pleased to meet ya."

"Which dessert may I serve you?"

"Not interested in anything sweet here but you. My children need a new ma. Heard you had no place to go. I'll treat you fair if you don't sass me, and I'll even give you a brat of your own."

"And if I do sass you?" The nerve of him offering her a "brat." Any father who referred to his children in such derogatory terms needed to be sassed.

The man raised his hand as if to slap her, and Emily stepped back far enough to be out of his reach. "I will pass on your proposal. Cake?" She held up a piece, but Mr. Collins left with the three children.

The next man in line didn't look her in the eye, his focus instead on the bodice of her dress.

"Pie?"

The man looked up, shook his head, and walked away.

Mrs. Morgan was next in line. "I enjoyed your playing this morning. Do you play other instruments?"

"I have a passing knowledge of the violin."

"Have you considered teaching music?"

"No, I am not that accomplished."

"You might think on it. What isn't accomplished in Boston becomes virtuous out here. May I have a slice of cake, please? Thelma makes the best in town."

"That is what everyone keeps telling me. I can't wait to try it." Emily placed a slice on Mrs. Morgan's plate.

"You may need to hide a piece for yourself."

Soon only a few pieces remained. Mr. Collins returned with the youngest child for cake. "Would you care to go for a ride tonight?"

Not any night. Ever.

A man behind him pushed the child aside. "No fair, Collins, you've already had two wives. I wanted to ask her."

Mr. Collins whirled on the first man, knocking his child to the ground.

"Gentlemen, please!" Emily's interjection went unheard, as did the cries of the child. "Gentlemen!" Emily squatted and waved to the child to crawl to her under the table. Before Emily could stand, the child flung its arms around Emily's neck, forcing her to pick it up or stay crouched.

"Mr. Collins!" Still, the men paid no heed. A third joined them, claiming he had seen her first.

"Mr. Col—"

A whistle cut her shout short, and a heavy hand landed on her shoulder. "Sirs, what Miss Wilson has been trying to tell you is she can't possibly spend time with you as she's agreed to stroll along the river with me."

The fighting men stopped and, as one, glared at the newcomer. Mr. Collins frowned at the child in Emily's arms. "Aubry, leave the lady alone."

Aubry? Or Aubrey? Emily set the child down, still no wiser as to the gender. The child crawled back under the table, and the men dispersed. Emily turned to the man beside her, who removed his hand from her shoulder. "And you are?"

"Dr. Aidan Palmer. TJ, I mean the sheriff, asked me to break up the fight. You are under no obligation to even talk to me or take a walk this evening."

Why hadn't the sheriff come himself? "Do you regularly break up fights by lying?"

"I can't say I do, but it worked with no fists flying." Dr. Palmer smiled. "And if you agree to let me call, then there was no lie."

"Is this how you do all your courting? First scare off the competition?"

The doctor appeared to be several years older than some of the other men, though no gray speckled his hair. Perhaps it was the tiredness in his eyes that aged his face. "You may have noticed by now that eligible women are in short supply in Hiramsville."

"Does that mean you are going to propose too?"

"Too?" The doctor's eyebrows pinched together.

Emily deposited the last slice of pie onto a little girl's plate. "'Too,' as in 'as well' or 'also,' as in the number of proposals I've received since the sermon ended."

The doctor raised a brow. "More than five?"

"Not yet."

"You haven't broken the town record. Have you eaten?"

Emily shook her head and cut a slice of cake for another cowboy.

"Where is your plate? I'll fill it for you before the only food left is pickled beets and boiled potatoes."

"Thank you, Doctor. Mrs. Reese has my plate. She is under—" Emily searched the churchyard.

"The pecan tree in her usual spot. I'll see to it. Any food you are not fond of?"

"Not that I can think of."

"Even pickled beets?"

"I don't know. I've never tasted them."

Dr. Palmer chuckled. "Then I will only put the smallest one on your plate."

Emily smiled as the doctor hurried across the yard. Possibly there was a decent man in town after all, aside from the sheriff himself of course.

⬗◆⬖

"You what?" TJ nearly spit his iced tea across the doctor's kitchen table.

"I said I was calling on Miss Wilson this evening."

"I asked you to break up a fight."

"Which I did. Miss Wilson's evening plans were, as you guessed, the subject of the fight. I realized if she had plans for the evening, it would end the commotion."

TJ set down his glass. "So Doc, you are calling on her to stop a fight?"

Aidan smiled. "That, and I think she is a lovely young woman who's had a rough start in this town."

"Her introduction to Hiramsville could have been much worse. I don't understand how some of those gossips can spread Belle's lies."

Aidan drained his glass. "I believe a conversation with Miss Wilson will be very pleasant. And maybe it is time I try to find a wife. It has been years…"

…Since the worst day this town had ever known. "I thought you said there would never be another woman for you."

Aidan leaned back and crossed his arms. "Never is a longer time than I thought. I thought you would be glad for me. You aren't concerned about this woman just as a sheriff, are you?"

"Of course, it is just as a sheriff. I am responsible for the rumors destroying her reputation. Do you think half of those men would have tried to get her attention if they didn't think she was one of Belle's girls? If I had gotten her away from Cline quietly, this would not have happened." The words were mostly truth. Friend or not, the doctor didn't need to know how Emily's presence affected him. Increased pulse, errant thoughts, the desire to hide her from every man in town, and not only the disreputable ones.

"You aren't the cause of the problem. Belle would still be on the warpath, no matter how you got Emily away. Had you managed it before Cline had seen her, then maybe she would have escaped with her reputation and be on a train back to Boston. But that wasn't possible. You know as well as I do that the rumors about Miss Wilson started in Belle's parlor. Collins would still have tried to get her attention, as well as most of those men. A single woman in these parts who isn't one of Belle's or Harold's is rare as a hen's tooth. The local girls barely get their first dance before they are snatched up and married off to some young man still wet behind the ears. Men of our age have few choices."

TJ turned the truths of the doctor's statements over in his mind. "But if I'd gotten to Emily first…"

"How? Maybe if Rose had lived longer, you would have been able to arrest Belle and her men, or she could have had another clue to Miss Wilson's identity. Maybe if I had helped her escape months ago when I thought something was wrong—" Aidan stood so fast his chair slid across the floor. "If you want to blame someone, blame me. I could have rescued Rose, but I didn't. I could have understood her message." Aidan leaned on the table, his face pale.

"But—"

"Don't! It's my fault." Aidan escaped into the interior of the house, slamming the kitchen door behind him.

TJ wiped his hand over his face, surprised the outburst hadn't come a week and a half ago. Rose might not have let Aidan take her away, or she would have been killed sooner and they would never have known of Miss Wilson's arrival. There were too many factors to guess the outcome. Until Palmer stopped seeing his dead fiancée in the face of every woman who met an untimely death, he'd never be happy.

TJ washed both glasses and let himself out the backdoor. If Emily could heal the doctor's soul, TJ wouldn't get in the way.

Emily dried the last dish and returned it to the cupboard.

"Thanks for your help, but it still isn't your place."

Thelma laid the wet dishcloth over the side of the sink. "Nonsense. You deserve as much of a Sabbath rest as we do. So I'll share in your work and you can rest too."

Thelma slipped off her apron. "Let's go find us a cool spot. Looks like there is a breeze out there."

The shade of the large oak kept the sun away, but the temperature didn't drop as Emily expected it to.

Becky fanned herself with her apron. "If June is already this hot, I don't want to live through July."

Mrs. Reese clucked her tongue. "You'll scare Emily off with that kind of talk. Speaking of which—do you have any light cotton or linen blouses? You'll be wanting them, especially if you decide to take in laundry."

Emily regretted not keeping her old summer dress. "I have one or two. I figured I would purchase some fabric tomorrow and make another, like the one Becky wore yesterday."

Mrs. Reese nodded. "Becky, is there any more of the calico in the drawer?"

"At least enough for a blouse. There is also a length of linen and some muslin."

"Tomorrow, show it to Emily. If there is something useful in there, there is no point in her spending her money on cloth."

"Thank you, Mrs. Reese. I'll be happy to pay you for it." She had spared Emily another visit to the mercantile.

Mrs. Reese waved her hand in dismissal. "I have a terrible habit of buying far too much when I go into Fort Worth or Dallas. Mr. Tarr marks his fabrics up too high. Besides, after his refusal to see the truth about you, I have no desire to patronize his store."

"Where will you shop?"

"I rarely need to purchase anything. We have our garden, chickens, and I get my milk from Donny's mother. I haven't lived these many years in Texas to not know how to be self-sufficient. If we need anything, I can always make my purchases over in Acton. I may well take my buggy over this week anyway, so Mr. Tarr knows I refuse to shop with him. He'll have a hard week of it if the other women follow my lead."

"Because you refuse to shop there?"

Becky laughed. "Mrs. Reese is the most respected woman in the county on account of her husband. Half the women join the church sewing circles so they can be invited to tea. Once old watching-out-the-window—"

"Rebecca." Mrs. Reese frowned.

"Sorry, ma'am. After we come back in the buggy with parcels, all the women will magically know Mrs. Reese snubbed the mercantile on account of you, and they will do the same."

"Not magic. Human nature."

"That and the Alamo."

Emily tilted her head and pondered. "I thought everyone respected you because you have lived here so long."

"I've lived here so long because of the land grant the Republic of Texas gave me because I am an Alamo widow. One of the few left. Mrs. Crockett received her grant on the other side of the river. There are few as famous as her husband, other than maybe Mr. Bowie. Now that she has passed, people look at me like I am some kind of hero. We'd only been married for a year, and I was carrying our son, when Mr. Reese went to join the fight. Texas deemed they should reward me, and that is enough for most people around here. 'Remember the Alamo.'" Mrs. Reese waved her cane like a flag.

"You don't enjoy the attention, do you?"

"Not in the least. But I have learned to use it to my advantage. I can help women such as yourselves and occasionally get things moving in the right direction. Thanks to the money I've invested over the years, most men will listen to me too. If I had the right to vote—" Mrs. Reese shook her head. "Until then, I do what I can. Thelma, write a list of everything you need. We are going to Acton tomorrow."

The conversation died, and the women became absorbed in their own tasks. Mrs. Reese wrote what looked like a letter, while Becky and Thelma opened novels. Emily set Rose's journal on the table and unfolded the paper she'd transcribed the first few pages on. So far, she had learned little other than Cecilia's life before she became Rose. The first several pages turned out to be a substitution code. Three forwards for the consonants and two back for the vowels, excluding *Y*.

The first entry, *Kvohioxaer aw o duuo oaoc. A lozu o nef ejjuv ar Lavoqwzappu*, translated to "Graduation is a week away. I have a job offer in Hiramsville."

May 10, 1878

Roger kissed me tonight. He hasn't asked me to marry him, but we spoke of working for a year. Parker county schools offered him a teaching position. I am looking for one and have a lead in

Hiramsville. I will be more than thirty miles from him. I hope to find something closer.

First kiss. Emily closed her eyes. How many times had she sat in her dorm's common room and listened to her friends giggle and whisper about their first kiss? Was it truly as wonderful as they claimed? Of course, half of the time there were tears and broken hearts to follow. Some of her more pious friends vowed not to kiss until they were married, a notion Emily didn't share. What if his kiss made her skin crawl, like Barbara said about her first kiss when she was thirteen? An avowed flirt, Barbara kissed any man who looked at her twice. Emily held few illusions about her marriage prospects, but she did want to experience a kiss. Maybe the doctor…but instead, the sheriff's face filled her mind.

Trying to stop that thought, Emily shook her head and refocused on the journal.

June 2, 1878

I am taking the teaching job in Hiramsville as I can find nothing else. Roger asked me to come to his parents' home in Fort Worth before I start.

July 1, 1878

Roger proposed. We will not make it official until Christmas, as being married will make it impossible for me to work. Most teachers cannot even be courted. He gave me a cameo to mark our agreement. I have had a wonderful time with his family. His mother is very much like mine. I cherish every day I have left with his family. I must leave for Hiramsville in two weeks. I am surprised that it is so early, but Mrs. Leblanc writes there is an orientation for new teachers.

July 15, 1878

I leave in the morning. I can hardly bear to leave Roger. He kissed me again. Our third kiss.

The writing changed, or, rather, the code changed. The only part that wasn't coded was the date: July 28, 1878. But it was the last date Emily could find in the book. The code translated to gibberish.

einrat sius ej eudrep sius ej

Emily stared at the new writing. Cecilia had changed her code. No longer was it simple to decipher. No longer was the fine hand light and loopy. It could only mean one thing. Cecilia arrived at Belle's and the worst had happened. Why else change so drastically?

Emily covered her mouth to suppress a gasp and closed the book.

"Emily?" asked Mrs. Reese.

The lie fell from her lips. "I just noticed the time. I need to prepare to go on a walk with Dr. Palmer. Excuse me."

The doctor wouldn't arrive for another hour or more, and smoothing her hair would not take more than a second, but Emily hurried up to her room. She tucked the journal into a drawer and sunk down onto her bed, covering her mouth to keep her words in and the bile in her throat.

"It could have been me." She rocked back and forth for a moment. She'd be arrested a hundred times rather than live that nightmare.

Taking a deep breath to calm her racing heart and the myriad of emotions clamoring inside, Emily retrieved the journal from her drawer. She rubbed its worn cover and studied the drastic change in handwriting. Emily straightened her shoulders and stood staring at herself in the mirror. "Cecilia, you prevented my ruin. I'll do my best to see your killers convicted." Resolved to do her part, she took the journal and returned to the shade of the outdoors.

<hr>

The sheriff's office was quiet. Only one prisoner sat in the cells above, waiting to be transported to Dallas. Ma came in from the parlor. "I am going over to Mrs. Reese's. She asked for a recipe last week, and I forgot to take it."

"I'll escort you."

Ma raised a brow but didn't comment.

When no one answered their knock on the front door, Ma circled the house, and TJ followed. They found the four women sitting in the shade of the trees lining the west side of the property. Mrs. Reese looked up from her writing. "Ah, Harriett, come join us. TJ, will you get two extra chairs off the porch?"

As there was only one answer to that request, TJ hurried to get the extra chairs. When he returned, he found that Emily had given up her seat for his mother. He set the new chairs a few feet from the other women in the shade of the pecan tree Mrs. Reese had planted years ago. He greeted each of the women. Emily held up the journal and nodded at the newly placed chairs. "Do you have a moment, Sheriff?"

The papers sticking out from the journal caught his attention. "Yes, ma'am."

TJ indicated for Emily to choose her seat. He pulled the other chair closer to her before sitting. "Was everything in your trunk?"

"Yes. Nothing was touched. I don't have a lot of valuables, just my grandmother's sugar bowl. It was made by Paul Revere. And my mother's silver hairbrush. I don't think I could sell it. My father brushed my mother's hair every night with it."

"Your father brushed her hair?"

"It's a family tradition my great-grandfather started the day he got married to my great-grandmother. They passed it down to all of their children." Emily paused for a moment. "Everything else was there. Books, clothes, shoes. The trunk was my father's. We have the same initials. I'm so glad to have it back."

Emily opened the book and handed him the transcribed pages. "She'd planned a future. Before she came here, she had a future." Emily paused and blinked several times. Unable to keep all the moisture back, she wiped away a tear.

"She was engaged to a man named Roger. That is as far as I've gotten. She changed the code or cipher, or whatever she used for the entry after she was supposed to come here to teach for Mrs. LeBlanc." Emily put her fist to her mouth and blinked a few times.

TJ waited for her to compose herself.

"I'm sorry, Sheriff. I am very emotional after reading her entries."

"You don't need to finish this." Maybe she'd learned enough to help him decipher the rest of the book.

Emily turned the pages of the book. "I do need to finish this. I want to. She saved me from—" She waved her hand over the book. "I owe it to her to see if there is something in her writings that will bring someone to justice for her death."

"But—"

Emily shook her head. "We had so much in common. Her parents died, and she was raised by a grandmother. We both attended colleges with a strong Christian basis. Yes, there were differences. Cecilia Pruitt was in love and engaged. Do you understand how much worse that would be?"

No answer came to mind.

"If you hadn't rescued me, no one would care. My uncles might not even notice that I never wrote. As it is, if the truth were known to my aunt, she would find vindication of all the nasty things she called me over the years. I would mourn the loss of an imaginary, faceless future. Cecilia's future had a face and a name. I owe it to her. I need to finish the translation."

TJ closed his eyes and rubbed his forehead. Of all the mistakes he ever made, asking her to translate the journal was the worst. No woman raised the way she was should ever know of the depravity he suspected many of Belle's girls endured. Not that he had witnessed any of it, but he'd been forced to listen to the ravings of drunken men as he escorted them to cells. Occasionally, Harold or Belle would have him arrest one of their patrons for attacking one of the girls. Most of the women survived on whiskey and opium. TJ didn't want to know more. As long as the taxes were paid, he couldn't stop the surrounding evil.

Opening his eyes, he met Miss Wilson's gaze. "I shouldn't have asked you. I was only searching for—" Cecilia's killers? A way to end the city's depravity.

Emily brushed his arm, warmth radiating from where she'd touched him. "Some women I went to school with are headed to Africa and the Orient to convert the natives. Some are marrying preachers to help watch over their flocks. I was taught to make the world a better place, and if reading this book can make Hiramsville a better place, then I fulfill the motto of my school: *Surgo Ut Prosim*."

"*Surgo Ut Prosim*?"

"I rise to serve. At graduation I spoke about how we can serve in the world and improve this mortal place, wherever God has placed us." There was a certain dignity in her voice, the same as the reverend used when quoting a favorite scripture. "When it comes time to leave Hiramsville, I will leave it a better place. Now, if you will excuse me, I have to prepare for a caller." Emily nodded, said something to the other women, and walked, no, floated, across the lawn.

TJ followed her with his eyes. Never had he seen a more dignified woman. Not that he would tell Ma or Mrs. Reese that. He whispered the motto under his breath. It embodied every lesson his father had ever taught him. *"Surgo Ut Prosim."*

awn crept over the trees lining the Brazos River. Emily pulled an empty cart she'd found tucked away in Mrs. Reese's barn along East Street to the square. A dog sniffed at the door of the mercantile, and roosters greeted the dawn from all directions. A lamp still burned in the hotel's window, but otherwise the town still slept. The alley at the back of the hotel was almost as wide as a street. Emily stopped at the kitchen door and knocked twice.

A heavy-set woman with coffee-colored skin answered. "You here for the laundry?"

"Yes, I am."

"Come in, and I'll show you the linen closet. Next time you need not knock. Takes me away from breakfast preparations."

Emily followed the cook into a side room.

"Count what you take—sheets, towels, pillowcases—and mark it down here. Note any rips or tears." The cook pointed to a ledger. "When you bring it back, the numbers should match. If you fix the damage, note that. If it was not repairable, put it on the red shelf and mark it in the book. Mr. Davis pays by the piece. He expects all sheets to be crisply ironed,

111

towels folded like the ones on the clean shelf. Don't forget to sign the ledger." The cook looked Emily over head to toe. "I'm assuming you can read and write?"

"Yes, ma'am."

"Good, I won't have to do it for you. Mr. Davis insists on using the new Ivory Soap. Make sure you mark how many cakes you take. If you use too much, he'll charge you. The table linens must be done separately. Use an indigo bag in the rinse. There are some next to the soap. If you have questions, come ask. I better get back to the bread."

"Thank you. I'm Emily Wilson, by the way."

"I'm Hannah, just Hannah, sometimes Big Hannah, but I don't cotton to that name much."

"Thank you, Hannah." Emily sorted through the laundry. There were ten sheets, eight pillowcases, two dozen towels of various kinds, and ten tablecloths. None had holes, but wine stained one of the table linens and coffee another. While marking the ledger, Emily wondered if the new soap would be more effective than the remedies she had learned "helping" in her aunt's home. She made three trips out to the cart, waved goodbye to Hannah, and returned the way she'd come.

Donny walked along the edge of the road, a bag over his shoulder. "Morning, Miss Wilson. You sure is out early."

You sure are. Emily was not his teacher or his mother. She forced herself not to correct him. "Morning, Donny. What are you doing out here at the crack of day?"

"Finding stuff. Sometimes people drop pennies and such. Last month I found a whole dollar near Harold's place. He told me to keep it. Once I found Ma a real nice thimble, but she asked the sewing circle ladies at church if anyone had lost one, and four of the old hags claimed it. They must have missed the not-lying part of the reverend's sermon."

"You shouldn't call them hags. It is rude. All of those women could have lost thimbles as they are very easy to lose and they all look very similar." Emily looked at Donny thoughtfully and asked, "Do you always seek an owner for your finds?"

"Ma says I have to, except for the pennies or when it is impossible to guess."

"So you hope for pennies?"

"Or dimes with dried mud on them."

Emily smiled. "I'd wish for a double eagle with dried mud."

"Ma would make me give it to the sheriff if I found one of those."

"You have a smart mother. I won't keep you. I need to get back and start this laundry. The water should be boiling by now."

"If you see any pennies, will you tell me?"

"I sure will." Emily continued down the street. Smells of early morning coffee and bread drifted from a few of the houses she passed. She turned at the corner which led to the alley behind Mrs. Reese's. Before dawn, Becky had helped her set up the wash area by lamplight in exchange for Emily doing the household laundry too. Emily set aside the cake of Ivory and used a scoop of the soap Becky had flaked while they read on Saturday. If she had a stubborn stain, she'd try the Ivory. No point in getting charged for using too much or taking the time to flake it now.

The washhouse, a tiny closet at the back of the summer kitchen, was long enough for two large washtubs and a wringer, which sat on a low table next to the tubs. According to Becky, the wringer "worked wondrous" when it worked, or ripped everything to bits when it didn't. Emily hoped she could manage to keep it working.

Since the beginning of time, laundry was largely mindless work. Emily let her mind drift to last night's short walk with Dr. Palmer. They hadn't reached the square when Donny had run toward them yelling, "Doc! Doc!" and Dr. Palmer had left Donny to escort her home. The walk had been pleasant enough during the ten minutes it lasted. If the doctor asked, she would be available again. According to Becky, he was quite the catch, but no woman had ever gotten him to propose since…Mrs. Reese had scolded Becky for gossiping, and Emily never learned what the "since" was.

A few of the women at the college were always trying to convince some young man to propose by using a new perfume, conjuring up new compliments, or scandalously padding a corset. A few had taken things further, forcing a man into marriage by evading the chaperones or allowing more than a quick, chaste kiss good night and getting caught. Some of her fellow students, including Barbara, had spent more time planning a trap for a wealthy merchant's son than on writing essays or studying coursework. In the end, such plans usually came to naught.

The doctor, like other men, shouldn't be treated as a game where the winner won a husband by trickery. After all, wasn't that what Aunt Melba had done? Neither husband nor wife was content in that marriage. Emily longed for a love story like her parents', where both parties had found joy. Some of her friends, like Amanda with her impending nuptials, seemed to have found that too. Perhaps love did exist outside of novels. If Dr. Palmer became a friend, then something more, that would be the way of it. But there was little chance of a love match. The few moments they had to speak yesterday, he'd showed the same kind of interest her cousin Percy showed—kind and brotherly. Her heart failed to beat the irregular beat Amanda described. Perhaps it took time.

Making an effort to see Dr. Palmer again wouldn't be the same as entrapping him, was it? He was handsome, kind, and intelligent, and she'd rather wash laundry for one household than a hotel. Emily shook her head. She never expected to live in a place where men proposed to her so often. Not that she'd accept them when she didn't know their names. The doctor was nice and polite. If feelings developed later, maybe, but she would have to think of the doctor more often than she did the sheriff.

Emily dropped the towel she'd been scrubbing back into the water, splashing her dress. Where had that thought come from? She only thought of the sheriff because he'd rescued her. And they were becoming friends too. Right? Absolutely nothing more. She simply would not think of him again for the rest of the day.

⎯⎯◆⎯⎯

Every chair in the barbershop sat empty—unusual for a Wednesday afternoon. TJ tapped at the doorjamb, rousing Pete from his chair.

"Afternoon. Do you have time to give me a haircut?"

Pete climbed out of the barber chair. "Shave too?" Laughter tinged his question.

"Not today. Adding a shave is tempting fate. How many times have you had me all lathered up when trouble came calling?" TJ sat in the chair.

"Five or six times at least. Good thing you don't wear a mustache or you would have lost half of it that time those boys got lost in the caves."

"The way their ma was screeching, I was sure something had killed them." TJ laughed. "Almost as good as the time little Molly got her cat stuck under the mercantile steps."

"You should get a shave. The interruptions make for good stories." Pete ran a comb through TJ's hair.

"One of these days it will be a real emergency, and it won't be so funny." Like the fire that killed Pete's father in the first barbershop. They sat in silence as Pete trimmed around TJ's ears.

"Speaking of trouble…there is some packaged as pretty as can be."

TJ looked out the window to see who Pete meant. Miss Wilson walked by, with Donny pulling her little cart.

"You may be the first man this week who hasn't mentioned her in their conversation." Pete moved to TJ's left, blocking the view.

"You mean Miss Wilson?"

"That's the one. Half the single men in town have been in to get a shave. As near as I can tell, she won't give any of them the time a day since she is an "uppity Northerner"—their name for her, not mine. I think it has more to do with her courting the doctor than it does being uppity. He came in yesterday and managed a shave without a catastrophe occurring. I'm glad he is looking to court again. I keep telling him what happened with my sister wasn't his doing. My family had a run of bad luck." Pete stepped back and handed TJ a mirror.

"So there is more interest in Miss Wilson than usual?"

"When was the last time we had a respectable, unaccompanied woman come to town? Although the respectable part has been debated."

"She…um…None since last fall, with the new schoolteachers." TJ thought better of defending her honor at this point.

"Precisely, and they were both engaged by Christmas and married the day school finished. There are rumors she came to work for Belle and you arrested her?" Pete fished for more information.

"I've heard those myself. Miss Wilson came to town to teach at a nonexistent women's academy. When the position offered turned out to be quite different from what she envisioned, she declined employment."

Pete nodded. "Heard her playing in church and figured it must be something like that. I wish Palmer the best with her."

Despite Aidan being one of his confidants, TJ couldn't bring himself to wish Dr. Palmer the best. TJ paid Pete and checked the street before exiting. Donny and Miss Wilson had disappeared into the alley behind the hotel. TJ walked that direction, hoping he appeared natural. He checked the area to see if anyone else had taken unwarranted attention in Miss Wilson's activities, but everyone appeared to be minding their own business, and none of Belle's men were about. TJ leaned against a post and waited for Donny and Miss Wilson to emerge from behind the hotel. Mr. Collins exited the newspaper offices and looked toward the alley. The printer rarely left his office in the middle of the day.

When Donny and Miss Wilson emerged, Mr. Collins rushed across the street to meet them.

TJ moved to intercept the man before he could cause a problem.

Donny squinted at Emily. "It ain't—"

"Isn't."

The boy scowled. "That too, ma'am. Riding a horse on ice. Isn't possible."

Emily laughed. "Are you calling me a liar?"

"Yes, I—" Donny's reply was cut off by Mr. Collins grabbing his shirt.

"Don't talk to your elders like that, boy." Mr. Collins lifted Donny off the ground by his shirt. Donny wiggled and kicked.

"Mr. Collins, let him go this instant!"

Donny landed a kick to Mr. Collins's knee. Mr. Collins roared and drew back his free arm. Emily dove between Mr. Collins and the boy and shut her eyes, waiting for the blow. Mr. Collins grunted. Donny gave another yell, this time in triumph.

Emily looked through squinted lids to see the sheriff holding Mr. Collins by an arm twisted behind his back. "You owe the lady and the boy an apology."

"I need not apologize to him." Even with his arm twisted behind him, the odious man managed to look down his nose at Donny.

The sheriff lifted Mr. Collins's arm further. "Sure you don't have something to say?"

"Miss Wilson, I shall call on you at half past seven, where you can formally accept my proposal."

Emily kept her arm around Donny's shoulders. "Why, I never—"

Still holding Collins's arm, Sheriff Morgan spun the man around. "Miss Wilson said she is not accepting your suit."

"Why not? I have less laundry than the hotel, and any woman desperate enough to work for Belle will find my place much more—"

Sheriff Morgan stepped closer to Mr. Collins until only a few inches separated them. "That is enough. I suggest you be on your way." The sheriff let go of Mr. Collins, who took two wobbly steps.

Mr. Collins turned and straightened his printer's apron. "Miss Wilson, until tonight."

"No, I—"

The sheriff stepped in front of her. "That would be a very bad idea."

Mr. Collins crossed the street. Emily glared at both men's backs, infuriated. Which was worse—overbearing widower or overprotective sheriff?

Emily picked up the handle of the cart with a jerk. "Come on, Donny. I'll see if Thelma has some gingersnaps for you."

"I can pull the wagon for you, Miss Wilson." Donny ran to keep up.

"I know you can—"

"Miss Wilson."

Emily didn't stop for the sheriff.

"Miss Wilson." Sheriff Morgan reached for the cart handle.

Emily spun around to face him. "What?"

"I will escort you home."

"No. Thank. You. Sir. Donny is my escort." Emily pulled the cart after her.

Sheriff Morgan took the cart handle from her hand.

Emily stood in front of the wheels. "Sheriff, I appreciate you rescuing me from Miss Belle. However, in other aspects of my life, I can look after my own affairs."

"But he would have hit you."

"And it would have been over. I can handle a punch. I am not delicate. I believe Mr. Collins would have either stopped before he hit me or been remorseful enough to stop pursuing me. As it is, he will continue to bother me because you answered for me. He needs my answer, not yours." Emily held out her hand. "My cart, please. I trust you can let me do my work."

"You mean I should have stood there and let him hit you?"

Emily took a deep breath. "I do appreciate not needing to nurse a black eye. But you spoke for me when I could have told him myself that I have no interest in him. I thank you for keeping us from physical harm but not for interfering in my affairs."

"I see." The sheriff nodded to Donny, waiting for him to take the cart handle. "A gentleman wouldn't allow a lady to pull the cart when he was walking with her."

Conceding his point, Emily gave Donny a nod and glared at the sheriff before resuming her trip home.

Conceited, wretched man! How dare he answer for her? Emily wished for a place to scream. Instead, she kept her grumblings inside. "Donny, back to that ice. Sometimes it is thick enough to drive a wagon across. Last winter it snowed two feet in a single day."

Donny shook his head. "It doesn't seem possible—not that I am disrespecting you."

Emily ruffled Donny's hair. The boy didn't deserve to feel her anger over the sheriff. "I never thought you were. I am very sorry Mr. Collins treated you so poorly. Let's go find what Thelma made today."

A niggling feeling in her heart made her wonder if she had inadvertently disrespected the sheriff. After all, he had only been trying to help.

⟫◆⟪

Women! TJ watched Miss Wilson and Donny until they turned the corner. If he hadn't stopped Mr. Collins, the man could have injured her. Did she expect him to stand by and let it happen? Not to mention if Collins had hit her, he would have had to arrest him, and where would that leave the children?

Fuming, TJ returned to the office, hoping and praying that the rest of his day would go smoother.

As he started up the steps to his office, Aidan drove his buggy around the corner and pulled his horse to a stop. "TJ, will you do me a favor? I need to go to Lipan. Their doctor was in a buggy crash, and I don't think I'll be back before sunrise. Will you give my apologies to Miss Wilson? I was going to visit her tonight. Thank you." The doctor hurried his horse and buggy on before TJ could answer.

Rubbing the back of his neck, TJ turned and headed back the other way on the boardwalk. Pete was right. The woman was trouble in a pretty package.

mily set her crocheting aside and stared out the window, hoping to see Dr. Palmer's buggy. The clock read ten past seven. No doctor and, thankfully, no Mr. Collins. As she was about to turn away from the window, the sheriff came around the corner. Emily's breath caught. He better not be coming to protect her from Mr. Collins. Sheriff Morgan stopped in front of the house and looked up before entering through the gate. He must be remembering their previous encounter and unsure how he would be received. Squaring her shoulders, she turned and readied herself to hear what the reason for his visit might be.

Emily met him at the door, determined to be civil. "Sheriff, what brings you here?"

"Dr. Palmer left town on an emergency. He asked me to convey his apologies." He wore a fresh shirt. The ends of his hair around his face were damp and his face looked freshly shaved.

"That must be the way with doctors."

"I also wanted to apologize for this afternoon."

Emily opened the door wider. "Will you come in and sit for a minute? I must apologize too."

He removed his hat and entered the house. As he passed, Emily inhaled the same scent she'd noticed when they met that first night—soap, leather, and a woodsy scent the breeze sometimes carried from the west. He waited until she sat in her chair before sitting across from her and setting his hat next to him.

"Sheriff, please excuse me for my poor behavior. I know you were only trying to protect me."

"Miss Wilson, there is no need to apologize. You were correct. I shouldn't have answered for you. I hate to see anyone ill-treated."

"I see that. Upon reflection, I realize you were only trying to keep him away from me. I presume this is why you dressed up to deliver a message?" As angry as she had been earlier, Emily couldn't help but smile.

"Only if you want me to stay. I know Mrs. Reese is at a woman's society meeting with my mother and Thelma. I assume Becky is around?"

A thump sounded from the hallway.

"Fairly nearby, eavesdropping."

Footfalls retreated to the kitchen. The corner of the sheriff's mouth lifted in a half smile. "If you think it proper, I would like to stay. After witnessing Mr. Collins's rage this afternoon, it feels wrong to leave the two of you to face him alone."

Emily checked the time on the parlor clock: 7:20. "I think you could stay for a half hour on one condition."

The sheriff's brows rose.

"As long as I can resolve things with Mr. Collins by talking, you promise to stay out of it."

"I won't stand by if he raises a hand against you."

"I wouldn't expect you to. If I meet him at the door, you can stand just inside where he can't see you. There are enough rumors flying about town. I don't want one about me courting the doctor *and* the sheriff circulating. Even if Dr. Palmer knows the truth of it." Of course, the doctor was only courting her in word, not action.

For the briefest of moments, Sheriff Morgan tipped his head to the left. "I can agree to those terms as long as you try to get out of the way if he becomes violent."

"I'll do that. Becky, you can serve the lemonade now. And bring three cups, then you won't need to listen at the door."

Red-faced, Becky curtsied in the doorway. "Yes, Miss Emily."

Emily covered her mouth to keep from laughing.

"I've never seen her act like a proper maid before." TJ said with a smile.

A giggle escaped her. "Me neither."

"I heard that." Becky entered the room with a tray and set it on the low table. The tray held three glasses of lemonade and an assortment of Thelma's cookies.

When the sheriff smiled, the skin near his eyes crinkled.

A wagon stopped near the front gate as the clock chimed the half hour. Mr. Collins.

"Becky, go back into the kitchen, please." Emily straightened her skirt and nodded toward the entryway. "Sheriff, before he sees you, please."

Emily sat back down and waited for Mr. Collins to knock. He pounded.

As sedately as she'd been taught, Emily crossed the parlor. The sheriff stood with his back to the wall next to the door. He reached out and touched her hand, and a new calm filled her.

When Emily opened the door, Mr. Collins yanked the screen door open. She'd neglected to set the hook after the sheriff had come in. Not that it would have helped.

"Mr. Collins. I am not—"

"I say we get married this Saturday. If you need, I'll give you two weeks."

"No."

"What?"

"I am not marrying you. The doctor has *asked* to court me. You have only *told* me things. I wish you a good evening."

"Now, you listen here—"

Emily held up a hand. "Mr. Collins, I am trying to be polite. Perhaps that doesn't work in Texas. I said no. Now, please leave."

Instead, he stepped closer. "You should be glad I am willing to take you."

"Good night." Emily closed the door.

Mr. Collins stopped it with his foot. "I've got a good house and the paper. I told you that you can even have another child if you wish. What more can you want?"

Emily leaned on the door to try to close it. The sheriff moved. Emily put out her hand to stop him, her hand landing in the center of his chest.

"Respect, Mr. Collins. If I am to ever marry, at the very least, I want respect." This time she was able to close the door fully, probably due to the look of shock and surprise crossing Mr.   Collins's face.

As the sheriff reached over and threw the bolt, Emily's eyes briefly met his before she dropped her gaze to where she had placed her hand. Before she could remove it, he covered it with his own.

⋙•◇•⋘

TJ looked at their hands over his heart as he listened to the departing wagon. If only Aidan wasn't courting her. He dropped his hand, and Emily did the same. "I guess I should leave."

Emily took a step back. "At least finish your lemonade. It has ice in it." She led the way back into the parlor. "I'll never take ice for granted again. Donny doesn't believe me that it gets so thick one can skate on it and even drive a wagon across a frozen lake."

Once she sat, TJ resumed his former seat. "I've read about that. Considering I've never seen ice thicker than my little finger, except out of the machines, it is hard to believe.

"You've never been north?"

"I haven't ever had a reason to."

Emily sipped her lemonade. "When I was younger, I wanted to travel to all the places I read about, including Texas."

"Why Texas?"

"The books made it sound so exciting. Cowboys and Texas Rangers fighting the bad guys."

"What about sheriffs?"

Emily laughed. "I guess I got my very own sheriff to rescue me, didn't I? Too bad I can't brag about it to all my friends. I could never explain Belle to them."

"Hmm, your very own sheriff, Hiramsville might disagree."

"Well at the time... England, I want to go to England. But it will take years of teaching to save up that sort of money. My father took me to Canada when I was ten. It was much like Massachusetts, only some people spoke French. I suppose that is why I learned it."

"You speak French?"

She held up her fingers, pinched together. "*Un petit peu.*"

"I speak some Spanish."

"That would be more useful so near Mexico." Emily glanced at the clock.

"I should leave. I think the two of you should be safe. You did well with him tonight. I think he should leave you alone now."

She walked him to the door. "Thank you for coming."

If Aidan hadn't already asked to court her, TJ would act upon the temptation to bend down and kiss her on the cheek and tell her exactly how much he admired her for the way she'd handled Mr. Collins, the gossip, and being stuck in Hiramsville. Instead, he stepped out the door and put on his hat. "The pleasure was mine, Miss Wilson."

14

Emily groaned. The rooster had interrupted a perfect dream. No point in trying to sleep in for a few minutes now. The faintest tinge of pale yellow lined the horizon. The sooner she started the laundry, the faster she could finish. This was only the second week, and already she felt as if she'd been working for a year.

The letters she'd intended to write Sunday afternoon still needed to be written. The long nap she had taken after church had pushed them to later. Which didn't happen, and now she was behind. They must get out by tomorrow morning.

The rooster crowed again. Emily climbed out of bed and put on her work dress.

Donny sat in the cart she used to haul the laundry.

"Why ever are you here so early?"

Donny shrugged and scrambled out of the cart. "Can we hurry? It rained Saturday night, so I'm likely to find a muddy dime." Nodding her assent, they were soon on their way to collect the hotel's laundry.

The rest of Monday proceeded, as did every other day. Wash, rinse, ring, iron. Repeat, repeat, repeat.

Later that afternoon, she'd fallen asleep writing the letter to Uncle Carl and cousin Percy, creating a huge blot on the page and the same on her face. Thelma had her scrub it with a quarter of a lemon dipped in sugar, and now only the faintest shadow of color remained. After dinner, as the women of the house sat in the screened-in porch, Emily started a new letter.

Monday, June 30, 1879

Dear Uncle Carl and Percy,

I am well. The job I was promised was quite different in reality. In short, the school does not exist. Since I refused to take the alternative job presented, the proprietress demanded her money she'd spent on my ticket. Thanks to your generous graduation gifts, I was able to pay the woman and get my trunk back, which she held as collateral.

A kind widow whose husband was killed at the Alamo is allowing me to live in her home. She claims that in return, I need only to act as her companion. So far, that role has included reading in the evenings. She includes the cook and the maid in our evenings, so it is very comfortable.

Presently, I work as a laundress and am looking for better employment. After my experience with the misrepresentation of this teaching job, I am cautious about accepting any other advertised positions.

I know Percy is asking why I don't return to Boston. At the moment, I lack sufficient funds and have vowed never to live with Aunt Melba again.

I am not without friends here. There is a ten-year-old boy you would find quite amusing. He has taken on the role of my protector and walks me to and from the hotel, where I gather laundry to wash, each day.

As always,

Your niece and cousin,

Emily

She debated for a time about adding more details but didn't want to alarm them. Uncle Carl would insist Percy come fetch her.

Dear Uncle Harlan, Aunt Melba, and Barbara,

I am well and safe. The job is demanding, but I have secured a lovely room with a widow. Texas is hotter than anything I have experienced. The widow has a screened-in porch where we spend many of our evenings as the bugs thrive in the summer heat.

It isn't like the books and newspaper articles. No shootouts with outlaws. I haven't seen any Texas Rangers. Barbara, you will be gratified to know that the sheriff is every bit as handsome as in those novels you read. He has a scar on his cheek, making him look dangerous as well.

Yesterday, I was asked to play the church organ on a weekly basis. The old organist has problems with her vision. The reverend was pleased to have someone to play. The hours of lessons and practice have paid off.

The work is different from what I expected. The heat is bearable. I will write again soon.

As always,

Emily

The short letter was hardly worth the postage. Everything she wrote would be analyzed for secret meanings. Barbara would whine about the hours she practiced, and Aunt Melba would stew about whether the church roof might fall in. Including the part about the handsome sheriff was mostly to taunt her cousin. Since the incident with Mr. Collins on Wednesday, they hadn't spoken. Dr. Palmer had stopped by, and they'd talked, but when the doctor brushed her arm or squeezed her fingertips upon their farewells, her heart never raced as it did when the sheriff had covered her hand with his.

Emily pulled out another piece of paper and started her last letter.

Dear Amanda,

I hope you are well and married. It must be so exciting to start your own housekeeping as a minister's wife.

My teaching job was not what was promised, as the school was a house of ill repute. I hope that is not too shocking, but as you are in Texas also, you might understand these things. I was fortunate the sheriff rescued me before I was tricked, or worse, into working in such a place. Presently I am living with a kind widow and working as a laundress. Fortunately, life with my aunt prepared me for such a job.

I am seeking better employment. If you learn of any teaching positions at a real school, I welcome the referral. I believe I have enough money to purchase a ticket to Austin if needed. Please do not tell any of our Bradford friends. I can only imagine my aunt's reaction if she were to learn I narrowly escaped becoming a fallen woman.

I have made a few friends, but please do write soon.
Your friend,
Emily

PS. I think this town could use missionaries more than the
Indians or the wilds of Africa.

Emily looked over her letters. She debated about amend-
ing Uncle Carl's with the truth about the job she didn't take,
but one of them might slip up and tell it to Uncle Harlan,
though she'd given enough clues that Percy might guess.
That Amanda knew at least part of the truth of the situation
was necessary. Her husband might have contacts in the
Austin area.

Emily addressed the letters.

Becky looked up from her sewing. "I like quiet nights like
this. Are you going to read?"

"To ruin the quiet night?" asked Mrs. Reese.

"I must bid you all good night, I'm worn out from the day
and wouldn't be able to focus on any words to read." Emily
punctuated her statement with a yawn.

"It's late. We should all go in." Mrs. Reese gathered up her
knitting and her cane. The others followed.

⬤◆⬤

The square lay silent. The hammers of the builders working on the courthouse had stopped their pounding over an
hour ago when the thermometer outside of the barbershop
had inched above 105 degrees in the shade. Businesses on
the north and east sides of the square dropped their awnings
to give the few patrons some shade. TJ ambled along the
boardwalk, hoping there was still some cold left in the iced
tea and contemplating the profitability of investing in one
of the new ice machines from the company in Waco and
then selling the ice.

The post-office door flew open, and a woman barreled out.
TJ put out his hands to catch her before they collided. "Beg
your pardon, Miss—"

The woman looked up through tear-filled eyes.

"Miss Wilson? Bad news?"

She shook her head. "Sorry, I wasn't looking…"

"What happened?"

"Do you mind if we keep walking?"

TJ didn't have much choice. His first instinct was to march into the post office and search for the guilty face, but after last week's ill-met attempt to help Miss Wilson, he waited. They turned the corner at the south side of the square.

"My apologies for nearly running you down. I should have looked where I was going." Miss Wilson gave him a half smile from under the brim of her hat.

"What happened at the post office?"

"The postmaster wouldn't accept my letters. Said he didn't need a Yankee spy sending secrets north."

TJ bit his lip to keep from laughing. "Mr. Penny's never gotten over the war. He is one reason the Independence Day celebration is nothing but a minister reading the Declaration of Independence and the church hosting a picnic."

"No parade?"

"I've never seen one."

"I've never celebrated an Independence Day without a parade. When I was little, I remember the two last soldiers of the Revolution from our town sitting in carriages decorated with red-white-and-blue buntings. There were speeches and fireworks. The entire day was one long picnic. This heat would make marching in a parade unbearable." Miss Wilson fanned herself with her three letters.

"The veterans of the last war are divided in their feelings over the United States. Most of them are Texans through and through and consider that good enough. I can take your letters in and post them."

"Who's to say they'd make it on the train? I hope I can make it over to the Acton office before it closes."

No fool would walk the six miles to Acton in this heat. Even horses had to be watchfully ridden to keep them from failing due to exhaustion, though the short ride rarely caused any problems as long as the horses weren't pushed too fast. "I am expected for dinner at my sister, Abigail's, this evening. I could leave now and deliver your letters."

Miss Wilson ceased her fanning and sorted the letters. "I would be ever so much obliged if you would. My Uncle Carl will worry if he doesn't receive a letter soon." She handed him the letters and extracted two dimes from her purse. "Get yourself a couple sticks of candy with the extra two cents. You can put it in your collection for Donny."

"You don't need to pay me."

"Call it a gift, then. After I overreacted last week, I need to do something to make you see I have a sweet side." Miss Wilson gave him a smile sweeter than any candy he'd ever tasted.

"I thought we already agreed on this. All is forgiven. I should have let you say your piece. But I don't regret preventing him from hitting you. If I had to put him in jail, his children would have suffered."

"Oh, I hadn't thought of that, and I am glad not to have a black eye." She smiled again.

If it was anyone other than Aidan trying to court her, TJ would try to edge him out. "May I escort you home?"

"I don't require it, but I'd like your company. If we're lucky, we can get a glass of lemonade from the cellar. I've never been in one so cool."

"Mrs. Reese built her cellar in a portion of one of the natural caves under this end of town. Caves stay much cooler than the dug-out cellars."

They turned down the street leading south.

"Do many people have caves under their houses?"

"Only about five I know of, all near the cliffs. From this side of the river along the cliff, there are several shallow cave entrances. I used to explore them with GW and Abigail. We loved to play in them on hot summer days."

"There weren't animals in them?"

"Not that ever bothered us." They rounded the corner, and Mrs. Reese's home came into view. Ma sat under Mrs. Reese's trees with several other women from the sewing circle. TJ decided that avoiding the circle was worth missing out on lemonade. "If I am going to get these to the post office, I should leave now."

Miss Wilson glanced toward the women and nodded. "Thank you again."

TJ tipped his hat and refrained from looking back. He didn't want to risk coveting his dear friend's girl.

Tonight, not two minutes after Dr. Palmer arrived to commence their Wednesday night of courting, Mr. Collins pulled up in his wagon. The odious man brought his children with him, bathed and well-groomed, which, though the manipulative nature of his actions galled her, simultaneously alleviated some of her worries regarding the little ones being well cared for. He balanced the youngest on his hip as he joined Dr. Palmer and Emily on the front porch. Aubry wore a dress that could have been for any young toddler not yet old enough for pants. It lacked the bows and ribbons of a girl's dress. So far, no one she'd asked knew the gender of the child, only that Mrs. Collins had died of childbed fever after delivering a fourth child last January. The child didn't outlive the mother.

"Emily I've come to—"

Dr. Palmer stood and put a hand on Aubry's head. "Is your child ill? Or one of the others?"

"No, they is as right as rain as you can see. Get out of my way so I can talk to Emily."

"As you can see, I am calling on Miss Wilson." Dr. Palmer emphasized her name. "If you would be good enough to wait your turn."

Disliking anyone speaking for her, Emily stood from the chair near the door she'd been occupying and joined the men. "Mr. Collins, the doctor is courting me. I am not entertaining offers from anyone else at this time." Not that anyone seemed to mind. This week she'd only received one proposal outside the hotel on her way to deliver laundry. Donny's presence to and from work kept most of the men who saw Emily on the street in line. What woman would accept proposals from strangers?

Mr. Collins glared at the doctor for a minute before returning to his wagon with the children. Emily tried not to look at the disappointed faces of the children. She and Dr. Palmer had conversed several times, never getting much further than the comparison of the weather and foliage between Massachusetts and Texas.

Donny ran down the street waving a paper. "Doc Palmer! Doc Palmer!"

Moments later, the evening of courting ended with a quick apology. Emily retreated to the side of the house and onto the screened porch, joining the other ladies of the house in sewing.

The doctor was a nice man, and handsome, but there wasn't that "little something" that existed in every book she'd ever read. Perhaps it was only in books. Keeping him around as a buffer against Mr. Collins wasn't fair to either of them.

The sheriff tapped on the screen door.

"Come in, TJ," called Mrs. Reese.

He took off his hat and hung it on a peg on the wall. "Good evenin', ladies. Ma." He kissed his mother's cheek. She must have come to have a nice chat with her friends. TJ would use the same excuse if asked, but deep inside, his motives had more to do with Miss Wilson and the constant draw he felt towards her. "Nice breeze off the river."

"Before I built this place, I walked all over my property in the evenings, searching for the best breeze and view. I am fortunate this spot was only a few acres from the north end of the grant land. I sold off everything to the north and built my cabin, then replaced it with this house a few years later. I've never regretted the location."

"You chose well. I saw you were all out here, so I stopped by to tell Miss Wilson I posted her letters yesterday before closing." His eyes twinkled when he smiled, and Emily's breath caught.

It must be the heat. "Would you like some lemonade? You didn't stay long enough yesterday to get some." Emily poured the last three drops into a glass. "Oh no. Wait here, and I'll get more."

Thelma looked up from her knitting. "There is more sitting on the ice blocks in the back section of the cellar. You'll want a candle from the kitchen."

Emily was half out the screen door when Mrs. Reese banged her cane on the chair. "TJ, go help the girl. That cellar door is hard to lift in one of those narrow-skirted dresses."

Heat rose to Emily's face as TJ's glance lingered a half beat on her straight skirt.

"Yes, ma'am." TJ followed her around to the cellar entrance and reached for the door.

"Oh, the candle. Wait here." Emily hurried to the summer kitchen, cursing the narrow skirt, which was just as impractical as the wide ones her mother had worn years ago. At least in those, they could pick up their hoops and run, as long as it wasn't through a doorway. Emily lit a candle in a holder and returned to the cellar, cupping her hand around the flame.

TJ took the candle from her and led the way into the cool depths. At the far end of the room, he opened a door to a second storage area cooler than the first. "Hold the candle, and I'll find the lemonade."

The air felt wonderfully refreshing. On the next hot afternoon, she'd be tempted to sneak down and read a book. TJ lifted a pitcher, then moved the sawdust to cover the ice to keep it from melting.

The ice was so clear and uniform. "What lake do you get your ice from in the winter?"

"This isn't lake ice. It is made in a machine. Mrs. Reese gets it shipped here in late spring. I've pondered buying one of the contraptions and setting up an ice business here."

"I thought you were the sheriff."

"This is only a temporary job. I could get voted out. I have some land south of here that I'm building a house on, and I'll go back to farming or such."

"Have you ever been a farmer?"

"Pa was. Even when he was the sheriff. The old jail didn't have room for the five of us to live in." He stepped close enough that Emily could feel his warmth.

Realizing the impropriety of the situation, she stepped back until she wasn't blocking the doorway of the ice room. "I could see how an ice business could be very profitable in the summer."

The sheriff turned around and closed the door. "I think it would be. I'd enjoy driving the ice truck around in the morning. Only the hotel, café, Judge Granger, and Mrs. Reese have iceboxes. So many more could benefit from them."

"I hadn't realized. I thought many people had them."

The sheriff's rich laughter filled the cellar. "That only happens in a place where wagons can be pulled on ice."

Emily climbed the stairs to find the cellar door shut. She pushed it open a few inches, only to have the heavy door slam back down. She turned to the sheriff. "How did that get shut?"

He set the lemonade on a shelf and joined her on the narrow stairs. "Possibly a stronger wind caught it and closed it on us. Careful with the candle."

His arm brushed against hers, and Emily had to check to make sure she hadn't accidentally lit her sleeve aflame. Moonlight flooded in as TJ cautiously pushed the door open. Emily blew out the candle before the warm breeze could and exited. TJ handed her the pitcher, turned, and closed the door. Their fingers brushed as he slowly took the lemonade back, and Emily found herself in a scene from her novels. She'd only ever imagined what it felt like for the heroine to stand under the moonlight, the stars shining overhead, while the hero looked on. She stepped back. This was where she should be standing with the doctor. What she was supposed to feel with him, not TJ. The tingling of the fingers as their skin made contact. Wanting to run away and draw nearer to him at the same time.

Choosing propriety and protecting her heart, Emily hurried to the safety of the screened-in porch before she said or did something foolish.

⟫•◆•⟪

For the past two days, TJ had avoided Aidan and Miss Wilson. Of all the men TJ knew, Aidan deserved a good wife. Even if she was the woman TJ couldn't stop thinking about every free moment. Which he wasn't doing now, since he'd ducked into the jail rather than watch her pull the little cart into the alley behind the hotel as she'd done every afternoon for the past two weeks. Thelma must have added something to his lemonade. Nearly forty-two hours later, he still could feel Emily's hand tremble as they'd touched and see her blush in the moonlight. He shook his head and retreated to his desk.

A half hour later, Donny ran into the office and handed TJ a folded piece of paper. "Doc said to deliver this quick."

"Thanks, Donny. Did he pay you?"

The boy nodded and held up a nickel.

"Have you swept the sidewalk in front of the jail today?"

"Remember, you paid me for it this morning."

TJ pulled a three-cent piece out of his pocket. "Go help Miss Wilson take the cart back to Mrs. Reese." Emily's consistent schedule made her an easy target for Belle's men. Considering he'd followed her three mornings this week without her notice, it would be easy enough for Bart or Cline to do the same.

"I'd do that without your money. She's real nice. She sneaks me one of Miss Thelma's cookies every time I help her." Donny took the money. "If I take your money, would it be wrong to have a cookie?"

"That depends on if you know why I want you to help her." Not all the reasons, just the ones sheriff-job related.

"Same reason I am. Because you're worried Belle's men might follow her and make trouble."

"Have you seen them following her?"

Donny nodded, his too-long hair bouncing off his forehead and into his eyes. "Bart watches her, but he stays on the other side of the street. You better read the doctor's note. He told me to hurry." Donny pocketed the coin and ran across the street to the hotel.

TJ unfolded the note. His friend's untidy scrawl made it difficult to read.

Someone you want to meet. Use back door. Room 3. ~P

Until that moment, TJ never thought of Aidan as being cryptic. Out of habit, TJ checked his gun belt before putting on his hat and walking the two blocks to the small clinic. He circled the building and entered through the back door as instructed. The door to room 3 was shut. TJ raised his hand to knock and listened. Hearing nothing, TJ opted to open the door. A man lay on the thin mattressed bed. Where his left leg should have been, a patch of red marred the sheet. Thick whiskers covered his ashen face. TJ took a step closer. The room smelled of whiskey and death. The man exhaled but didn't open his eyes. Behind him, the door brushed the floor.

Aidan shut the door before speaking. "Recognize him?"

"Can't say I do."

"I wouldn't have either had I not found the tattoo." Aidan moved the sheet aside, uncovering the man's left bicep.

TJ stepped back. There wasn't a lawman in the state for the past twenty years who hadn't read a description of the infamous tattoo—the word *kills* drawn in the fanciest hand with twenty-five hash marks under it. Only there were more hash marks than reported.

"Thirty-seven"

"What?" TJ stopped counting and looked at the doctor.

"There are thirty-seven marks there. This one is only a few days old, still red around the edges." Aidan pointed to a mark surrounded by reddened flesh. "There is more." The doctor let the sheet drop back in place and moved the sheet covering the right leg, exposing the thigh. *Law* was etched in a coarser hand and embellished with swirls. Below the word, six stars had been crudely tattooed, each marked by a set of initials underneath. The fifth had the initials M. M.

Matthew Morgan.

Pa.

Sheriff.

The room spun.

Aidan clamped a hand on TJ's shoulder and pushed him

into a chair. "Put your head down and breathe deep. I nearly did the same when I realized who my patient was. He's lost a good sixty pounds."

An eternity later, TJ raised his head. "How did you find him?"

"I stepped out into the alley an hour or so ago and smelled the gangrene. It's a smell you never forget. The war reeked of it. I took the leg, but I don't know if it will make much difference. There are forty-two people's loved ones who'd argue I shouldn't have tried to save him at all, but I am a doctor. I realized who he was before I started the amputation. I was tempted to not even do it. I owe Cathleen that much for what he did." Far more than the families of the forty-three dead would sleep better tonight knowing Cole Pike lay immobile, his leg gone. There were the women and girls who were spared the cut of his knife or the lead ball of his gun for a worse fate. Women that included Aidan's dead fiancée.

The doctor was wrong. TJ wanted Cole Pike to face justice for his crimes. For terrorizing Hiramsville. For killing his father. "You did the right thing."

"I wish I hadn't. He might have died within minutes. No one would ever know I killed him. But then I'd be a killer like him. Cathleen wouldn't have wanted that."

Both men gazed upon the outlaw who'd ripped holes in their lives, families, and futures. The murderer lived. Each breath was followed by another. If there was mercy to be had, surely the next breath would be the man's last.

"Can I take him to the jail?" *Out of our sight?*

"Not sure how you'd get him up to the second floor, and I need to monitor him. I gave him laudanum for the pain. I don't think he will wake up soon, but I'll feel better if he has a pair of those handcuffs keeping him chained to the bed."

TJ carried only one of the three pairs the sheriff's office owned. Placing one end around Cole's right wrist, TJ linked the other to the iron bed frame. "Does he have any weapons?"

"No, I cut off his clothes and put them in the crate in the corner. There isn't a gun. There are two knives, though. Makes me wonder if someone dropped him off."

"If so, they may try to get him back. I don't want to endanger your other patients or the citizens. We need to move him out of here." TJ would need to get his mother out to Abigail's for the night. No way would he let Ma sleep under the same roof as his father's killer.

"We can move him if he survives the night. You or Jerome can guard him here. I'm sure half the men in town will stand in line to be deputized to have a turn guarding him."

Cole's ruthlessness had touched half the town. "And deal with another murder? I'll contact the Rangers and get him moved. Can't do his trial here anyway as he is likely to be hanged. Best if we don't have a lynching."

"Agreed." TJ studied the room. "Let's remove anything Cole could use as a weapon, and I'll get a wire off to the Rangers and find Jerome. Do you have any other patients here?"

"Nope. I finished stitching up little Brian Bird's arm. Got caught on barbed wire and made a mess of himself. I sent Mrs. Bickford home as soon as I realized who Cole was." The nurse had lost her husband in the posse who'd tracked Cole's gang.

Aidan gathered all the knives and saws onto a tray.

"Lock up, then. Dr. Jones is in town. He can handle things for the rest of the day." TJ dragged the bed away from the cupboards. The outlaw didn't even grunt. "You sure you didn't knock him out forever?"

"I don't think so. He'll come around before we want him to." Aidan left the room with the instruments he had gathered.

TJ also exited the room. "I'll be back in ten minutes. I know I don't need to tell you this, but if he wakes, stay away from him."

"You know I will."

Emily tucked her two dollars of pay into her pocket. Five days of backbreaking laundry and she'd made less than the three dollars she had been promised after the deductions for soap and a table linen that had an unreported tear in it. Mr. Davis blamed the wringer and charged her, even though Emily repaired the tear, which was no longer than her little fingernail. A nail much shorter than it had been Monday morning. Her hands remained raw despite copious amounts of balm. There had to be a better job.

Donny waited for her by the cart in the alley. "Need any help today?"

"No. I am not taking any mending home tonight."

"Then what is that?" Donny pointed to the tablecloth Emily carried over her arm.

"A minuscule victory." Emily reasoned if she had to pay for a new tablecloth out of her wages, the old one should be hers. Mr. Davis had argued until she pointed out he couldn't use it for dinner if he charged her for the cloth, claiming it was unusable. A bit of embroidery and the cloth would be better than new.

"Can I pull your cart to Mrs. Reese's?"

"Do you know what I really need you to do?"

Donny shrugged his shoulders.

"I need a jar of the best hand cream the mercantile sells." Emily sorted out a dime from her pay. "Or at least what you can get for ten cents."

"I'll take the cart, and you can go to the store."

Emily smoothed her hair back. "I am a persona non grata in the mercantile. Do you know what that means?"

Donny shook his head.

"It means they won't serve me as a customer."

"Oh, because Mr. Tarr insists you are a dove, right?"

"Something like that."

"My ma makes soaps and hand creams. Hers are better than anything that old store sells. She even sells them at a lady's store in Dallas. They smell nice too, if you're a girl." By the time he finished his sales pitch, Emily was sure he stood a full inch taller.

"I think I should buy some of your mother's cream."

"I can go get some now, and I'll even beat you to the house!"

Emily handed Donny the dime, and he scurried off. As she pulled her nearly empty cart out of the alleyway, she collided with someone running down the street and struggled to remain upright. Strong hands clasped her upper arms and steadied her.

"I thought Donny was going to help you." The sheriff dropped his hands.

"Pardon me. I must not have been looking." Emily narrowed her eyes, encouraging the sheriff to apologize.

"No, it was my fault. I was rushing. Where is Donny?"

"He ran an errand for me. How did you know he would be with me?"

"Never mind. When you see him, tell him both Dr. Palmer and I want him to stay home for the rest of the evening. It would be best if you hurried to Mrs. Reese's and stayed there the rest of the night too." The sheriff tapped the brim of his hat and rushed up the street.

Emily watched with narrowed eyes as he turned the corner to the depot. As disturbing as his ominous warning was, she found that the fact he knew Donny had been with her bothered her more. He had only spoken a few words to her since last Wednesday night, mostly along the lines of "Good day" or "Miss Wilson," always accompanied by the tip of his hat. Emily turned down the street, her arms still tingling where he'd held her. She had done her best to forget him this week. That was hard to do when he'd followed her to the hotel and back from a distance, as if he didn't want to be seen. As she continued on her way to Mrs. Reese's, Emily tried not to think on the sheriff and all the conflicting feelings she had about him.

True to his boast, Donny met her at the house. He held two small glass jars. "Here ya go. This one is a special salve Ma says to put on at night and anytime you are wearing gloves. The other is a cream that smells like verbena."

"Those have to cost more than a dime."

Donny shook his head. "Ma sold them to you for the same price she sells to the stores. She also wants you to sit with us at the Independence Day picnic tomorrow at noon. She wants to meet you."

"Tell her I am delighted by her invitation and I'll be there. Also, I bumped into Sheriff Morgan. He told me to tell you neither he nor Dr. Palmer need you the rest of the evening and to stay home."

"Doc told me not to come back for the rest of the day?" Donny's lower lip stuck out in a pout. "I knew that man was trouble. He smelled like a dead skunk. Doc sawed his leg off."

Bile rose in Emily's throat. She covered her mouth.

Emily dropped her hand. “You should listen to the sheriff and stay home tonight.”

“Are you staying at Mrs. Reese’s?”

“Yes, I am. I have no reason to go into town on a Friday night. And neither do you.”

“But I earn my best money Friday nights, watching horses and such.”

“If the sheriff asked you to go home, I am sure he has a very good reason. Would it help if I asked you to go too?”

Donny studied her for a minute and made a face. “I’ll go home, then. Night, Miss Wilson.” He took off at top speed and disappeared around the corner. Poor Mrs.—Emily had no idea what Donny’s last name was—she had her hands full with him. A good handful, but still a handful.

Emily put the cart away and went upstairs to get the journal. The next time she saw the sheriff, she wanted a reason to talk to him long enough to figure out why his presence affected her so.

Aidan stood at the sink in the workroom washing the instruments. He didn’t look up when TJ entered through the back door. “He’s still sleeping.”

“I got a cable off. If there’s a Ranger available in Fort Worth, they might make the evening train. If they don’t, I hope they ride out anyway.” TJ set his hat on a chair. “I wish this hadn’t happened on a Friday. If Belle is still holding a grudge, Jerome will have a miserable night arresting all those drunk men.”

“It will be worse if word gets out Cole is here.” Aidan dried his hands.

“I need another deputy for Friday and Saturday nights. But most of the candidates are former soldiers and ten years older than I am. I can’t have a deputy who won’t listen.

People only voted for me since they couldn't vote for Pa."
TJ rubbed the back of his neck. There might be a man or
two he could recruit for the night.

"That isn't the reason most people voted for you."

"That's right. They voted against Cline." TJ poured a glass
of water and drank it swiftly.

"Cline is Belle's man, and the law-abiding citizens didn't
want more of her type here, even if her trade brings in tax
revenue. You do a good job."

A groan in the other room had them both running to check
on the patient.

"My leg! My leg!"

The doctor entered first. "Don't pull at the bindings."

"It burns!"

Aidan tried to restrain Cole's left hand, but the outlaw
lashed out, knocking Dr. Palmer back against the wall.

"I thought you said he was weak." TJ moved around the
foot of the bed.

Cole tugged at the handcuff shackling him to the bed. "Let
me up. What did you do to my leg?" His voice decreased in
volume, ending in a whimper.

Aidan poured a half spoonful of laudanum. "I had to amputate."

"You cut it off?" The outlaw tried to sit up but collapsed.
"But I feel it. My leg hurts."

"Would you like something for the pain?" Aidan stepped
closer to the bed but stayed out of range of Cole Pike's free arm.

"'Course I would," snapped Cole.

TJ quickly moved to restrain the arm. "Speak nicer to the
doctor. He saved your life."

"For what? The gallows? I won't be here that long." A thin
layer of sweat covered Cole's pale face.

"You are in no condition to be moved. All your thrashing
has caused your wound to bleed again." The light glinted off

the reddish-brown liquid. "Take this. It will help with the pain while I stitch you back together."

TJ pulled another set of cuffs from his pocket. He should have come straight in here when he'd returned. After fastening Cole's other hand to the bedstead, TJ stepped out of the way.

"It's probably poison." Cole clamped his mouth shut.

"Laudanum. Not enough to kill you, just let you sleep." Dr. Palmer held the spoon to Cole's lips.

"Always the good doctor." Cole drank from the spoon. His face contorted at the taste. "He'll come for me, you know. Won't let his father die alone like the sheriff here did his father."

"Close your mouth, Cole." TJ stepped forward.

Aidan grabbed TJ's arm in time to keep him from knocking the hateful man out with his fist.

"And if I die here, he'll make you pay. Same way I made the doctor pay for—" Cole Pike's eyes rolled back into his head, and his mouth hung open, releasing one fetid breath after another.

"I wish it *had* been poison." Aidan slammed the spoon on a table near the door and left the room.

Silently, TJ agreed. He double checked to make sure Cole was out before leaving in search of the doctor.

Aidan sat at the workroom table, a cup in front of him. "Cold coffee. What I would do for something stronger."

"The same thing I would." TJ sat at the far side of the table. "Should I get the judge? It might help to have a witness if Cole talks again."

"It's Friday night. I doubt you could extract Judge Granger from Belle's second floor if you had a small army. Judge Canday won't step foot on this side of the river unless he needs to be in court. Besides, it wasn't a confession. Everyone knew he shot your father when he tried to stop Pike's gang. As for me—" Aidan blinked, then drank the cold cup of coffee in two gulps.

A confession wouldn't change things, nor erase the pain, or allow Cole Pike to hang more than once. All it would do was to shorten the trial. A speedy trial would be a blessing.

"I'd better restitch that leg." Aidan set his coffee cup on the table.

TJ followed the doctor back into the sickroom, the smell causing him to gag. Aidan removed the remainder of the old dressing. "I thought I cut off his leg high enough, but the remaining flesh may still be infected. The gangrene may have been too far gone."

"How did he have the strength to fling you into the wall?"

Aidan shrugged. "I saw it in the war. Some men would awake violently and with the strength of an ox, but after a moment, they were as weak as a newborn lamb. He may have lost consciousness on his own in a few more minutes." The doctor rarely talked about the war. He'd enlisted at seventeen and was assigned to the medical corps. Much of his knowledge came from reading one of two books the doctor he served under kept in his trunk and from watching and learning. After the war, Aidan had completed his education and received his degree. Unlike other veterans, he wasn't given to commiserating over a whiskey at the saloon. Perhaps it was why he didn't look as old and worn as the other soldiers.

"If he doesn't fight his restraints, this should hold the next time he wakes." Aidan re-bandaged the leg over the new stitches.

They retired to the doctor's office, neither wanting to be in the same room as Cole.

"Have you seen Miss Wilson this week?" asked TJ, raising the subject of the second worst thing they could discuss.

"I stopped by Wednesday evening. She is adjusting to the heat better than most Northerners. I was worried with all the laundry she does that she might suffer more from the heat." Only the doctor could make a social call sound like a medical inquiry. "And what about you, have you seen her?"

"Just in passing. Making sure Belle doesn't send her men after Miss Wilson." TJ didn't elaborate about stopping by the house on Wednesday too. The few minutes in the cellar's cold room with Emily had no cooling effect on his increased thoughts of the pretty northerner.

"Mr. Collins tried to call on her again on Wednesday night. Belle's men aren't the only ones you should worry about. Although Miss Wilson didn't give him even a moment to plead his cause. She—"

Someone pounded on the front door. "I'll see who is there."

Four Texas Rangers, including TJ's brother, stood on the porch. "Glad you made such good time."

"You're sure it's him?" GW removed his hat, as did the other Rangers.

"He has the tattoos to prove it." TJ explained all he knew and took the men back to the room where Cole lay.

GW pulled TJ aside. "Three telegrams in two weeks. We need to talk, little brother." TJ hoped his brother hadn't told anyone of the cryptic wires he'd sent.

"When can we move him?" asked the shortest ranger.

"Tomorrow, if he survives the night. I may have been too late with the amputation. His fever is higher than it should be," said Aidan.

"Do any of you know if Cole has another son who rides with him? When he was awake earlier, he was threatening that his son would be coming to get him and bringing retribution if he died." Silence answered TJ's question. The only son anyone knew of had died three years ago, triggering the unfortunate events leading to so many deaths.

What would Cole's gang start next if he didn't survive tonight?

TJ sent a note to the reverend advising tomorrow's picnic be canceled. Hiramsville wouldn't see another death at the hands of Cole's gang if he had anything to do with it.

The salve Donny's mother made did wonders for Emily's hands, erasing much of the redness. Perhaps her skin would heal after all. Emily pinned up her braid. She refused to work on Saturday, as she needed one day to concentrate on finding a better job. She tucked twenty-five cents into her bag. That should be enough to pay for a copy of the Dallas and Fort Worth newspapers, a few sticks of candy, and the ferry ride to the other side of the river and back.

Mrs. Reese always took her breakfast at the table in the nook overlooking the river. Mrs. Morgan sat opposite her, both looking up as Emily entered the room. Emily's eyes darted to the clock. Seven thirty was early for a social call, even among friends.

Emily poured herself some tea and took a boiled egg and a fluffy biscuit from the sideboard. "Good morning. I'm walking over to Acton today. Do either of you need anything?"

"Walking? It is six miles. What do you need that badly?" asked Mrs. Reese.

"I need the newspapers, and I can't buy a thing at the mercantile."

Mrs. Morgan set her teacup on the matching china saucer. "Mr. Saunders sells them at the station. No need to go all the way to Acton. Although you should wait to go to the station until the eastbound train has left."

"Why? I don't want to be late for the Independence Day picnic. I told Donny I'd sit with his family."

"Same reason I slept here last night. Dr. Palmer has Cole Pike in his office. Four Rangers rode into town last night to take him into state custody. The doctor wouldn't let him move until this morning." Mrs. Morgan's eyes were puffy and tear-stained.

Emily looked from one woman to the other. Strain pulled at the edges of Mrs. Reese's eyes. "I beg your pardon, but I don't understand. Why did you spend the night here? And who is Cole Pike?"

Mrs. Morgan's mouth pulled into a grim line. "He is the man who murdered my husband."

Mrs. Reese patted Mrs. Morgan's arm. "Seven years ago, one of the most despicable gangs of outlaws ever to roam Texas made the caves on the peak their home after the Comanche moved out of the area. Cole Pike was their leader. They terrorized the region for years. Several times, the Rangers tried to root them out and caught part of the gang, but never Cole. Three years ago, with the help of an old Indian who knew the caves, Matthew Morgan led a posse, including GW, TJ, and several Rangers. They caught the gang. But something went wrong. Cole escaped, but his son was shot and later died from the wound. A month later, Cole rode through town, firing his gun. Matthew Morgan tried to stop him and hit Cole on the shoulder. Cole fired back, and Sheriff Morgan was killed. Cole came back to town only once, six months later. No one from Hiramsville's seen hide nor hair of him since." Mrs. Reese took a sip of her tea.

Mrs. Morgan continued the narrative. "Until yesterday. The vermin showed up at the back of Dr. Palmer's, his leg so full of gangrene the doctor had to amputate. As soon as the doctor realized who he had in his surgery, he contacted TJ. The Rangers came in last night. The Rangers want Cole to face trial as much as every person in this town does. GW and TJ didn't want me around to see Cole—as if he wasn't in all of my nightmares—so they brought me down here late last night. For my safety, they claimed. But I think it was to make sure I didn't put a knife through the outlaw's heart." The force behind Mrs. Morgan's words was enough to drive a knife through the heart of a stone statue.

Mrs. Reese poured Mrs. Morgan another cup of tea. "It has been a very long night. Memories no one wanted to recall resurfaced and such. Anyway, until the eastbound train leaves the station, we are under orders to stay here. TJ is worried word will get out that Cole is here and he'll have a mob to deal with."

"Oh, then I'll wait before doing my errands. Do you need me to do anything, Mrs. Reese?"

"Not this morning. With Mrs. Morgan here, I have all the companionship I need."

"I've worked for you for two weeks now, and other than reading a few books and washing a bit of laundry, I've done very little to earn my room and board." Emily swept the crumbs she'd dropped into her hand.

"Nonsense. You have been here for me to talk to each evening. From what I've read in those English novels, a lady's companion mostly sits next to her employer and listens to her complain. I would find that very dull. Why don't you run along before I fire you?" Laughter followed Mrs. Reese's threat, taking any sting out of it.

Emily returned to her room and opened the journal. Her efforts from last night didn't offer anything more than eliminating another possibility. There must be a different way of looking at it. Emily set the open journal on the chair and walked around it. She squinted. Tried reading upside down. Out of desperation, she picked it up and held the book in front of her mirror.

Je suis—I am.

French! Cecilia had written the words backward and in French.

.einrat sius eJ .eudrep sius ej

Je suis perdue. Je suis tarnie.

"I am undone. I am tarnished." Perhaps the equivalent of "I am ruined." Even knowing that the worst things had happened, Emily was not prepared for the feeling of loss. If the writer still lived, Emily would have pulled her into her arms for a good cry.

I know backward writing is too easy to decipher, but I am too stunned to think. They call me Rose. A beautiful name for something so terrible. There is no school. Belle—that is what they call Mrs. Leblanc—put something in my food. When I woke up. . . I wish I was dead.

They had drugged Cecilia. Exactly what TJ assumed. Was it enough to be evidence? The next entry was written a week later.

Daisy says I am lucky for now. Only one man may—Daisy tells me to take opium, that it will help. Daisy says, Daisy says, Daisy says. I don't want to listen! I want to leave.

The handwriting in the next entry was wobbly.

I told Belle that Roger would rescue me. She laughed and of-fered to give him a free night as soon as I am available. For now, they lock me in my room because he is out of town. Only Belle has a key. I think they put something in my food every meal as I never quite feel myself. But I can never be me again.

Emily shuddered. Belle had slipped something into Cecilia's food. That would be evidence the sheriff could use.

I must keep my wits about me. I may read. Nellie brings my food now, but she must watch until I eat it all. I know they drug my meals. I heard him arguing with Belle, saying she was giving me too much. I don't fight him anymore. Belle tells me I must pretend to hate it and fight him. I do hate it, but I don't like it when he slaps me.

The next several entries were similar. Whoever 'he' was, Cecilia Rose—Emily couldn't think of her as only her before or after name—hadn't identified him.

I tried to sneak a letter to Roger to ask for help, but Belle found it. She told him. He beat me—says I am his. I reminded him of the emancipation proclamation and he laughed.

Emily turned the pages, searching for something that was proof, but not wanting to read about the life Cecilia Rose endured. She pulled out a second handkerchief, as the first one was too soaked to be of use.

Roger came. All the shame I feel came with him. I told him I had been tricked and drugged. He called me all the names I call myself and more. He will not take me away. He said, "If I loved him, I would have killed myself." He is like every other man who comes here.

Emily closed the book. She could read no more.

⬤◆⬤

The first gunshot came from behind, catching Jerome, who drove the wagon, in the arm. The second was in front of them and hit the dirt at TJ's feet. TJ grabbed Aidan and hauled him into the nearest building as shouts and gunshots filled the air.

The butcher came out from his back room.

"Get back and take the doc with you!" TJ waved the butcher back.

In the street, the Rangers took cover. Jerome jumped from the wagon and rolled for cover, leaving the wagon in the street. Cole's rescue party was more likely to get their leader killed at this rate, not that the outlaw was likely to live out the week since his fever had climbed throughout the night.

TJ strained to see the location of the shooters. Above his head, something thumped. TJ ran to the back room. "Who's upstairs?"

The butcher glanced at the ceiling. "There is no upstairs."

"How do I get to the roof?"

"There is a ladder in the alley." The butcher pointed to the back door.

TJ eased the door open. Two horses stood tethered behind the next building. Five feet to the left, a ladder leaned against the wall. TJ climbed the ladder until he could see onto the flat roof. A man knelt behind the false front of the butcher shop, reloading his guns using one arm. His other arm hanging limply at his side. TJ scanned the other roofs for the owner of the second horse and located him on the roof of the newspaper building next door, which was a story taller. If TJ came out on the lower roof, he'd be easy pickin's. The gunman in front of him stood. TJ aimed for the man's leg and fired, hitting his mark, and the man dropped his gun and yelled. The man on the higher roof paused. TJ aimed for his shoulder and missed, and the shooter spun around and stepped forward. It took the gunman a moment to spot TJ, and as the outlaw raised his weapon to fire, a bullet from the street side of the building blasted through his chest and the outlaw fell to the roof.

The sounds of gunfire from the street ceased.

TJ climbed onto the roof, watching both men, his gun trained on the man in front of him, who held his leg with his good arm.

"Put your hands above your head." TJ quickly moved to kick the man's gun out of the way.

"You busted up my leg!" moaned the man on the butcher-shop roof. No sound came from the man on the roof next door.

"Stay still, and I'll have the doctor look at it." TJ whistled a shrill note and was answered by one from below. Good. GW was alive. Another whistle sounded—GW's all clear. They'd used it a thousand times playing along the Brazos as children. Two boxes lay stacked against the wall of the newspaper building. TJ leaped up on them, peering onto the higher roof. The second shooter lay facedown in a pool of crimson. TJ whistled again. "GW, I could use help up here!"

GW joined TJ a few minutes later and nodded to the man holding his leg. "So that is why he stopped shooting."

"I think the other one is dead up on the next roof, but I am not sure."

"Here are some handcuffs." GW tossed TJ the cuffs and scrambled onto the next roof. "Did you shoot this one too?"

"No. Someone from the street did." TJ cuffed the outlaw and tied the man's bandanna to stanch the bleeding leg.

"One of these men must have shot Cole."

It took a moment to process what GW was saying—that one of his own men had shot the outlaw. "Shot Cole?"

"Right through the heart."

"I thought they were trying to rescue him."

The shooter laughed. "Save Pike? Why would we do that if we can have all that was his?"

No honor among thieves. "Who's we?"

The man clamped his mouth shut and didn't open it again until they'd hauled him down from the roof to where Aidan could remove the bullets, and then only to scream.

The Rangers boarded the noon train with a new prisoner and Cole's body in tow. Promising to return for the search.

Jerome stayed in Hiramsville to recover. Aidan reassured TJ that the bloody shirt was worse than the graze of the bullet.

Ma, who'd come running minutes after the gunfire died down and stayed to help the wounded, was talking to GW farther down the platform. They turned back and joined TJ.

"I'll be back soon." GW hugged Ma. It was obvious from her frown that his promise didn't satisfy Ma. "I still need to tease little brother about his false arrest. Can't tease him by letter."

They watched the train leave. Chances were that GW would be back soon but not to see Ma. Someone had killed Cole Pike, and it hadn't been to serve justice, and there wasn't a Ranger out there who knew the area like GW.

They were halfway back to the jail when his mother stopped and turned back to the depot. "I told Emily I'd get her the latest newspapers."

Emily. He hadn't called her that yet. He enjoyed hearing the name. TJ stopped his mother. "Let me take you home, then I'll take her the newspapers. I have the latest ones on my desk. She won't even have to pay for them."

Ma patted his arm. "You are so kind."

If only Ma knew his desire to see Emily Wilson had more to do with selfishness.

18

As much as she didn't want to read the journal, Emily felt compelled to finish it. As the heat of the day filled her room, she moved out to the screened-in porch. Harder than reading the words was transcribing them.

~

He hasn't come in days. I am glad. When he does, he's crueler than the guards.

~

He doesn't want me anymore. I must work with the other women.

~

Belle came today with my pay. A hundred dollars. After she deducted my room and board, she deducted my taxes. What kind of wicked town would tax a woman abused daily by all who meet her? Then she took money out for my gowns. There were only two dollars left. She took that back, saying I owed for the doctor. I don't know why I must pay the old man to leer at me.

But Belle says it is the law. She tells me I must work harder if I am to pay her off. I want to yell. But she had C with her. I think he enjoys hurting me.

The "old man" must not be Dr. Palmer. He might be in his mid-thirties, but there wasn't a speck of gray in his hair. Emily had only seen Doctor Jones at a distance. He was at least fifty. Days passed before the next entry.

~

It is true. If I take some of Daisy's opium, I do not mind the men as much.

~

How can I pay Daisy and Belle? I must stop the opium. I cannot feel my mind. It works almost as well to recite mathematical equations. One cannot feel when computing the area of a triangle. I won't recite my favorite books. They can't have that. I give them Hamlet.

Cecilia's lettering lacked its previous beauty.

I caught Belle in my trunk. Despite her name, she knows no French, but I need a new code. If she finds this book...

The next page, full of numbers, was indecipherable. Quite possibly the code was a book cipher. Cecilia was a teacher and must have arrived in town like Emily, with half a trunk full of books. But what book provided the key?

The screen door banged. Sheriff Morgan set a stack of papers on the table. "Afternoon, Miss Wilson. Ma asked me to bring you the newspapers. I brought all the ones I had at my office from this week. Here is your quarter back."

His fingers brushed her hand, and the quarter fell to the porch, rolling into a crack between the floorboards.

"I'm sorry," they said in unison, their hands still touching. TJ pulled back. "I have another quarter."

"No, I got my papers."

"I could climb under and get it. Or wait until the next time Mrs. Reese asks me to chase cats out from under there." He gave her a half smile.

"Donny will be happy to retrieve it." Emily sorted the papers to cover her reaction to his nearness. "*Matrimonial News*? Is this for me or you, Sheriff?"

The sheriff's face reddened, and he attempted to snatch the paper away.

Emily held the mail-order bride paper out of his reach. "So, it is for you. Would you like me to write you a recommendation? I can attest to the shortage of proper females here and affirm that you are a gentleman even when arresting a woman under false pretenses." She folded the newspaper and handed it back to him. His face grew pinker. The last time she had had this much fun had been…she couldn't remember. She'd teased cousin Percy, but not like this.

"I don't need the paper. Abigail sends both GW and me copies on a regular basis." He shifted his weight and avoided her eye.

"So you have no wish to wed?"

Impossibly, the color in his face deepened to a bright apple red. "I need to return to my duties." The sheriff tipped his hat and turned.

Emily sprung out of her chair and grabbed his arm. A bolt of electricity like that which she'd read about with Benjamin Franklin's kite shot up her arm, yet she couldn't let go. "Please, I shouldn't have teased you. If you have time, I've decoded a significant portion of the journal." He turned to face her, and she found the strength to remove her hand.

She scurried back to her chair, afraid a second touch might deliver a lethal shock.

The sheriff looked at her for a long moment before he nodded and removed his hat. "I should not have overreacted. No one other than GW has teased me like that for years. Have you found any evidence?"

Emily handed him the transcribed papers. "She rarely uses names. If you could figure out who the 'he' is that she talks about, you would have a valuable clue." She sat silently, watching the sheriff as he read. His face became harder, then drained of color, his scar more pronounced.

He set the papers down. "My humblest apologies, ma'am. I should have never allowed you to keep the journal."

"Do you know French?"

"No."

"Does Dr. Palmer?"

"I don't think so."

"You would have needed a translator anyway. And as I told you last time, Cecilia Rose saved my life. She saved me from the life she was forced to live."

"Cecilia Rose?"

"I couldn't call her Rose, and Cecilia, the old her—" Emily waved her hand. "She didn't want to be Rose. Although that is the only name you and Dr. Palmer knew her by."

The sheriff thumbed through the journal. "Why aren't you screaming in mortification? These writings aren't for a proper lady."

"It is shocking, but I am not as naïve as some. Bradford educates missionaries and wives of preachers. We were told of the depravity in the world. It would not do for a missionary to faint the first time she ran into something not discussed over society tea—whether it be natives of Africa or the islands only partially dressed, the squalor of the slums, or the depravity of the Wild West. I admire Cecilia's attempt to not lose herself in her world. She saved me from that world. I will see this through."

His face softened. "Still, I cannot ask it of you."

"No, you are too much of the chivalrous knight for that. Hiramsville's own Sir Galahad." Emily clamped her lips shut lest any other inane thought find its way to the surface.

"I am far from being a Knight of the Round Table. You give me far more credit than I deserve."

"I don't think I give you enough." Emily waved her hand to dismiss the subject. "I do have a new obstacle. Cecilia Rose changed to using a book cipher. I need to know what books she had access to. Were there other books among her things?"

"A book cipher?"

Emily turned the journal so he could see it. "Each set of numbers is a word in a specific book. Page, line, and word. In order to read what she wrote, I need the book she used."

"What about these sets of four numbers?"

"I think she may have had words she had to spell out, so the last number is the letter in the word. But without the book, there is no way to tell."

"Donny said there were books in her trunk. I think he gave some to Nellie and took others home. Do you need the books or the titles?"

"I need the books. Two editions of the same book are likely to have words on different pages or in different places."

Sheriff Morgan rose. "I'll get them to you as soon as I can." He left with a nod.

Emily rubbed her hand as she had wanted to all during the conversation. It still tingled from touching him. What had happened? Perhaps she should ask Dr. Palmer the next time she saw him. No, better write Amanda. The doctor was trying to court her, and she didn't have those reactions to his smile or touch.

A knock on the screen door pulled Emily from her thoughts, causing her to realize that more than a few minutes had passed since the sheriff had left. She glanced up to see who it was, then beckoned the doctor in. Time to test her theory. "Is it near sunset already?"

Dr. Palmer took off his hat. "I've come to apologize and to cancel our outing. I've come to realize something this past day and a half." He kneaded the rim of his hat as he sat down in the chair opposite her. "I am not ready to court a woman." The poor man's leg bounced as if it were trying to propel him away.

Emily sat stunned. In all the books she ever read, there had been a flowery speech, small talk, or hurled accusations. "Dr. Palmer, we went on half a walk, had one pleasant conversation, and exchanged but a few words on the street. You are under no obligation to me."

"I do not offend you?"

"No, we hardly know each other." Emily paused, studying him a little closer. "Please do not be offended, but you seem to be under an inordinate amount of strain."

Dr. Palmer clamped his hand on his knee, stopping it from bouncing. "I'm afraid lack of sleep and too many pots of coffee have not helped."

"Understandable. If it eases your mind, I am not sure I am ready to be courted." *Unless it is the sheriff.* "My first adventure into the world has not gone as planned. I still want to prove that I do not need to be shuttled from one caretaker to the next. I want to teach." *I want to find love, not just be convenient or an answer to desperation,* she added in her thoughts.

The doctor released a long breath and pointed to the newspapers. "Are you seeking a new job?"

"Yes, although I am nervous about finding another one like the offer I received from Belle."

"Will you allow me, as a friend, to make inquiries about any offer you might receive? I know a great many other doctors, and they know doctors…so I could inquire in most any town in Texas and parts of the South."

"Thank you, Dr. Palmer. I am glad you would consider me a friend."

"Friends. Does sound nice, doesn't it?" His warm smile did nothing to change her heart rate.

Emily gave him a genuine smile. Despite losing a suitor, she felt no pain. Friends were what they were destined to be.

———◇———

Finding Donny took TJ longer than expected. Who would have figured Donny to be home on a Saturday afternoon? Especially when the picnic was canceled after the shootings. Neighbors cautiously traded extra cake for fried chicken and bread for cucumber salad or gathered in small groups at one another's homes.

Mrs. Owen looked up from her mending. "Sheriff, do you need my boy? I'd like him close today."

An understandable request. "I have a quick question for him."

"He's in back fixing the lean-to roof."

Donny hopped down from the low side of the roof when he noticed TJ approaching. "What do you need, Sheriff? I can't help you today. I'm fixing the shingles." Donny's chest puffed out in pride.

"Do you remember what books were in Rose's chest?"

"Only the children's books and readers. Nellie kept most of 'em. I have four."

"I need to borrow the ones you brought home. I'll bring them back in a few days."

"Why?"

"They might have a clue in them."

Donny took off running around the house, calling for his sisters. "Francis! Elizabeth! Where are those books?"

Donny returned with an armful of books and a pair of sad-eyed little girls following in his wake. TJ knelt and pulled two peppermints out of his shirt pocket. "I need to rent the books for a few days. Can I leave this as a down payment, and when I return the books, I'll pay the rest of the rental?"

The girls looked at the candy, then at Donny, who looked at his ma, who nodded at her children. At his mother's nod, he answered. "Sheriff Morgan is a good man. If he gives you his word, he'll bring them back."

The girls took the candy and ran for their mother's skirts. Mrs. Owen smoothed their hair. "You need not rent the books."

"Ma'am, I believe I do." TJ winked at the girls, who giggled and ran back to the front of the house.

"You already pay Donny—"

"Exactly what his work is worth to me. Now, what are the girl's favorite colors? I think some new hair ribbons might be the correct form of rent payment."

"Pink!"

"Yellow!" The girls answered almost at the same time, their voices coming from around the house.

"I'll see what I can find. I hope I don't need to go all the way to Dallas for such colors. I've never in my life shopped for ribbons for two such beautiful girls."

The little girls giggled.

"Good day, Mrs. Owen. See you at church, Donny." TJ tipped his head and resisted the urge to tell the boy to take care up on the roof.

At the Bull's Eye, Nellie shooed him away from the back door. "Come early tomorrow and I can help you, Sheriff. Belle's mighty busy today, and everyone's on edge because of the shooting. Cline will have my hide if he sees me talking to you."

TJ left. Getting Nellie in trouble would not help in the long run.

Mrs. Reese, Becky, and Thelma sat at the table in the screened-in porch when he arrived back at Mrs. Reese's house. Aidan must have already come to call on Emily and whisked her off on a ride.

"I brought books for Miss Wilson. Will you see that she gets them?" TJ set the stack of books on the smaller table.

"She's down by the river if you want to tell her yourself." Mrs. Reese's knitting needles clicked a steady beat.

"No, I wouldn't want to interrupt." TJ set his hat on a vacant chair near the door.

"Interrupt what?" asked Becky.

"Her walk."

"Hard to interrupt someone walking alone," Thelma muttered.

"She's alone?"

Mrs. Reese nodded.

TJ clenched his jaw to keep from yelling at the women. What had they been thinking to let her go alone? Between Belle's men and the unknown killer, it wasn't safe for any woman to walk alone near sunset anyplace in Hiramsville, especially near the river. "Which way did she go?"

"She took the path over there." Becky pointed across the yard.

Nodding at the ladies, TJ grabbed his hat and sprinted across the yard. The path zigzagged back and forth down the face of the thirty-foot canyon wall leading to the river.

At the bottom of the drop, the path split. He scanned in both directions. TJ ran south around the bend where the trees gave way to the water. A woman walked along the path. "Emily!"

TJ exhaled. She was safe.

He closed the distance between them. "Emily."

"Is something wrong?" She tilted her head to look at him.

"Not anymore." TJ breathed out, trying to catch his breath as he also reached for her hand to tuck it in his arm. Thrilled when she allowed it.

"You ran down the embankment and yelled my Christian name, and nothing is wrong?"

Not wanting to return to the house, TJ guided her along the path in the direction she had been going. "It isn't safe for you to be down here alone. Belle would do anything to get you back, and there is a new outlaw in town, and I don't know who he is."

"That's why you've been lurking in the shadows and following me. You've also had Donny following me, haven't you?"

She realized he'd followed her. TJ swallowed. "Yes."

Instead of yelling at him, she smiled softly. "Thank you."

"Where is Dr. Palmer, anyway? I thought he was supposed to come calling. Another patient emergency?"

Emily sighed. "I assume he is at home. He isn't courting me anymore. We agreed we are better off as friends. Dr. Palmer would make a very good big brother, and I am not the person who can heal his heart."

"But I thought—" TJ couldn't finish the thought. He was too aware of the blue eyes peeking up at him from beneath long lashes, and of her nearness, and of the scent he recognized as hers from the moment he arrested her. Lavender and a hint of lemon. He looked across the river, afraid if he kept looking at Emily he might never be able to move again.

She tugged on his arm. "Are we going to walk, or are you going to stare out into the river?"

"Sorry, I rarely get the chance to escort, I mean—Thank you for not getting upset." He moved his right foot, then the left.

"Upset about what?"

"Me following you, paying Donny to keep an eye out." He paused and lifted their linked arms. "Allowing me to take your arm and escort you without asking your permission."

A bird called from high in the tree branches above them.

"I didn't mind, but I wish you had spoken to me. I have been careful. Bart's been watching me from a distance. I suppose you know that."

"I didn't want to scare you by warning you too much."

"Mrs. Reese has given me several stern warnings and even offered to send me to a friend of hers in Flower Mound. But I want—no, need—to not rely on charity."

"Did you find any promising job leads today?"

Emily shook her head. "Not for a teacher. I'm not venturing to another town to tend a store."

The trail ended at a sandy shore where the river made a slow bend. "I learned to swim here when I was five or six. GW threw me in and screamed snake."

"You are afraid of snakes?"

"Just the poisonous ones."

Emily moved closer to his side and studied the ground around her feet. "How can you tell the difference?"

"The easiest way is behavior. If the snake flees, it is probably harmless. If it stands its ground or attacks, it is usually venomous."

"Not color or markings?"

"There are differences, but if you are close enough to spot them, you're probably too close."

Emily extracted her hand from the crook of his elbow and rubbed her arms.

"Cold?" TJ moved to slip off his jacket and realized he only wore a vest.

"No. Only thinking. Snakes are like people. You can tell their nature by their actions. But I don't think snakes plot to bite. People do. Sometimes they run and yell at you."

TJ placed his hands on her arms and moved his thumbs in slow circles. "I'm sorry if I scared you running down here like I was charging a dragon."

Emily tilted her head and looked into his eyes for an eternity of heartbeats. "You've never scared me. Not even when you arrested me. There is something safe about you." She reached up and traced his scar, her eyes avoiding his.

There was nothing safe about the riot of emotions surging through his heart. Her touch was the exact opposite of the cut that had left the mark on his face—soothing in a way he had no words to describe. He longed for more.

Emily stood on her toes and brushed her lips over the spot where the scar met jawbone. Immediately, she dropped her head, hiding under the brim of her hat. "I shouldn't have done that."

TJ traced the line of her arm up to her shoulder and over until he found her chin. He lifted it gently with one finger until he could see her eyes and brushed his thumb slowly along her jaw bone, her eyes widening at the gesture. "Why not?"

"It isn't proper. I remember my mother kissing my father's scar, and I—" Emily's cheeks glowed pink, and her voice came out as soft as a hummingbird's flight. "I wondered—I shouldn't have been so bold."

In response, he bent slowly, watching as her eyes dropped to his lips, then fluttered closed. Before their lips met, her straw hat stopped him with a jab to the middle of his forehead. TJ pulled back and rubbed a spot above his eyes.

"Oh no!" Emily's fingers smoothed his brow, pushing his hat away. "I'm sorry! I didn't realize...I never—" She blushed a deeper pink.

TJ loosened the bow tied under her chin and slipped her hat off with one hand. For good measure, he removed his own, dropping it to the ground and lifted her chin with his free hand. TJ brushed her lips with the softest touch. Once, twice, three times, before lingering long enough for her to return his caresses. He pulled back and leaned his forehead against hers. Searching her eyes, he whispered reverently and sweetly, "Miss Wilson, may I court you?"

"Yes, but I think you should call me Emily." With a light blush dusting her cheeks, she returned her lips to his.

The setting sun cloaked the path in shadow. Emily took TJ's hand as he helped her along the steep turns.

I've become one of them.

Those girls from school who threw themselves at men and thought of nothing but the next kiss. The ones she looked down on as they giggled and blushed about this ball or that outing. The ones willing to walk thirteen miles on a Saturday just for a chance to see the men at the college on the north side of the Merrimack River. The ones who primped more than they studied. She knew what happened to them. They gave their kisses and enjoyed their flirtations. Then, when the Johns, Williams, and Herberts chose a wife, they were the ones left behind. They were the ones crying inconsolable tears and eating boxes of sweets, yards of licorice, and every Fry's Chocolate Cream bar they could buy.

She'd sought to never join their ranks. But the softness in TJ's eyes when she'd touched his scar intending to smooth out the worry she'd caused had pulled her in. It had been so long since someone had cared enough to worry about her. Rounding the last corner, her boot caught on a rock, but TJ's arm encircled her before gravity could exert its pull, enveloping her in the scent she hadn't been able to place the first time he'd accidentally held her. It was Texas, sunshine, hard work, and mesquite.

"Careful." He held on until she nodded.

If only he had issued that warning twenty minutes ago, before her world had tilted with his kiss. Emily's feet were planted on solid ground, but everything inside was being tossed to and fro. He'd offered to court her, but that was the proper thing to do after sharing a kiss that begged for more. How did one go about letting a man out of his obligation gracefully? It tore her insides apart thinking of not courting him, but she didn't want to be an obligation for a man. She had held onto hope that there would be a growing attraction and desire on both their parts to find love when she found someone she wanted to court her. Now doubts began to swirl in her mind, causing her to question her earlier emotions.

At the top of the cliff, TJ stopped near the base of an ancient oak. "I still would have asked to come calling."

"What?"

"I wanted to call on you before, but I wouldn't get in Dr. Palmer's way."

"Oh." Men were strange creatures.

"What I am trying to say is I don't want you to feel compelled to…"

Wasn't that what *she* was supposed to say? Emily shook her head. "I shouldn't have—"

His hands moved from hers to cup her elbows. "Perhaps not according to some etiquette book. In case you haven't noticed, we don't use too many of those out here. I would have asked before the doctor had if Mrs. Reese hadn't warned me off at the church picnic. My only regret of the evening is not taking you on that walk in the first place."

"What about the rim of my hat?" That part hadn't been pleasant. It never occurred to her that wearing a proper hat was a way to protect one's virtue. And for a minute, she regretted that the hat had fulfilled its chaperone duties so well—until he'd removed it, his eyes never leaving her face.

A half smile played at his lips. "No, I don't regret the hat."

"Why not? It hurt you."

"It gave me a moment to think before I acted."

"Oh." Stranger and stranger still. She hadn't been thinking at all, at least not of anything more than what kissing him would feel like.

TJ tucked her hand in the crook of his arm, and they crossed into Mrs. Reese's backyard. He leaned over and whispered, "If you want to back out, you have a few moments."

Emily turned to see if his face was as sincere as his voice. Her breath caught at the open longing in his eyes. "No."

He pulled back, but Emily tightened her grip. "I mean, no, I don't want to back out. I would very much like for you to court me. People won't think ill of me for getting a new beau so soon, will they?"

"Likely not. Someone is still bound to propose to you after church tomorrow, even if I am at your side." He pulled her closer as they crossed the lawn.

TJ held open the screen door. The women, recently joined by Mrs. Morgan, stopped their conversation.

Mrs. Reese set her knitting in her lap. "I see he found you. Harriett was telling us some of what happened today. If I had known we had another possible new threat in town, I would have never allowed you to go walking alone near the river. Although, given Belle's disposition, I shouldn't have let you out of my sight in the first place."

Emily hung her hat on a peg and sat in the chair TJ held out for her. "Do you think she would try to harm me?"

"I saw Cline watching your bedroom window the other night." Becky didn't look up from her mending as she spoke.

"What? Why didn't you tell me?" Mrs. Reese scooted forward in her chair.

"Didn't think nothing of it. Harold and his men are always watching me, but nothing comes of it."

Mrs. Reese said something that sounded suspiciously like words the dockworkers used. "How long have they been watching?"

"Since I turned sixteen two months ago. Harold saw me coming home from the mercantile and asked me if I wanted to come work for him. Of course, I told him no."

"He has no right! I settled this two years ago." Mrs. Reese pushed her chair away from the table, iron legs screeching against the boards.

Mrs. Morgan put a calming hand on Mrs. Reese's arm. "Don't confront him on a Saturday night. Wait until Monday morning, when his place is empty."

Emily looked from one person to the other, trying to sort out what she was hearing.

Becky turned to her. "You don't know, do you, miss? Mrs. Reese bought me right out from under Harold's nose. Then she gave me my pa's IOU so I belong to no one but me. She doesn't like me trying to work it off and forces me to go to school, but someday I'll pay her all $300."

"And I'll give it back to you in my will. Emily, in case you haven't noticed, I collect lost women. Most of them don't stay with me very long, only until they can get resettled with a new job and life elsewhere. There isn't a working girl on Second Street I haven't tried to help when I could. But I don't always have the opportunity."

"My pa done brung me to town and bought me a fancy new dress for my fourteenth birthday. I looked real pretty."

"Becky…" Mrs. Reese raised a brow.

"I mean, my father brought me to town…then he took me to dinner. Only it was to Harold's, but I didn't know what Harold's was. They played music and pulled me up to the stage. Everyone got all quiet. Then Mrs. Reese came marching in the front door and yelled at Harold and Pa to stop. Called them more names than a herd of cowboys. She plunked a money bag on the table, took some papers from Harold, grabbed me by the wrist, and took me out of there. At first I was angry with her, then Thelma sat me down and gave me a slice of cake. I ain't…I mean, no one ever gave me a cake for my birthday before. Then Thelma told me about what my pa and Harold were doing. Miss Callie lived in your room then. She was always crying, probably on account of—"

Mrs. Reese cleared her throat. "Thank you, Becky. I think Miss Wilson has the general idea. I paid off her father's debt on two conditions—that the man never show his face in Hiramsville again and that Harold let it be known that Becky was under my protection until she turned twenty-one. Apparently I need to remind him what that means."

During the conversation, TJ reached under the table and took Emily's hand in his, passing on a strength Emily didn't realize she needed. She didn't dare look at him, knowing she would blush.

TJ gave her hand a light squeeze. "Becky, when did you see Cline?"

"Thursday night. I wanted some water. I saw him leaning against the tree out there. He lit a cigarette, and I saw his face plain as day."

Emily shuddered.

<hr>

No one spoke. The desire to envelop Emily in his arms consumed TJ, but that would have to wait for a more opportune time. He rubbed his thumb over her knuckles to reassure himself she was safe. "Have you seen anything else peculiar?"

Becky squinted up at the ceiling. "Donny's been around more than usual. Judge Granger stopped his carriage twice in front of the house. The first time, I thought he was going to call, but he didn't get out, which was good since I hadn't finished dusting the parlor. The second time he didn't really stop, just drove by all slow, like he was looking for something."

"Why would he come here? He knows I don't like him, and vote or no vote, I'll use my influence to keep him out next election." Mrs. Reese relaxed again in her chair.

Thelma and Ma pursed their lips but made no observations.

A few ideas about the judge's motives came to TJ's mind, none of them good. "He wants to figure out a way to get Emily to swear out a complaint against me for the false arrest. He'd like nothing better to put someone who supports his ideas on taxes in the sheriff's office."

Ma's head jerked up. Mrs. Reese and Thelma looked from him to Emily and back. Emily's hand tightened on his own. He'd used her Christian name.

"Emily's agreed to allow me to court her." The words spewed from his mouth like too-hot soup. There it was. Out.

"What?" the three ladies asked in unison. Becky's mouth hung open.

Emily answered. "Earlier today, Dr. Palmer came by, and we agreed our future held nothing more than friendship. When TJ found me by the river, he very eloquently expressed his desire to court me. I've agreed. We'd planned to tell you the moment we returned."

Ma and Mrs. Reese shared a look and a nod.

Mrs. Reese lifted the tablecloth. "Glad you said something. Five more minutes of you two hiding your hands under the table and I was going to have to call you out, which

I didn't want to do. Dueling is so barbaric, and I am not as good a shot as I once was."

Ma laughed. "I was going to take the strap to him. He's grown since last time, but it worked before."

Emily blushed and dipped her head.

"I'm surprised it took him this long. Did you see him at the picnic? I thought he'd jump over the tables to keep all those men away. Someday I want a man to look at me like that." Becky sighed and went back to her mending.

The other women kept studying him and exchanging glances he didn't understand. This must be what a defendant felt like standing before the court. TJ tried to swallow. "Perhaps I should leave, start my evening rounds." *Let you ladies talk.* He dropped Emily's hand and stood.

"Three minutes."

"Pardon?" TJ asked Mrs. Reese to repeat herself.

"You have three minutes to walk around the house together. Stay on the porch. I'll hear if you stop for very long. Those boots have extremely loud heels." Mrs. Reese pointed toward the covered porch.

TJ helped Emily up and threaded through the chairs to the back screen door. Mrs. Reese held up her pin watch and nodded. They hurried out the door and around the corner of the house, where the lamplight didn't reach them.

Emily giggled. "What do you think she'll do if we take four?"

"Best we don't find out tonight. Unless you want a shotgun wedding."

"I don't think I am ready for that."

TJ pulled her close to his side. "I would prefer to marry when I wasn't under duress." He turned her to face him and placed a kiss on her forehead, glad she hadn't brought the hat. At a thump from the screened-in porch, TJ and Emily walked on.

"May I see you tomorrow evening?" They came to the porch swing. He held it so Emily didn't bump herself passing.

"Of course. It's tradition for courting couples to spend Sunday evenings together."

"Are you playing the organ again?"

"Yes."

"May I walk you home after church?"

"Please."

They reached the far corner of the house, where the next turn brought them to the street side. TJ lifted her fingers to his lips.

Emily placed her free hand on his chest. "Be careful tonight."

"I always try to be."

"I mean with the—"

He put his finger to her lips, then pressed another kiss to her brow. He figured they had ten seconds left. "Hurry!" He tugged her into a jog around the last side of the house.

Mrs. Reese held her watch. "Three seconds to spare. It wasn't necessary to run like a herd of buffalo across my porch."

Yes, yes it was.

20

If she could throw a baseball like cousin Percy, Emily would have aimed it out the window at the rooster's head. For the second morning in a row, that she would admit to, the feathered fiend had interrupted her dreams of TJ.

Monday was Jerome's day off, so today she would only see TJ in passing, if at all. Considering they'd spent four hours in each other's company yesterday, she couldn't complain. Becky had been a dutiful chaperone. The three minutes and thirty seconds Mrs. Reese had given them on a squeaky back-porch swing had hardly been long enough. Trying to kiss and keep the squeaky swing moving was as dangerous as kissing with her favorite straw hat on had been. Most likely exactly what Mrs. Reese planned. At least Becky had not stopped them from holding hands. Kissing muddled her thoughts too much anyhow. Mrs. Manning was forever telling the students to think more and kiss less during the courting period.

Few of the girls at school ever talked about things like the joys of handholding, or the way the soft tingles spread when one's hand was caressed, or the way one's heart could race.

185

Had TJ not already kissed her, Emily might be content to hold hands for a very long time.

The rooster crowed again. Time to stop daydreaming and prepare for the day. Emily climbed out of bed and put on her work dress.

When she came out of the house and around to her laundry shed, she found Donny sitting in the cart she used to haul the laundry.

"You are early again."

"The sheriff said you knew I was looking out for you, so I figured I'd be out here instead of in the bushes waiting to meet up with you accidentally." He scrambled out of the cart and set a burlap bag on the table. "These are all the books Nellie kept from Rose's trunk. She said there was a Bible too, but she put that in the Church's poor box, along with some of Rose's old clothes."

"Thank you. I'll return them as fast as I can." Emily moved the books to the shelf that held the irons.

As predicted, she didn't see TJ except from a distance all of Monday.

Tuesday morning, he sent a note with Donny.

Emily,

I fear you are going to find me somewhat inconstant for the next week or two. Everyone is upset about the shooting. Today I am riding around some farms to the south to see if I can learn more. I should be back this evening.

I look forward to supper tomorrow night. Please don't venture off on your own.

Affectionately,

TJ

Emily smiled and tucked the envelope in her pocket. It wasn't an eloquent love note, but it was hers.

⬥

TJ threw off the sheet covering him. The late-night cable on his office desk bothered him. Two of the Rangers were returning to Hiramsville on the morning train. There was no other information. He would be fortunate to see Emily in passing again today. Monday he'd nodded at her from across the street as she'd returned her laundry. Tuesday they'd exchanged a few words when her cart had caught in the mud left by the afternoon rain. Tonight, she'd invited him to dinner at Mrs. Reese's, but the cable that had arrived minutes before midnight changed that. How could he court a woman if he could never see her? But his Ma and Pa had made their marriage work, even with Pa's unpredictable work hours, as had Jerome and his wife.

A second deputy would help solve the problem. Every week for the last year, he and Jerome had discussed the ramifications of hiring even a part-time deputy. Another deputy meant a bigger budget. Which meant more taxes. Which came back to the brothels and was a major part of the reason he needed another deputy. What he wouldn't give for the Temperance Society women he'd read about in the papers to take up residence in Hiramsville. Although most local women sided against the brothels and saloons, their voices were not heard by the city council. The preachers and ministers had some impact, but not enough. TJ loathed asking for a second deputy, but what other choice was there? The Rangers might fill in a few gaps for now, or their arrival could create a bigger need.

The clock in the parlor chimed five times. TJ sat up. There was no point in trying to sleep anymore. His Wednesday had officially started.

For the hundredth time since last weeks' shooting, TJ walked the area, looking for some clue he'd missed. As it was still before six, the shops remained closed. Hiramsville's butcher's shop escaped damage from any bullets, but the newspaper office had a new hole through the sign near the roofline. TJ crossed the street and studied the two-story building. The shot that killed the gunman on the newspaper's roof must have been incredibly lucky, as it was close to impossible to make the shot from any place along the street. The gunman would have had to be leaning over the building. TJ closed his eyes. From the ladder, he hadn't had a good view of the man, just a general impression of where he'd stood.

TJ circled the butcher shop. The ladder still leaned against the building. Despite yesterday's rain, bloodstains marked the center of the newspaper building's roof. Standing at the edge, TJ replayed the events as he'd witnessed them from the ladder and counted off the paces to where the outlaw had fallen. Unease filled him. The fatal shot hadn't come from the street. It had come from above. The only spot higher in range was the hotel. Whoever shot Cole must have turned on his own men and started shooting them from the hotel.

He scanned the windows. The third-floor corner room or the roof were the most likely options. TJ climbed back on the top of the ladder to test that perspective. The false front to the butcher's office obscured the third-story window, but not the roof. Since no one had shot at him when he'd reached the top of the ladder, the hotel shooter must not have seen him, meaning he had to be in the third-floor room.

An outlaw who'd turned on his own gang? Unusual. TJ returned to the street, where the creek of wheels caught his attention. Emily and Donny pulled the laundry cart up the street. TJ lengthened his stride to greet them.

"Morning!" He tipped his hat. "May I walk with you?" TJ took the cart handle from Donny.

"Please do." Emily's smile warmed him.

Donny crossed his arms. "If you walk with us, do I get paid?"

"You'll even get paid if you don't walk with Miss Wilson, since I'm here."

Donny ran off with a backward wave.

Emily laughed. "I don't think I've ever seen someone so eager to leave my presence."

"He doesn't realize how fortunate he is to spend time with you each day."

"I understand he spends time with you each day as well."

"If that's what you call talking my ear off and spinning in my chair."

"That is more than I've seen of you this week, though I'm not complaining. I understand it comes with the job."

"You might complain when I tell you I might not attend supper tonight as the Rangers are coming back into town this morning."

"Oh." Emily turned into the alley behind the hotel. TJ followed her into the building. Emily shook her head and shooed him back out. Five minutes later, she emerged with two large bags of laundry. TJ took the bags from her and tossed them into the cart while Emily disappeared back into the kitchen.

She returned with a smaller basket. "Don't throw those. They are lace curtains."

"Do you normally do curtains?

"This is the first time. I've never repaired them, either. There is a hole in one, and another looks like it has soot on it."

TJ pulled the cart back onto the main street. "May I walk you home?"

"Of course."

Walking a woman home by sunrise while pulling a cart wasn't as enjoyable as by sunset, but it beat not seeing her for another day.

❧

They walked the last hundred yards, no faster than a snail. Emily kept her steps deliberately slow, but inevitably, they reached Mrs. Reese's backyard.

"I need to get back and let Ma know the Rangers are coming. Before I do, may I look at those curtains?"

"Why?"

"It seems odd to only have two that need washing, and with the shootout on Saturday, I wonder if a bullet could have done the damage."

Emily pulled them out of the basket and laid them on the lawn.

TJ ran his finger around the edge of the hole and smelled the blackened edge. "Do me a favor and don't wash these today. Not until I can have the Rangers look at them."

"I can't start them until I wash the regular laundry, anyway."

TJ looked around the yard, then pulled Emily into the doorway of the washroom. He placed a kiss on her crown and stepped back. "I wish—" Instead of finishing his sentence, he leaned down and brushed a kiss across her lips. "I'll let you know as soon as I can if I must cancel tonight."

Emily watched until he disappeared before turning her attention to the laundry. Not what she'd pictured as court-ing—a man in his best suit sitting in the parlor, going to a concert or a play under the too-watchful eye of her aunt. Not that her aunt would have allowed such a thing until after Barbara was settled and not with a young man whose fortunes shined brighter than Barbara's intended. Yet Mrs. Reese allowed them a few moments of privacy here and there, and no one had to beg Uncle Harlan for the privilege of courting the unwanted niece. And then there were the quick kisses. Emily closed her eyes to replay the one he'd left her with. Instinct told her there wouldn't be another one like down at the river unless he proposed. Proposal? She bit her lip. Not yet, but maybe someday.

Emily poured boiling water into the washtub, splashing a little onto her faded skirt. Best part of courting the sheriff? Not always having to be in proper dress and discussing proper subjects. That was a puzzle. How was one supposed to know one's future spouse if they had to offer only proper opinions? She stirred the soap into the water and added the first of the sheets. Courting in the West may be unpredictable, but she preferred it to what she might have endured in Boston.

While wringing out the sheets, Emily envisioned the lemon cake she planned to make for after dinner. If only the Rangers didn't need TJ tonight.

21

ot meeting the train was a calculated risk since TJ didn't know what had brought the Rangers back to Hiramsville. The Rangers from last Saturday, or GW, would be recognized. If these were new ones, they could keep their identities hidden if they chose. TJ checked the clock again. The train had arrived a quarter of an hour ago. He should have gone to the station.

A man entered the office and removed his dusty hat, the sure tilt of his head and his confident gait labeling him as a Ranger. "Sheriff Morgan?"

TJ nodded. "How may I help you?"

"I have a letter for you." The man handed over a sealed paper addressed in his brother's semi-legible scrawl.

Doug will explain. For the safety of our family, listen
and get Ma to listen too.
-GW

Doug folded his arms in such a way as to leave the back of his left hand facing out. The scar traced a clean line from his wrist to the third knuckle.

TJ raised a brow. "And?"

"Is your deputy around?"

"I sent him to check on a case of missing cattle over near the peak."

"Is there someplace more private than this?"

TJ pointed to the floor above. "The jail is unoccupied. Want a tour?"

"I've heard about your second-story jail. GW claims it's inescapable."

"I hope so." TJ pulled out his keys, and the ranger followed him to the iron-barred door leading up to the cells.

"Lock it behind us." Doug preceded TJ up the stairs. "Nice facility you have here. I'm surprised you don't have residents."

"Judge Granger is more lenient than I'd like. Judge Canday spends most of his time waiting to be called before the Pearly Gates. He'll write out a warrant now and then and come to court if the case is small. Since capital cases are moved to the state, we rarely have prisoners over two to three days."

Doug toured the empty cells. "The isolation cell is a nice feature. If we get our job done here, we'll need it."

"So, what is your job?"

"To find Cole Pike's son. Appears that he had another son that we weren't aware of. Slim, the man you shot in the leg, is being tight-lipped about the identity of the son but confirms what you learned from Cole. The son is intent on revenge. In particular against the doctor and you, for reasons Slim couldn't, or wouldn't, divulge."

What more revenge could they have? Cole had killed TJ's father and kidnapped and murdered Aidan's bride. "Why us?"

Doug leaned against the wall. "Best guess? For putting him in a position to either rescue or kill his own father. Cole said he'd rather be shot than hang, so the son gave him his wish,"

"So, the son must have been the one shooting from the hotel."

"The problem is no one saw him. And the Rangers who looked at the hotel roof didn't see any evidence of anyone having been up there. But GW is sure someone had to be over there."

TJ pointed to the corner of the hotel visible from the small window. "He wasn't on the roof. He was in the third-floor room. I think he shot his own gang member—the one on the newspaper roof."

"How did you come to that conclusion?"

"I've been trying to retrace everything from the shootout. I was on the ladder to the butcher's shop roof. I shot Slim, then the outlaw on the roof of the newspaper building was hit maybe ten seconds later. Unless the shooter was leaning over the edge of the roof, a bullet from the street couldn't have hit him in the chest. The outlaw landed ten feet back from the front of the building. Since he only turned and fell, not taking any steps, he could not have been near the edge of the roof when the shot came. Which he wasn't, as he had taken a few steps toward me. Not even a stray bullet from the street could have hit him ten feet back. Therefore, the shot came from above. From where I stood on the ladder, I had a clear view of the hotel roof. I didn't see anyone, and, more importantly, no one fired a single shot at me. The false front of the butcher shop hid me from the view of anyone in the third-floor window."

The Ranger crossed his arms. "The ledger showed there were no rooms let on the third floor. The hotel manager was adamant about that. Do you have any other proof?"

TJ smiled. "The hotel laundress was given a set of lace curtains to launder and repair this morning. The black stain on them looks like gunpowder burns to me. I asked her to save them for last in case you thought they were worth inspecting. As you can see, there are no lace curtains in the corner room."

"So only two curtains?"

"Just one set. Normally the laundress doesn't wash any."

Doug studied the hotel through the window. "I'd like to see those curtains. But first, I gave my word to GW that I would see to your family's safety. Six of us are in the area. Two Rangers went to Acton to your sister's home. They have a letter like mine for her husband and her. GW suggested your mother go join them. My partner has already gone to speak with the doctor. Your brother wasn't sure who was threatened beyond you and the doctor. Is there anyone else? It will be easier to have them leave town."

"Jerome, my deputy, has a wife and daughter."

"Does the doctor have a girl? With what happened to his fiancée, GW wasn't sure if he did, but he thought someone mentioned he was courting. He said you didn't have anyone special."

"Dr. Palmer feels responsible for what happened to his fiancée. It will take an extra special woman to entice him to leave bachelorhood. The woman he saw for two weeks wasn't the one." TJ cleared his throat. "I recently started courting someone."

"Is it general knowledge?"

"Not sure. Miss Wilson came to town under extraordinary circumstances, so most people know I am protective of her."

"How extraordinary?"

"One of the brothel owners pretended to run a school and hired her to teach."

Doug shook his head. "I've heard of that happening, but they usually don't escape until—"

"I was warned by a dove who tried to escape. Someone beat her to death for her efforts."

"How come her killers aren't in your jail?"

"She didn't tell us who it was…"

Doug blew out an exasperated breath. "…and the courts aren't going to spend too much time on a dead prostitute."

"Pretty much."

"How long have you been seeing Miss Wilson?"

"Officially? Saturday night."

"Four days. She recently came to town. Can she go back to wherever she came from?"

"Not without funds."

"I don't have an extra man to guard her. Is there room at your sister's?"

TJ rubbed his neck. "Abigail is close to delivering another child, and their place is already bursting at the seams. With the addition of your men, I think sending Miss Wilson over would only cause more problems."

"I suggest you find a way to rid yourself publicly of Miss Wilson. Since you haven't been courting that long, it shouldn't be too hard to accomplish."

TJ stifled his reaction to Doug's suggestion. Doug must be like GW, one of those Rangers who never stayed in one place long enough to have a woman capture his heart. There had to be a way to keep Emily safe without hurting her.

⌐◆⌐

The wind changed directions, and the lower corner of the sheet Emily had pinned up slapped her face. She ducked around the cloth to the other side to see three men on horseback at the edge of the property. TJ dismounted first. Smoothing her skirt, Emily walked over to meet him. "Sheriff?"

"Miss Wilson? May we see the curtains you showed me this morning?" TJ didn't introduce the other men.

"They are in the washhouse." Emily skirted around the drying sheets and tablecloths to the basket holding the lace curtains. The men followed her.

TJ looked around before speaking. "Miss Wilson, this is Mr. Doug Thatcher and his fellow Ranger, Mr. Sherman. We'd appreciate it if you'd keep our visit quiet."

"Gentlemen." Emily handed them the basket with the curtains.

Mr. Thatcher lifted the first curtain out of the basket. "Do you mind if we look at this in better light?" The Rangers didn't wait for an answer before taking the curtain out into the sunlight.

Warmth radiated from TJ's hand where he touched Emily's elbow. "Can we talk in private for a moment?"

"I can hear you!" Thelma shouted from the summer kitchen.

Emily led TJ to the space between the second and third rows of laundry. "Will this do?"

TJ ran his index finger down the side of Emily's face, sending delicious tingles dancing across her skin. "Can you trust me?"

Leaning into his touch, she answered. "I already do."

"Even after I arrested you?"

"Well, not at that moment."

"What if I arrested you again?" His hand cupped her cheek.

Emily stepped back, breaking his hold on her. "What are you saying?"

"Could you trust me if I did something nonsensical again, like arresting you, or worse?"

Turning the question over in her mind led to several perplexing thoughts. "I think I would try to."

"Please, please do." TJ cupped her shoulders and held her in place until his lips found hers. He didn't linger and was gone before she could respond. The sheets fluttered in the wind, mimicking the vibrations of her heart. She touched her lips. Could she trust him? And what could possibly be worse than being arrested?

She took a moment to compose herself. The men were climbing back onto their horses. One of the Rangers had the curtains. She ran to them. "Wait! Where are you going with those?"

"The Ranger tipped his hat. They might be evidence."

She looked to TJ. "What am I to tell Mr. Davis?"

"Try to dodge his questions for a day or so. The Rangers will have an answer by then."

Emily placed her hands on her hips. "If he realizes they are gone, he will charge me, and they are worth more than I'll make this week."

The Ranger tipped his hat. "Don't worry about that, ma'am."

They rode away without another word or a backwards glance.

Emily turned back to her work with a newly churning stomach, sensing the lost curtains wouldn't be the worst thing she experienced this week.

22

"Where are the curtains I left for you yesterday?" Mr. Davis met her in the linen room.

The Rangers left with them. "When I picked them up this morning. I marked in the book they required an extra two days. They need to be mended and starched. It will take almost a week to clean and mend them properly." *The Rangers better have them back before Friday.*

"What am I to do with no lace curtains in the suite?"

"Don't you have an extra set?

Mr. Davis reached above her head. Emily squished back into the shelves to avoid his touch, only breathing again when he moved back and held out a bundle of yellowed lace. "This set was not washed properly. It will never do for the suite."

"Sir, if I am to repair the curtain, it will take at least two days longer than usual cleaning. However, I don't think it was dirt on the lace. I think the curtain is charred. I can't clean that."

He stepped closer, boxing her in against the shelves. "I will have to take it from your pay."

Emily sucked in a breath. He stood much too close for propriety. He stretched his arm to the shelf over her head again. Emily ducked under it, putting her in a corner of the room. "I am not the one who burned the lace. If you had examined it closely, you know the lace is likely beyond repair." Emily grabbed the ledger and opened it between them. "I wrote *soot* or *burn*. You only charge me for items I destroy, not your boarders."

Mr. Davis moved closer until his chest touched the ledger. To hide the slight quiver in her hands, Emily pushed the ledger into him and he stepped back.

Emily dashed for the exit. "Pardon me."

He latched on to her elbow with a bruising grip. "You'll be back tomorrow?"

"That is our agreement." Emily exited to the alley.

Donny waited by the cart.

"Miss Wilson, what took so long? I'm supposed to help Doc pick up his orders from the train. We had better hurry." Emily focused the emotions from her encounter with Mr. Davis on pulling the cart. The handle gave a curious wobble. Ignoring it, Emily pulled the cart into the street. In the distance, a train whistle blew.

"Miss Wilson?" Donny was clearly torn between his two obligations.

Emily leaned close to his ear. "Has anyone been following me today?"

"No, ma'am."

"Run along and help the doctor. There are plenty of people about their business this afternoon. I'll have no problem getting home."

A huge grin filled Donny's face. He took two steps and paused. "May I come by and get a cookie after I am done? I mean, make sure you got home?"

"Of course." Emily waved and continued on her way,

buoyed by Donny's smile. The handle to the cart wiggled again. Emily stopped to see what was wrong. One of the pins holding the handle was missing. Emily bit her lip. A blacksmith could fix it, but the only shop she'd seen was several blocks over on the other side of the Bull's-Eye at the end of Second Street. It would be better to send Donny with the cart later. Besides, she had a cake to make.

As she walked, she tried to make sense of Mr. Davis's odd behavior. Maybe he knew the Rangers had the curtains. She needed to speak with TJ tonight about getting them back or she would be charged. The last set of lace curtains Aunt Mabel purchased had cost seven dollars for the pair. The hotel lace wasn't as fine as her aunt's, so they might cost less, but still, that would mean two weeks without pay or depleting her savings.

The handle wobbled again. Emily looked back to be certain the last pin was holding. As she did so, a man grabbed her by the shoulders. She whipped her head back. "Let me g—Oh, TJ! You scared me."

TJ let go and stepped back, crossing his arms, his scar bulging, lips in a firm line. Pulled lower than usual, his hat hid his eyes. "What are you doing?"

⊰•◈•⊱

Emily gave him a half smile. "Going home."

"What did I tell you about running off on your own?" His building frustration at Doug's suggestion he end his relationship with Emily collided with the fear of seeing her pulling that silly cart down the street, not paying any attention to her surroundings. "Where is Donny?"

"Dr. Palmer needed his help, so I told him to go. I am perfectly capable of walking home alone in the middle of the afternoon." Emily tilted her chin up. "Now, if you will excuse me, I have dinner to go help prepare."

"Not for me, you don't."

Emily's eyes widened. "Work?"

"No. I am not coming."

"Why?" She searched his eyes.

TJ held on to the anger. If she saw how hard this was to do, he'd not manage it. Now was the best time. Three women stood in front of the mercantile, pretending not to watch. Near them, a man spent too much time adjusting his horse's bit. In the shadows a half block down lurked Cline. TJ pulled the handle of the cart from Emily's hand. "I've told you before what I expect. I don't have time for a woman who won't listen."

Uncertainty filled her eyes. "I listened. Donny barely left. There is a street full of people. I can walk home alone."

"I told you it wasn't safe." TJ jerked the cart forward. While the wheels didn't move, the handle did, slapping him in the calf. TJ jumped. "Why didn't you tell me!"

Emily blinked, her eyes watering. Pulling her into his arms was his first instinct. To ensure her safety, it was the last thing he would do.

"I was going to ask Donny to take it to the smithy." Her voice was calm but flat.

"Leave it here. I'll do it."

"No. Sheriff Morgan, I have no need of your assistance." She yanked the handle out of his hand and tossed it into the cart. Moving to the back, she bent and pushed it a foot before he blocked her way. Straightening, Emily placed her hands on her hips. TJ stepped aside, and Emily bent to push the cart again. TJ fisted his hand to keep himself from giving in and helping her. Emily pushed past him.

TJ refused to look back. The ladies near the mercantile turned their backs on him. Good. They would spread the gossip that might keep Emily safe. Would she understand it had cost him a bit of his heart? *Please trust me.*

Kicking the wheel of the cart didn't help. Emily bit her lip to keep from yelping. What had just happened? First TJ was upset she was walking alone. Now he'd left her to push the cart on her own? And his words cut her to the heart. This couldn't be what he'd warned her about, could it? Mean wasn't a word she'd equated with him until today.

Every slang word she'd ever heard crossed her mind. Quick footsteps came from behind.

"Miss Wilson! Miss Wilson!"

Emily turned to the sound of Donny's voice. "Doc didn't need me. How did you break the handle?"

"I didn't. The sheriff did."

"Why didn't he walk you home?"

Emily expelled a breath before answering. "He was busy."

Donny was too absorbed examining the broken handle to acknowledge her answer. "The blacksmith could fix this. Why didn't you take it there?"

"I only know of the blacksmith at the end of Second Street. I didn't think it wise to push it over there myself."

"I can take it there as soon as I see you home. I can't shirk my duties." Placing both hands on the back of the cart, Donny pushed it under a tree. "Don't worry. No one will bother the cart. The ten-year-old extended his arm, and Emily did her best to utilize it, thankful she had returned laundry and not picked it up, forcing her to carry it to Mrs. Reese's house. Once he grew another foot or two, Donny would make someone an excellent beau.

As soon as they reached the edge of Mrs. Reese's property, Donny ran off. Perhaps he was no more ready to be a beau than the sheriff was. Emily went to the outdoor kitchen to deliver the news that the sheriff would not be attending tonight's dinner, but found the room empty.

She entered through the back door and followed the sound of excited voices to the east parlor. A black Singer sewing machine sat in the center of the room. Becky held up scraps of fabric with a seam down the middle. "Emily, isn't it the most amazing thing! I can sew a dress in half the time. Mrs. Reese ordered it all the way from Boston, just like you."

"More like a quarter." Thelma stroked the top of the machine before turning the balance wheel, starting the machine in motion. Becky's mouth hung open as Thelma fed the fabric through the machine.

"Lookee here." Thelma held up a hemmed dish towel. "Ten minutes and it is all done."

"Have you ever seen such a wonder? I can make a nine patch quilt as fast as a wink." Becky sorted through a pile of scraps.

"Would you like to try it?" asked Mrs. Reese.

"It is very much like the ones they had in Bradford. I would like to finish the blouse I started on last night."

Becky dropped the fabric. "You mean you've used one?"

"They required us to take a class on domestic sewing." Emily sat in the one chair Becky hadn't sorted scraps on.

"Will you teach us, then?" asked Becky.

"Of course. We should have time after dinner."

Mrs. Reese looked up. "Aren't you entertaining Sheriff Morgan this evening?"

"Not today or any day after. He gave me a thorough set down in the middle of Main Street and left me to manage the broken cart on my own."

"What did he do?" Mrs. Reese's voice rose half an octave.

Thelma stopped trimming the threads on her new towel. "He had no problem talking to you out there in the middle of the laundry this afternoon. Looked right cozy."

"Thelma!" Heat rushed into Emily's face.

"I wasn't spying. Just looked up and saw your shadows,

pretty as a silhouette picture on those sheets. Almost made me wish I could draw it."

Emily closed her eyes. What had the Rangers seen? She pushed the thought aside before any more blood rushed to her face. "Well, whatever the sheriff's actions earlier today were, he made it quite clear he no longer intends to pursue me." The tears she'd blinked back earlier now found their way down her cheeks. Emily hid her face in her hands, then ran to her room.

onny stormed through the office door. "Sheriff, I'm ashamed of you! You told me to never be the cause of a woman's tears and to always lend a helping hand. Half the town is talking about your snubbing Miss Wilson. Nellie says you treat Belle's girls better!" As he spoke the truth of the situation, Donny's face grew red.

There was little TJ could do to defend himself. A boy wouldn't understand that TJ had acted out of concern and that the tears were necessary to Emily's safety.

"See my sliver? Did you even try to push that cart? Mama told me to work for good men. I'm afraid I can't work for you no more! You're as bad as Mr. Tarr, what with him not letting Miss Wilson shop in his store." Donny ended his rant with a huff and turned to go.

TJ grabbed Donny by the collar before the boy reached the door. He looped his other arm around Donny's waist, then wrestled the boy into the parlor. In the course of the struggle, TJ found it prudent to move his hand from Donny's collar to his mouth. TJ shut the door to the parlor with his foot and kept his hand over Donny's mouth so he could whisper in his ear. "Donny, you aren't going to understand this, but what I did was to help her. And I need your help more than ever, because I can't help Miss Wilson personally. I want to talk man-to-man with you, but I can't do that if you are yelling. I am dropping my hand now."

Donny spun around, his accusatory glare and crossed arms piercing TJ's heart.

"Remember how I arrested Miss Wilson to save her?"

No response.

"You thought I was crazy. And maybe I was. I can't explain what is going on now. But I can say this. It is best for Miss Wilson if the entire town thinks I'd like nothing more than to see her on the next train back East."

A head bob.

"I know I hurt her. Someday I hope to show her it was all a lie. Please don't quit working for me. You're the only one I can trust to keep a lookout for Miss Emily."

"You shouldn't hurt her."

"But what if the little hurt I caused saves her life?"

Furrows grew on Donny's brow. "I think you are dumber than our rooster, the one that crows at the moon."

"Maybe. That is why I need your help. Someone still has to look after Miss Wilson. I need you to do what you've been doing for the past two-and-a-half weeks. Keep an eye out for her. Look out for anything strange."

"You mean like Miss Wilson taking extra long to return today's linens and coming out of the hotel looking like my ma did when Mr. Porter tried to steal our horse for taxes?"

"Did Miss Wilson have a problem at the hotel today?"

Donny nodded.

Running his hand down his face did little to calm his heart. Doug's stupid idea of protecting Emily was already hurting both of them. "Did she say why it took so long?"

"No, but I heard Mr. Davis arguing with her over the lace curtains, though I couldn't hear everything."

TJ nodded. "Thank you. Now, I need you to do something else. When we go back out to the office, I need you to be as angry with me as when you came in. Then stay mad. If you have something to tell me, go to Dr. Palmer's. He will pass the message on."

Donny tilted his head and squinted. "Is this one of those things to keep Miss Emily safe?"

"Yes."

"I'll do it. She is my friend." The smile on his face turned to a frown. "But I think you are mean to treat her that way." Donny threw open the door and stomped out of the room.

Instead of following him, TJ retreated to the dogtrot by the kitchen, where he collapsed into a chair. He needed longer to compose himself. Bones opened one eye and raised his head for a scratch behind the ears.

"There you go, old boy. Did you know you have an idiot for a master?"

Bones tilted his head. TJ moved his hand to a spot behind the mutt's ear and scratched there. "I wish I knew if this would keep her safe." What would Aidan have done to keep his fiancée safe? A broken heart had to be better than the alternative. The Rangers would find their man in a few days. Then he could explain. He could send a note, but if it fell into the wrong hands, or if Emily let it slip…If only he knew she'd understood his cryptic request to trust him…but he needed to make it look real. Both of them acting might not fool everyone.

TJ buried both hands in Bones's fur and rubbed. Bones thanked him with a lick to the back of his hand before lying back down in the shade.

The chair creaked as TJ got up. "Oh, Emily, I am sorry," he whispered to the breeze.

Long shadows crisscrossed the yellow room. Emily pushed away her damp pillow. *Stop this pathetic crying! You are not a blubbering girl!* Shouting orders to her brain didn't work until she imagined Aunt Melba's sneer. Emily got up and crossed over to the washbowl. The water remaining from this morning's toilette had grown warm with the day. Dabbing her face with a wet cloth made her eyes redder. This would never do. *Crying over a man. Emily Ann Wilson, what is wrong with you?*

She checked her pin watch. Ten minutes wasted on tears. Well, maybe fifteen. That was enough. After all, he had warned her something might be different, but this was worse than being arrested.

"One week, TJ Morgan. You have one week to explain yourself," Emily promised her reflection. In the meantime, she'd avoid him.

Emily entered the dining room and slid into her seat as Thelma set a platter on the table. Mrs. Reese said grace. Conversation swirled around the table as did the aromas of the dinner. Emily smiled and nodded but didn't taste any flavors. When the meal was finished, she offered to do the dishes in Becky's stead. The offer couldn't be refused when there was a new sewing machine begging to be used.

Air moved through the screened windows, fluttering the curtains and giving the illusion of cooling the kitchen. Emily carefully dried each china dish before stacking it in the cupboard. Mrs. Reese entered the room and did the same. "Did you know that Mrs. Morgan packed up and went over to her daughter's for a few days?"

"I hope she has a nice visit."

"If all she wanted was a nice visit, she would not have packed her traveling case. Abigail's baby shouldn't arrive for another month at least. And the doctor wasn't called."

Emily turned the damp towel over in her hand in search of a dry spot. "Oh."

"Something odd is going on. Can't you feel it? Rangers coming to town…Don't tell me the men with TJ this afternoon weren't Rangers. I am old, not blind. Mrs. Morgan leaving to visit Abigail…The difference between TJ's tête-à-tête with you between lines of laundry and whatever he said when he told you he wasn't coming to dinner."

Picking up three dried plates, Emily stacked them in the cupboard. *"Can you trust me?"* TJ's question echoed in her head.

"So you don't think TJ was trying to rid himself of me?"

Mrs. Reese picked up the last glass. "I think he was, in a way."

"Then you think he was trying to end our association?"

"Yes, but maybe not to hurt you."

Old people were supposed to be wise. Emily found no logic in Mrs. Reese's statements. "I don't understand."

"Men have been known to do mighty strange things when they think they are protecting a woman. Especially one they love. If TJ thought you knowing him was endangering you, he might—"

"Tell me he didn't want to see me?"

"Precisely."

"Why wouldn't he tell me I was in danger and we needed to pretend to break up?"

"In all my years, I have learned one thing. What men call logic, women call nonsense. Give this a few days. You may find whatever he said today isn't as bad as it seems right now."

"Do you really think so?"

"Thelma wasn't the only one to see you standing between the rows of laundry. I was preparing to talk to you about the dangers of too many kisses."

"I don't think that is a problem at the moment." Emily forced a smile.

"No, but it could be again."

"So you are telling me to—"

"Wait him out. Stay away, and I think he'll come back again."

Mrs. Reese left the kitchen. A ray of hope remained.

———>•◆•<———

Alice's Adventures in Wonderland was the last book in the pile. Emily opened it to page seventeen, line five, word three and copied out the word *with*, then moved on to the next word and the next.

With eyes on me I must take care.

Emily bit her lip to hide her excitement. Out of fifteen books, this was the first time she'd pieced together a sentence that made sense.

He still chooses me over the others. He likes it when I read. D-i-c-k-e-n-s is his preference. If he is tired, he sleeps and I am safe from being hit.

Still no mention of the identity of "he," but initials were being used now. B, C, N, and D, all showed up regularly and had to be Belle, Cline, Nellie, and Daisy.

Everyone else has Sunday free, but I am expected to read to him and join him for dinner. It's as if for one day he dreams I am someone else, something else. But Monday always comes. Only touches me if angry.

~

B learned I play the piano. It keeps me downstairs.

~

N made rabbit for dinner

~

I am going to run.

~

C found me. Says he is done with me.

~

I heard children laughing today. It is hard to remember joy.

~

Nice d-o-c today. Help?

~

Ran again. Hurt everywhere. C says next time I d-i-e.

~

Emily set her pencil on the papers. The sentence stared back at her. It was only a threat. Was it enough? Not unless there was proof indicating C was Cline.

A yawn overtook her. Emily put the papers and the journal in her dresser drawer and checked the time. Three hours passed since she started. She needed to get word to the sheriff about the contents, even if she didn't want to see him.

No one had been in the kitchen or linen room of the hotel, so Emily hadn't needed to use the lie she prepared to cover for the still-missing curtains. Donny leaned against the alley fence.

"Do you have time to walk with me to Dr. Palmer's?" Emily balanced the empty basket on her hip.

"Sure, but he isn't there. He got called out an hour ago."

That wouldn't do at all. While washing the tablecloth with the wine stains, she'd thought of passing on the information about Cecilia Rose's journal through the doctor. Actually, the journal, the book key, and the notes.

Emily hadn't finished, but she had deciphered the last page to be sure the key hadn't changed.

If I die and she is safe, then it is not in vain.

The words cut her to the heart. Once she realized that Cecilia Rose knew she might die to save her life, Emily couldn't bring herself to translate the pages in between.

"Perhaps Dr. Palmer has returned." Emily handed the empty basket to Donny to put in the repaired cart.

"I ain't got nothin' better to do." He pulled the cart in the direction of the doctor's office.

Judge Granger came out of the bootmakers. They slowed to let him pass. "Donny. Miss Wilson." He nodded and came back. "A moment, Miss Wilson." The judge stepped between Emily and Donny. "I need a new laundress. I understand from Mr. Davis your work is quite good. Would you be willing to take mine as well?"

He stood closer than necessary for such a conversation, and Emily stepped back. "I am seeking other employment. I think it is best to not take on more customers."

A smile pulled the corners of his mouth under his mustache, and his eyes darkened as his gaze dropped from her face, then flicked back up. "What I really need is a new housekeeper. I pay seven dollars a week, with Sundays off. You could start on Tuesday."

Behind him, Donny vigorously shook his head and mouthed "No!"

"Thank you for the offer, but I am looking to use my teaching degree."

Once again, Judge Granger moved closer than necessary. "I will leave the position open until I return. Tonight, I am leaving for Waco. I'll be back late Monday. Give me your answer then. I promise you I'll make it the best job you can find."

The underlying threat sent a shiver up Emily's spine. Cornered by the building and a water barrel and unable to retreat any farther, Emily sidestepped to get around the judge and closer to Donny, who beckoned her to him. "Again, thank you for your offer, but—"

The judge tripped over the cart handle, landing in the water trough next to the raised sidewalk.

"Blasted kid!" Judge Granger jumped out and brushed off his pants. "Now I need to go change before I leave for the station. Make no mistake, boy. Your mother will hear about this!" He took three steps away. "Miss Wilson, do consider my offer." He rushed down the street.

Donny lifted the handle.

"You did that on purpose!" Emily covered her mouth to hide her laugh.

"Yes, ma'am. He was starting to scare you, and you don't want to work for him. Nellie says he is the devil himself." He covered his mouth. "I'm not supposed to repeat that."

"Don't worry. I won't. Let's see if the doctor is in." Emily helped Donny put the cart in an out-of-the-way spot.

The office was open, and Mrs. Bickford, the nurse, sat at a desk.

"Is Dr. Palmer in?"

"He returned a moment ago, Miss Wilson. Which one of you needs the doctor?"

Emily started to raise her hand as if still in the classroom. Quickly she lowered it. "I do. It will take only a moment."

Mrs. Bickford narrowed her eyes. "You can leave a message with me."

"I am afraid I can't."

"Are you ill?"

"No."

"The doctor is a busy man."

"I understand, and I wouldn't bother him if the matter weren't of some urgency."

"Have a seat."

Emily and Donny sat on the wooden bench. Mrs. Bickford made no move to leave her desk or inform the doctor of their presence. Battered copies of *Popular Science Monthly* and *Home Companion* lay on a nearby table. Donny flipped through the science periodical and stopped at an illustration of a penguin. "This bird doesn't fly. It swims. It also lives in a very cold place that always has ice and snow and no summer. We had snow two winters ago, but it was gone in a day. Do you think they are telling the truth?"

"Where I lived in Massachusetts, we received several snowstorms each winter. Some left more than two feet of snow. I can imagine there must be a place on earth as cold as Texas is hot. As for a bird that swims, I have read enough accounts about it that I think they must be real." Emily picked up a copy of *Home Companion* and flipped through the pages.

Footsteps sounded in the hallway. "Mrs. Bickford, I am going to close—" Dr. Palmer stopped talking. "Why didn't you tell me I had patients?"

"Because they are not ill."

"Miss Wilson, Donny, how can I help you?"

Emily stood. "If I could have a moment of your time? I have a matter I must discuss with you."

"Come back to my office." He frowned at Mrs. Bickford before leading Emily down the hall and ushering her into a tiny room crowded with a desk and bookshelves filled to bursting. "I apologize. Mrs. Bickford is under the assumption that all unmarried women who arrive here unchaperoned are here for nefarious purposes—mostly chaining me in matrimony."

"I didn't come completely unchaperoned."

"A ten-year-old boy?"

"Who not twenty minutes ago ended an unwanted conversation between me and a man twice his size and twice my age. However, that is not why I am here." Emily pulled the paper-wrapped package from her apron pocket. "This is not a gift. I have been working on the translation of Cecilia Rose's journal. She used three separate codes or ciphers in it. A simple replacement code, writing French in reverse, and a book cipher. I told TJ—I mean the sheriff, that I would decode the entire book. Early this morning I skipped to the last page to make sure she did not change book ciphers."

Emily took a deep breath to calm her nerves.

Dr. Palmer poured a glass of water from a pitcher on his desk and handed it to her.

Emily took a sip. "Thank you. The problem is the last line is about me. At least I think it is. She knew she might die trying to help me. She writes several times about a nice doctor and a bad doctor. I am assuming you are the nice one as T—er, the sheriff, told me she came to you before she died. I know you are a busy man, but I need someone to give this to who can finish what I started."

Dr. Palmer untied the package. "Lewis Carroll. Not the author I would have pictured her choosing."

"I think she chose it because he wouldn't have asked her to read it to him."

"Who is *he*?"

"I don't know. He isn't Cline or Bart. But I think if you and the sheriff can figure out who he is, you'll know who ordered her killed. I don't think Belle oversees the business." Emily felt heat creeping up her face. Cecilia's life as Rose was a topic she should know little about. Discussing it with an unmarried man was far beyond propriety. Oddly enough, it hadn't bothered her to discuss the book with TJ. "I should leave now. I trust you can get the information to the sheriff." Emily stood and reached for the door handle.

"Miss Wilson, you did the right thing to bring it to me and not to TJ. I can see you are hiding a broken heart. But I diagnose it as curable."

"How do you know?" The question slipped out.

"My heart was shattered years ago. I recognize the symp-toms."

"Is there a tincture or a tonic for the cure?" One girl in the room across the hall in her dorm had bought a love potion once. Could there be a reverse of it? Not that the love potion had worked…

"In your case, yes. Trust him. Trust TJ." Dr. Palmer gave her an encouraging smile. "Just trust him."

Emily left the office as fast as she could, before even Donny could follow her. The only way to process the doctor's statement was alone.

<hr>

"If I was a gentleman, I would throw down my glove and challenge you to a duel." Aidan dropped a brown paper package on the sheriff's desk.

"A duel? What did I do?"

Aidan ran his hand over his face. "Other than letting a woman decipher this? I read over her transcriptions. No lady should be subject to reading this. No man either."

"Emily returned it to you?"

"She asked me to finish it. Told me she tried, but she couldn't do it any longer. The look in her eyes—it was as if she'd learned her life long friend had died."

"I'm sorry." Arguing that he'd tried to take the book back was pointless. Emily had been adamant about continuing the translation. Aidan would never understand. He'd treated his memories of his fiancée as if she had been an angelic porcelain doll. Forgotten was the fiery woman who'd faced down an Indian in her smokehouse as a six-year-old and shot a snake before it could bite her younger brother at age nine. Most women were stronger than men allowed them to be. TJ shook his head. His thoughts sounded like one of the suffragette magazines Mr. Saunders from the telegraph office had confiscated from his wife and brought to him for safekeeping.

Palmer crossed his arms. "Don't tell me you're sorry. She deserves to hear it from you."

"I told her that she didn't need to finish it several days ago, but she wanted to keep working on it."

"You need to apologize for not taking it back, then."

"But I can't see her." Unless I close my eyes and see her stricken face.

"I know. The only reason I don't put my fist through your nose is I may be the only person in town who realizes how much you care for her. I would have done the same a million times to keep Cathleen safe."

TJ looked around, making sure no one was listening, and scowled at the doctor. "Did you finish the transcription?"

"No, I figured you could. The key is the storybook." Aidan turned to leave. "One more thing. I tried to give her a dose of hope. It will hold her only so long, though." The doctor shrugged and left.

TJ stared after his friend.

Hope. If only he could find some for himself.

⟞◆⟝

The parlor clock chimed a quarter after the hour. TJ closed the journal. The clues he hoped to find were not there. Belle had a partner. A silent, powerful, brutal partner. Never would he have guessed at Belle having a partner. Over the past couple years, he'd gotten a feeling for which men frequented her place rather than Harold's. None of them seemed like the type to be Belle's partner. Rumors that the Pike gang had used the building that was now Belle's place before Cole Pike shot his father were still whispered about every now and again.

Could Cole Pike be the mysterious *he*?

TJ read back over Emily's translation. Her tiny, neat handwriting was hard to read in the dim light.

The clock chimed twice.

A yawn opened TJ's jaw uncomfortably wide. He gathered up the books and papers and locked them in his desk drawer. He checked the front door. Jerome had left hours ago. The Rangers slept across the street in the hotel. The floor above remained empty, as it often did on Thursday nights. It hadn't been three weeks ago. Had she only been in town such a short time?

TJ retired to his room. Friday was the busiest night in town. With any luck, in twenty-four hours the Rangers would learn the identity of Cole Pike's son.

Not even the smallest of breezes moved the air. The last of the linens hung limply from the lines. Emily tucked an errant hair back into her headscarf and wished someone would invent an ironing machine. It would be so much easier to roll the table linens through a hot press, much like the wringer. The wringer helped. If she had to twist each sheet dry, she'd never finish the ironing. She wiped a bead of perspiration from her brow. Growing up, her grandma would share stories from a year where there was no summer. What Emily wouldn't give for a day or two of that year, especially after working out in the heat all day.

Becky ran out of the house waving several papers. "You have two telegrams and two letters."

"Telegrams?" Emily reached for the papers. One of the letters was from Amanda; the other was from a school in a town she'd never heard of. Both telegrams originated in Boston.

"What do they say?" Becky bounced on her toes.

"Becky, come back in and leave Emily alone to read in peace." Mrs. Reese stood on the back porch with her hands on her hips.

Emily retreated to one of the chairs in the shade of the large oak.

> Inheritance mistake. Letter to follow. Come home.
> Carl & Percy Wilson

The second telegram informed Emily she could pick up one hundred dollars at the Western Union office, sent by Percy Wilson.

It should take another week or more for the letter to get here. No point in rushing off before an explanation came. It would take that long to make arrangements for tickets even with the money. Emily turned over Amanda's thick letter, then tucked it in her pocket to read in the evening. The other letter was an offer to teach at a small Christian college, indicating Amanda had recommended her. Odd it referred to Amanda's maiden name. Emily added the job offer to Amanda's letter to wait for later.

The ironing couldn't wait. Or could it? Mr. Davis would take the money for the missing curtains out of her pay and claim she owed him the money anyway. Why bother finishing? She'd owe more than she would make.

Emily hurried into the house.

Becky stopped polishing the silver. "Bad news or good news? Mrs. Reese says telegrams are always one or the other."

Thelma and Mrs. Reese looked to Emily for an answer.

"I am not sure. The first telegram claims there was an inheritance mistake and to come home. It is from my uncle Carl and cousin Percy, who have always been kind to me. A letter is coming to explain. I suppose it will be here by next Friday. The second one informs me I can pick up money at the Western Union office so I have funds to travel."

Becky's smile faded. "Are you leaving us just like that?"

"I'm not sure. I won't leave until I receive the letter. I've also received a job offer from a school, upon my friend's recommendation, that I would like to inquire about, so I don't know. I wasn't prepared to have options." Then there was TJ. Despite being ignored for two days, her heart told her to not be hasty.

Mrs. Reese nodded. "If they got their letter on today's train, it could be here as early as Wednesday or as late as three weeks, I would think."

"This brings me to my next dilemma. I fear I am about to do something terribly wicked and return the rest of today's linens without ironing everything or even letting them dry all the way. I'm sure Mr. Davis will charge me for the lace curtains the Rangers took."

Thelma clapped. "Bravo. After the way he treated you earlier this week, he deserves to have them returned unwashed and unironed."

"I wish you would stay here in Hiramsville with us," said Becky.

Emily put an arm around Becky's shoulder. "I'm not entirely sure what I can do. However, I believe I can safely quit doing laundry and pay Mrs. Reese back." No one mentioned TJ, but she wouldn't leave until she'd spoken with him. Maybe he would give her a reason to come back.

"Don't you even think of paying me a penny! But I do agree entirely about quitting the laundress job." Mrs. Reese fanned herself. "It is a wonder you survived the heat this long."

"I thought Texans didn't complain about the heat."

Mrs. Reese scowled and fanned herself faster.

"I'm going to put these upstairs and change my blouse, then I will deliver the laundry as is."

Emily set the letters and telegram on the dressing table and caught a look at herself in the mirror. Yanking the cloth off her head didn't help matters. She still looked like she needed to be hung out with the sheets. If she was quitting, she'd do it in style. Emily ran back downstairs and filled her wash pitcher with cool water. After washing, she pinned up her hair and put on the dress she'd worn her first day in town.

Mrs. Reese met Emily at the bottom of the stairs. "Whatever you do, don't let that man goad you into paying him for the curtains. Tell him the truth—the Rangers have it. They can pay."

Emily nodded. A few of the sheets were still damp, and half the tablecloths sported a wrinkle or a dozen. The quick folding job she gave them wouldn't help matters. As she piled the laundry into the cart, Emily dismissed the thought of waiting for Donny, as she was nearly two hours early.

As she pulled the cart out of the yard, she hummed "The Yellow Rose of Texas."

❖

Mr. Davis folded his arms. "I don't have to answer you. You stole those from the washerwoman. Maybe *she* burned them."

Doug and the other Ranger glared at the man. TJ tried another tack. "So, you are saying it's normal for those you employ to shoot guns around your laundry?"

"Certainly not. You know how much shooting goes on around here on a weekend." Mr. Davis raised his chin.

"Mostly at the Bull's-Eye sign. Unless you are in the habit of loaning curtains to Belle, I'd say it is highly likely they were shot last Saturday during the shoot out."

Doug leaned over the counter. "Just tell us which window these were in, and we will be on our way."

"Northeast corner. The big window. Now I suppose you want to see the room. Too bad the judge is out of town and you don't have a warrant."

"That is a problem with some of these county judges. That is why we have a warrant from the state." Doug pulled a paper out of his pocket and presented it to the manager. "Would you like to give us the key or take us up yourself? We also need to see the register."

The manager pulled out the book and shoved it at Doug's partner. "I'll take you up. The register won't help. The suite wasn't occupied last Saturday."

"Thanks for your help, Sheriff." Doug's partner thumbed through the book.

There were worse things than being dismissed by the Rangers. TJ headed to the kitchen to talk with Hannah.

"Smells like pie day."

"If you're looking for a handout, Sheriff, I have nothing for you. Not after you treated that little girl so poorly. She is the sweetest thing to ride into town in years. First she's gotta deal with Belle and all them rumors. Then them folks who won't talk to her because she is a Yankee. Not that she understands that. And then you go and set her down in front of the entire town, insulting her intelligence. Uh-uh, you aren't getting one of my pies even if you pay me a gold double eagle." She held up her rolling pin.

TJ jumped out the back door and returned to his office to puzzle out the journal. Maybe it would have a clue about the outlaw's son. Then he could court Emily again.

⟞⟝◆⟞⟝

"Good afternoon, Hannah. Is Mr. Davis around?" Emily pushed the back door to the hotel open with her hip.

"You're early, child. He is upstairs with those Rangers. If it wasn't payday, I'd tell you to skedaddle on out of here. He is madder than an armadillo caught in a hog trap."

"Since I am sure he will charge me for the lace curtains, I won't stick around long. I'm not returning after today, and

I am not too worried about being paid." Emily returned to the cart in the alley for another load of sheets.

Hannah dusted off her hands. "I'm surprised you lasted three weeks. Nobody wants to work for less than they're worth. No matter how hungry people are, they got pride."

Emily wanted to ask Hannah if they paid her what she was worth.

As if reading her mind, Hannah answered, "Mr. Davis don't set my wages, or he would take half of them. The owner who lives in Dallas does. He says as long as I make my stew and apple pie the way he likes it, I am worth every penny."

After stacking the sheets and table linens, Emily tallied and cross-checked the ledger and placed it back on the shelf. Hannah pulled three pies out of her oven. Emily drifted over to the side table. "Those do smell divine. You are worth twice what he pays you."

"Oh, he pays me enough."

"If I was a thief, I'd be tempted to steal one of these."

"No need to do that." Hannah reached across the table and pulled a small tin from under a cloth. "This is my test pie. I always bake one to make sure my oven is working proper." Hannah gave Emily a fork and a nod.

The sweet peaches flavored with cinnamon stayed on her tongue as the flaky crust melted away. "I believe it is impossible for anyone to pay you what you deserve."

"It's mostly these good Texas peaches. Can't make a good pie with poor fruit."

Emily finished the little pie. "I am going to miss not seeing you next week. I put everything away and marked it in the book, but the lace curtains—"

A shout near the front of the hotel stopped her. Heavy footsteps pounded in the hallway. "Miss Hannah, tell me the moment—" Mr. Davis appeared in the doorway. "Why, Miss Wilson—just the person I was looking for. How dare you let the Rangers have those curtains! Leave and never let me see you here again! Don't even ask about your pay after the damage you caused!" Mr. Davis's face was as red as one of the apples in the basket on the worktable.

"I assumed you would refuse to pay me. The only reason I stayed was to inform you I will not be back." Emily nodded to Hannah. "Thank you."

As she crossed the room for the door, Mr. Davis grabbed her by the arm and spun her around, his fingers digging into her flesh. "I was nice to you when no one else was. You should kneel and thank me. No one else is going to hire you. Not with the bounty Belle's put on you. If I were a different nature of man, I'd drag you in there myself, especially now that the sheriff isn't sniffing around your skirts." He grabbed her other arm, yanking her so close she felt his breath on her face. "I don't see what is so special about you. Maybe I sh—"

A gun cocked. "Let the woman go, Davis."

"Why should I?"

"Because I'll arrest you for assault." A man slightly taller than TJ clamped a hand on Mr. Davis's shoulder. One of the Rangers from Wednesday.

The brutal hold on her arms eased, and Emily twisted away. She rubbed her arms to relieve the pain. Hannah wrapped an arm around her.

"Miss Wilson?" The other Ranger TJ had introduced spoke. He looked different without his hat.

"Yes?"

"Sorry about that." The Ranger dipped his head, not releasing Mr. Davis from his hold. "If you'll excuse me, I'm going to take him to visit the jail until he remembers how to talk to a lady. And who was in the third-floor room on Saturday." They exited by the back door, followed by the other Ranger.

"Child, why don't you take one of my pies home for your supper? After what Mr. Davis did, you deserve at least that."

Hannah wrapped the pie, tin and all, in a flour sack cloth. "Send Donny around with the tin later. And you'll always be welcome in my kitchen."

"Oh, thank you. We are going to enjoy this tonight." Emily took the gift and left the kitchen. What a day this had turned out to be. Emily whistled as she set the tin in the cart, but before she could take a step, she felt a cloth over her mouth and nose and smelled something odd.

heriff! Sheriff!" Donny's yell carried down the block. TJ moved in the boy's direction, hoping to quiet him.

As he got closer, TJ realized the boy was crying. He crouched to meet Donny's eyes.

"She's gone! She's gone!"

Mrs. Owen appeared healthy enough last time he'd seen her. Perhaps she'd only fainted because of the heat. "Are you sure? Have you seen Dr. Palmer?"

"No. But she could be there!" Donny whirled around and ran to the clinic, TJ followed quickly behind.

TJ reached the front door of the clinic as the door closed behind Donny.

"I need to see the doc!" The shout echoed off the walls.

Mrs. Bickford opened her mouth to answer, but Aidan entered the waiting area first. "What is wrong, Donny?"

"Have you seen Miss Emily? She's missing!"

The words jolted TJ. Blood rushed to his head as the room spun, and he sat down in the closest chair. "What?" His faint question went unheard as the doctor asked the same thing.

"She's gone. The laundry cart too. The peach pie Hannah gave her is gone too. But the tin was in the alley. The dogs were licking it."

TJ rubbed his head. "The Rangers saw her at the hotel less than a half hour ago."

Aidan laid his hand on TJ's shoulder. "Come back into my office so we can discuss this."

Once they were in the office, Aidan pulled a peppermint stick out of a jar and handed it to Donny, then poured glasses of water for TJ and himself. "Donny, start at the very beginning."

"But we need to find her now!"

Aidan knelt down in front of Donny. "First we need all the information you can give us. Tell the sheriff everything that happened, even things that don't seem like they have anything to do with Miss Wilson."

Donny sucked the end of the candy. "Well, I went to Mrs. Reese's house. Becky told me Miss Wilson had received two telegrams and some letters. Something about an in-her-hair-dance?"

"Inheritance?"

"Yes, that is it. And Miss Wilson was going to quit doing laundry and go back to Boston. Becky was all crying and carrying on, blubbering about how much she would miss Emily."

TJ attempted to swallow the water in his mouth. Emily leaving? He forced his throat to relax so the water wouldn't come back up. "Did Becky say when she was leaving?"

Donny's mouth screwed up as he thought. "No, but Miss Thelma told her to stop wailing 'cause nothing was settled and Miss Wilson wouldn't leave until she got a letter."

"So we will rule out that Emily left on her own." TJ took a deep breath. "Then what happened?"

"I hightailed it up to the hotel. When I got to the alley behind the hotel, there were mongrel dogs fighting over a pie of Miss Hannah's. It was one of her peach pies. Have you ever tasted one? Don't tell Ma, but Miss Hannah's is the best in town. Ma's is the best out of town. Sure is a pity to let the dogs eat it. I shooed them away and took the plate into Hannah. She wasn't in the kitchen. She was up front, but she came back to the kitchen before I could even ask for one of the ginger cookies she always keeps for me. I gave Miss Hannah the tin and told her where I found it. She got a funny look on her face and went and looked in the alley. She told me she done give the pie to Miss Wilson. Nobody in their right mind would throw away one of Miss Hannah's pies."

Aidan and TJ nodded in agreement. The gift of one of Hannah's pies was never taken lightly. It meant you'd met Hannah's approval and belonged in Hiramsville.

"So we searched the alley. Miss Hannah had me look all up and down, but I couldn't find Miss Wilson or the cart she used to haul the laundry. Miss Hannah was sure she had it. Then Miss Hannah told me Mr. Davis said there was a bounty on Miss Emily's head. Just like those outlaws. Only I know there ain't one because Miss Wilson ain't an outlaw. You were only pretending."

TJ took a deep breath. Logic was his friend. Running up and down the street like Donny did wouldn't help him find Emily. "Is there anything else you remember?"

"No, sir."

"Donny, I want you to listen very carefully. Dr. Palmer will take you home. I want you to stay there."

"I don't need to be walked home. I am not some baby."

"No, you are not. However, there is a reason the Rangers are in town, and I don't know if Miss Wilson is mixed up in that. Anyone who lives here knows you are my friend and Miss Wilson's. I want you to stay home so I can look for Miss Wilson without worrying someone might try to hurt you." If Cole's son had Emily, no telling what might happen.

Aidan leaned forward. "Donny, you are the man in your house. A man's first responsibility is to his family. You need to make sure your mother and sisters are safe."

"You can take me home." Donny paused. "Do you think we can take some peppermint sticks to my sisters? I ate this all gone and forgot to save some for them."

Aidan pulled four candies from his jar and handed one to TJ.

TJ pocketed his peppermint. "Donny, because you are the man in your family, I'll tell you when things are safe. In the meantime, I don't want you coming back into town unless you are with your mother and sisters."

"I'll do that, Sheriff. You will tell me as soon as you find her? I don't want Miss Wilson to leave town, and I need to tell her to stay."

I do too. TJ nodded. Nothing would be right until he found her and convinced her to stay.

⬥◈⬤

Pain filled Emily's head. Her mouth felt like she'd drunk a cup of dirt. Something tugged at her wrist as she tried to wipe her eyes.

"Shh. Don't make a sound," an unfamiliar female voice whispered from her side.

Emily blinked. "Where—"

A small hand clamped over her mouth. "Hush. You don't want them to know you are awake. They'll give you something to sleep again, or worse. Drink some water. Just a sip or you'll bring it all back up."

She pressed a glass to Emily's lips. A flickering candle sat behind the woman, casting her features in shadow.

While she drank, the voice explained, "You're upstairs at Miss Belle's. You are safe enough for now, as long as she thinks you are sleeping."

Belle's! Emily's hands flew to her stomach. Her traveling dress was still buttoned, the fabric of the long narrow skirt weighted against her legs. The bustle dug into her back. She experienced a moment of relief before heavy footfalls sounded on the other side of the wall. The glass disappeared.

"Close your eyes."

A key scraped in the lock, the door opened, and two people entered, the door closing after them.

Belle spoke. "Still out, I see. Just as well, thanks to that fool's poor timing. We gotta keep her here until he gets back on Monday. Cline, when she wakes up, you can tell her what will happen if she tries to run. Nellie, get back to the kitchen and prepare a tray. I don't want you up here again unless I tell you. That little urchin you are so fond of, realized our guest is missing, and the sheriff is out searching. If you say a word, I'll let Cline and Bart both take a turn at punishing you. Understand?"

"Yes, Miss Belle."

Emily hoped no one noticed her jump at the mention of Nellie's name.

"And, Nellie, same for the boy. Not a word, or he'll be sitting up here too."

"Yes, ma'am." The door opened and shut.

"Cline, I don't need to tell you she better not have a bruise on her or a single thread out of place. He is most insistent he be the first to touch her, and he will inspect every bit of her."

"He always does."

"Don't look so glum. I'll reward your forbearance. I am not allowing Bart in here after today's debacle. He doesn't have your control. And we don't need a repeat of what happened last time I let this girl slip through my fingers."

The door opened and shut again. Someone, probably Cline, sat with a grunt in the chair next to her. Which was safer—to try pretending to wake up or continue to fain sleep?

"You can hear me, can't you? There are two ways this can go. You can obey Belle and be a good girl, or you can give me a reason to punish you. I'll do things that don't leave a mark. Cline's hand brushed up her arm. Emily kept her eyes closed. The hand moved to her shoulder, across the collar bone, and down the row of buttons.

Emily's eyes shot open. "Stop!" The ropes on her wrists prevented her from pushing him away with any amount of force.

Cline removed his hand. "I knew you were awake. You're shaking. Good, you believe there are ways I can hurt you so he won't know. You probably heard I need to explain things to you. Belle's partner is out of town. It is unfortunate for all of us as Bart grabbed you too early. Belle is under strict orders that her partner is the first one to be with you. Which is sad for me because I must sit here with all this lovely temptation. For you it means you have three days to anticipate your new life." There was a gleeful tone to his words. Out of place with her situation. "The problem is, you're one of those women who thinks. If we give you too much time to think, well then—" Cline shrugged. "You think of things you are not meant to." He reached to smooth the hair out of Emily's eyes.

She shrunk back but was helpless to prevent his hand from brushing her forehead. Rubbing her face in maggots would be less disgusting. From his smile, Emily had the distinct impression Cline knew exactly how much his touch bothered her and was using it as his weapon.

Cline sat back and filled a glass with amber liquid from a decanter on the bedside table. "It's a kindness that Belle will give you her potion in the food. Don't worry. No magic. Mostly opium. It keeps you from thinking and me from doing anything we'd both regret to keep you in line."

"Why? Why me?" It was difficult to form the words with her head still pounding.

"When he read the first letter you sent to Belle, he decided he had to have you. I'm not sure why. I don't know why he chooses any of the ones he keeps. Perhaps it was all the book learning Pa insisted he get. But being he owns the majority stake in the Bull's-Eye, Belle does what he wants. We all do."

The word *he* echoed in Emily's brain. This had to be the same *he* from the pages of Cecilia Rose's journal. She had three days to figure things out. If she knew who *he* was—
"You keep saying *he*. Who is this mysterious man?"

"You'll know soon enough. But knowing may make the anticipation worse." Cline swirled his cup in slow circles. "Yes, yes. I think knowing his name might help you do your job better. After all, he doesn't treat his women like any dove. He treats them special, and he doesn't share. You could almost think of yourself as a kept woman. The judge spares no expense. If you play your cards right, anything you want could be yours. He could keep you for himself for years."

Someone charged with upholding the law was responsible for her kidnapping and what happened to Cecilia Rose? Emily squeezed her eyes shut and took a deep breath. This had to be a nightmare. "The judge? Which one?"

Cline laughed. "It's not the old geezer who lives on the other side of the river, is it? He has no use for a woman at his age."

Judge Granger owned a brothel. She tried to picture him as Cecilia Rose's captor. Unfortunately, the image was conjured far too easily. The way he'd studied her the other day when he'd offered her a job—no wonder he'd been so anxious to make her his housekeeper.

"Oh, I see you're overthinking. This is very bad. You're not thinking of the diamonds he could give you. You're thinking of the other part. I hope your dinner arrives soon. If it doesn't, I'll have to resort to a bit of ether. That's how Bart brought you here. Do you remember now? Somebody's hand on your face holding an itchy cloth and a sickly smell?"

Emily gagged, and her stomach flipped.

Cline laughed. "I see you remember. Ether is effective but risky. Give a woman too much and she might never wake up. And that would be a shame."

Somebody scratched on the door. Cline answered. Nellie stood there, holding a tray. Cline took the tray from the girl and shut the door without a word. "Your dinner is here. Nellie may be the ugliest girl in the world, but she knows how to cook."

Emily had never thought of a smile as evil, but the look on Cline's face must've mirrored Lucifer's when he convinced Eve to eat the apple in the garden of Eden. Emily weighed her choices. Either way, she was going to be drugged senseless. The way her stomach was rebelling, she had a fairly good chance of casting up the food and the poison. If they thought her subdued, they might not leave a guard with her. The thought of Cline watching her sleep made her even more nauseated.

Emily tried to push herself up and discovered that not only was a rope attached to her wrists, there were two others wrapped around her torso, binding her to the bed. They were loose enough that she could turn over.

"You've decided to eat? Sensible. So much better than the last girl. She kept fighting us. I'll loosen the rope around your chest enough that you can sit up. If you try anything—I mean anything, I will simply give you the potion. Eating lying down is dangerous. You could throw it up and die. And even I don't want to face the judge's wrath if that happens."

"I promise not to try anything." *Not yet.*

Somewhere between six and twelve hours later, she'd wake up. There would still be plenty of time to create an escape plan. They'd handed her two weapons: time and their fear of harming her. Judge Granger said he'd be back Monday night. She prayed she'd be gone by then.

As Cline untied the rope, Emily tried to watch him, but he stood in such a way as to block her view. With any luck, he didn't know half as many knots as the sailors who shipped her uncle's cabinetry down the Merrimack River. Pushing herself into a sitting position, Emily felt a tug on her legs. They must've used thirty yards of rope to keep her in the bed. "I need to use the necessary."

Cline smiled the evil smile. "There's a chamber pot under the bed. I can give you just enough rope to get to it. But I stay here."

"You'll watch me?"

"Not my favorite thing, but believe me, you ain't got nothing I haven't seen before."

Emily swallowed. "Perhaps later."

Cline's laugh was full of malice.

If taking Belle's potion would erase Cline's laugh from her memory, she would drink it all. Emily started with the bread, as it seemed like the most difficult thing to drug. The soup or drink would be easier. She smelled the cup before drinking. Weak lemonade. Emily ate all the bread and drank the lemonade before starting in on the soup. Before she finished, her eyelids drooped of their own accord. Holding the soup spoon became difficult. Cline's hand covered her own as he helped her ladle a few more spoonfuls into her mouth.

27

e can't stay to help you. They've called us back to Waco. The Rangers at your sister's place will stay for now at GW's request." Doug looked more apologetic than he sounded.

"How do you know her disappearance has nothing to do with the Pike gang?" TJ needed more than Jerome's help to find Emily.

"We don't," answered the other Ranger. "I find it mighty odd they have told us to come in right after we find evidence that could be a link to Cole Pike's son. Or should I say his oldest son? Slim indicated there may be more than one."

Doug rubbed the back of his neck. "Are you saying if we delay returning until tomorrow, you'd feel better about it?"

"I'm saying there is a missing woman and an order that makes little sense. I don't like either. At least we can try to find her. Even if we do catch the train, we will be staying in Fort Worth for the night."

"I'm not too keen on leaving town either. TJ, tell us everything you know." Doug sat down in the swivel chair behind TJ's desk.

TJ rehearsed everything Donny had told him and how Emily had come to live in Hiramsville. "I stopped by the hotel and questioned Hannah. She said just as Em—I mean Miss Wilson—left, there was a commotion up front. Hannah left the kitchen to solve the problem. She never saw Emily leave, but she also didn't see anyone else in the alley. I couldn't find any definitive tracks—too many carts and wagons going back and forth with the mercantile, hotel, and dressmakers all using the alley for deliveries. The most logical place is the Bull's-Eye. No way will a judge give me a warrant to go poking around on a Friday night."

"We could go change places with the Rangers out at your sister's. They are the only two left in the area, and I doubt anyone on this side of the river has met them. If they were to mingle with the rest of your out-of-town cowhands for a night at the Bull's-Eye..."

TJ nodded in agreement. "I have something that might help." He pulled out Rose's journal and the translations. "I've gone over this a half dozen times. I know there is something I am missing as far as Rose's death, but more importantly, it might help us to know what's going on at the Bull's-Eye."

Doug riffled through the papers and gave a low whistle. "I've never seen a journal all in ciphers before. Glad you found someone who could decode it."

Doug looked at the clock and handed half of Emily's transcriptions to his partner. "We have two hours before sundown. Can't make the trade too early if Belle has Emily. She'll be watching for trouble. Sheriff, go be predictable. Talk to the woman Miss Wilson boarded with, walk down alleys. Check back in an hour, and we'll see if we need to refine the plan."

TJ followed their advice. He wanted to talk to Mrs. Reese anyway.

An hour later, TJ had nothing to show for his efforts. He confirmed that she hadn't visited the Western Union office and that any funds that might be waiting for her were still in the safe.

"Good. You're back. We have a few passages we wonder if you can shed some light on." Doug handed TJ a page that had been transcribed.

Someone tried to grab N tonight downstairs. Never seen C and B move so fast. They hauled the man out. N very upset, afraid she got someone killed again. I think he is N's father.

"Any idea what she is talking about?" asked the other Ranger.

"It is hard to know. Nellie is Belle's cook. She is around sixteen. Nellie's mom was a prostitute who wanted better things for the girl. When Nellie was around ten, her mother decided to save her from the trade. She poured lye and who knows what on Nellie while she was sleeping. The right side of her face is terribly scarred. Nellie's ma already had one of those diseases the women get, and the man who ran the place turned her out. It was January. They found her frozen to death a week later. Belle took Nellie in and paid for all the doctoring. When Belle opened the Bull's-Eye, she hired Nellie. It is the one unspoken rule—no one bothers Nellie."

"What happens if someone does?" asked Doug

"I suspect that they never touch anyone again. What is the date on that?"

"January 5."

"We had an unidentified man show up dead on the road south to Glen Crossing about that time. Looked like a cougar attack, but Dr. Palmer found a bullet when I asked him to do a postmortem."

Doug took the paper back. "If 'he' is a partner with Belle, and she has only been open for…how many years?"

"Three. She worked for the previous owner, who is dead." Another victim of Cole's gang.

The other Ranger looked up from his reading. "Maybe he had a partner too. So, we are looking for a man who could have fathered a child near the end of the war."

"That would be half the town. A few returned before the war ended, injured or even as deserters. A handful, like my father, never went. We had our own battles to fight. There have been a couple of people in town who make remarks about Miss Wilson being a Yankee. I don't think they would have kidnapped her." TJ tapped his fingers on the desk. "No, they're mostly talk, and women are scarce enough around here that Yankee or not, they'll leave them alone."

"Here is something else." Doug handed a page to TJ

He and C are fighting again. Their father is coming to town.

"And two pages over." Doug pointed to another line.

They don't look like brothers. He is older. Different mothers?

"I didn't think the two were related. Rose writes about this father one more time." TJ searched through the pages.

Belle told me to take the night off and to stay in the locked room. His father is here, and there will be trouble. Everyone is angry. I wish there was a window.

"Wait. Locked room? That sounds like it isn't her usual room. Could there be a secret room?" asked Doug.

"If I read things correctly. Rose worked in two different rooms. The one was for the man she never uses a name for, the other for regular customers. When is the entry about trouble and the father?" asked the other ranger.

"Only a week before they killed Rose," said TJ.

"About the same time someone shot Cole Pike in the leg. There were no holdups or anything to indicate the law shot him. So he had to be shot by one of his own men or someone who wasn't one of his victims or a victim who managed to escape. Dr. Palmer said he thought someone had tried to take care of the leg but it got infected later. We also know someone dropped him off at the doctor's clinic. What if Cole Pike is the father of Cline and 'he?'" Doug crossed his arms and looked satisfied.

TJ pushed back from the desk. "That's a month between the night in question and when he showed up at Doc's. I guess it is possible, but that is a long shot. And I don't see any resemblance between Cline and Cole Pike."

"Family can be that way. GW doesn't look like he's your brother," said Doug.

"I favor our ma. GW got Pa's dark hair and eyes. I see your point. So we could be dealing with two sons, but according to Pike, only one would avenge him."

The other Ranger straightened his pile of papers. "If there is a secret room, or locked room, I'm going to assume Rose was safe that night as she doesn't write otherwise. All we know is it doesn't have a window. I assume the door is hidden. When they get upstairs, how are they going to find a room with no windows and a hidden door? How many entrances to the Bull's-Eye are there?"

"Officially, just the front and back. I've heard of a door from the theater next door, and I assume the building has a cellar. There is a chance there is a cave under there that could connect to anyplace in town. There are two or three accessible from the cliff above the river I explored with GW when we were younger. The drop is over forty feet in places. Mrs. Reese's cellar accesses one, but she blocked it off."

"I wish we had a few more men. If your sister's husband agrees, we could leave just one man on guard, but GW would shoot me if something happened." Doug shook his head.

"Dr. Palmer will help. He can look for an entrance from the theater. Jerome and I will have to be on our normal Friday-night rounds. We can go into the main bar and see if anything is out of place, but not much else."

"Well then, Doug and I will go switch places with the other men. Let's hope they find something."

When the men left, TJ retired to his room and prayed.

<hr>

Either Belle's potion wasn't as powerful as Cline believed or it delivered odd dreams to the accompaniment of "Camptown Races" and several bawdy songs Emily had never heard before. The door opened and closed a few times. Cline left and came back. Belle had been in, upset about something. Someone tightened the ropes binding her to the bed. Cline left.

Oppressive darkness shrouded the room. Emily strained to hear whether anyone was with her. All the noises came from the other rooms.

Emily regretted not using the chamber pot earlier. She strained at the ropes. No one said anything as one of them creaked against the bed.

She was alone.

As the darkness pressed in on her, Emily closed her eyes to pretend it wasn't there. The piano started playing again. It must still be Friday night. She doubted she'd slept through until Saturday. TJ would find her by Saturday night. He had to.

The music swirled around in her head, carrying her back into her colorful nightmares.

idan sat down across the desk from TJ. "I found the way into the Bull's-Eye from the theater. However, it looks like the door only opens from the saloon side. And the theater is missing a room."

"What do you mean missing a room?" asked TJ.

"In the theater up on the second floor there is a space, maybe ten by ten, with brick walls on three sides, with no door. The room is along the south wall, which meets the connecting wall to Belle's place. It wasn't obvious at first because there's a storeroom on either side."

TJ leaned back and rubbed his chin. "Where is the door that enters the Bull's-Eye?"

"It's at the back of the east storeroom." Aidan drew the floor plan on the top of TJ's desk with his finger. "I haven't been upstairs at Belle's for several months. But if I paced things off correctly, that door opens at the end of the hallway. I assumed it was a closet."

"So how would one access the brick room?"

Aidan continued to draw on the desk. "Assuming I'm correct about the door at the end of the hallway, access to the room in the theater is through the end room on the back side of the building. But there is nothing in that room."

TJ raised a brow.

"It is what they use as a sickroom. The only thing on the wall is the chimney from the kitchen. Makes the room insufferably hot, even in the winter. There isn't any furniture other than a narrow bed and a table."

"Is there a window?"

"A small one. Not enough to cool off the room."

"I think I know the window. They keep it closed, and I don't think I've ever seen a light on in it. How did you get upstairs in the theater, anyway?"

"Simple. I said I received a note that one of the actors needed headache powders. They took me back to the dressing rooms. Three of the actors claimed headaches." Aidan offered a half smile.

"So how do I get word to the Rangers to look in the sick room? I don't even know who they are. Doug thought it best if I didn't."

"I can't help you with that. I don't drink. The only time I go into the Bull's Eye is when I'm called there." Aidan yawned. "I'm going home. I delivered three babies this week. If I don't get some sleep, I'll be no help. If you need me later, come get me."

"Night, Doc, and thanks."

Aidan picked up his hat and left with a nod.

TJ exited to the kitchen, where Bones greeted him, asking for a rub behind the ears. Crouching, TJ obliged. "Too bad you were never much of a hunting dog."

⊰•◇•⊱

A loud thump woke Emily. More thumps and men swearing. TJ had found her!

The next thump shook the wall next to her bed. Emily

watched the door, waiting for someone to enter. Instead, she heard a faint groan and a scraping sound. Still, the piano played. The G and the A were flat. Emily rolled onto her side. It was too dark to study the ropes binding her. A key clicked in the doorknob, but the door didn't open.

"What are you doing?" asked Belle from outside the door.

"That's the second drunk I've hauled out of here tonight. I'm moving her to his room," answered Cline.

"You can't. Only he takes them in there. Anyway, I don't have a key anymore. He took it away after I put Rose in there when your father showed up."

"What can I do with her? One of the girls is bound to slip up. Place is real crowded tonight, and you've got more girls than rooms."

"Well, you can't be seen carrying her. She must stay here until closing. Then you can move her to the cellar. If the sheriff starts getting close take her down the back stairs. Have Nellie be your lookout. Don't let any of the girls see you."

Cline grunted. "She should wake up soon. Who do you want to sit with her?"

"Did you gag her?"

"No. You know some girls can't keep the food down with the potion in it. If I gag her, she might choke. Can't have her dying."

"Send Nellie up. One of the girls can use Nellie's room. I'll look in on her and give her a few more drops."

The door swung open. Emily squinted at the faint light.

Belle set the lantern she was carrying on the table. "Either you have the good sense not to scream or you're too dumb to try."

"I don't see how screaming will help me. Even if someone could hear it over the ruckus around here."

"The sheriff and his deputy have walked through the main room three times tonight. Just so you know, Bart will shoot either of them before they make it halfway up the stairs." Belle uncorked the decanter and poured some of the amber liquid in a glass. She took a small dark-blue bottle out of her pocket and added several drops. "But I doubt I can trust you to be quiet, even if it means the sheriff's death. Not that he isn't a dead man. My partner wanted to be the first to kiss you on those rosy lips. At least he knows who's at fault this time. Turns out the last girl he took was engaged. I didn't find out until later. My partner has a vindictive soul. He would prefer to kill the sheriff himself once you're settled into your new life, but he won't be too upset if I kill Sheriff Morgan for trying to rescue you." Belle swirled the glass, stuck her finger in it, then licked her finger clean. "This is a working girl's best friend, especially on a night like this when one man blurs into another and they don't stop to ask your name or take off their boots. If you're good to him, you won't have to use it for months or maybe a year or two. He doesn't share. Drink up."

"Please may I use the chamber pot first?"

Belle set the glass on the table. "I can untie you, but if you try to escape, I'll let Cline be creative in how he trusses you to the bed. Got it?"

Emily nodded. Belle released the ropes keeping Emily flat on the bed. The knots were basic. The bindings on her wrists and ankles remained in place. But there was enough slack that Emily was able to complete her task.

"Aren't you the sweet one. Can't relieve yourself without blushing. He is going to love that." The mocking tone in Belle's words stung. "Drink this before you lie back down. I don't want it spilling all over and you only getting half a dose. We are much too busy to watch you tonight."

A faint knock sounded on the door. As Belle turned to answer it, Emily tipped the glass into the mattress and poured out most of the liquid. She needed her wits about her.

Belle slapped Emily across the face. "That was a very stupid thing to do. Did you think I wouldn't see that? Nellie, get me a spoon. And send Cline back up."

Nellie scooted out the door. Emily tried to stand, hoping a client would see her through the open door, but Belle grabbed a fistful of her hair and pulled her back down.

"Tsk, tsk. I warned you not to try anything. Cline can be so creative."

Emily drank what was left in the glass and prayed for oblivion.

⸺⬥⸺

Two drunks sang "Clementine" at the top of their lungs as they wandered into the sheriff's office. One had a black eye.

"Sheriff? We'd like to report a crime. We stole this off our friend Doug." The man with the black eye pulled what looked like a coin out of his pocket.

TJ recognized it as the five-peso piece Doug had carved the Texas star into as a symbol of his job. He turned it over in his hands. "That is a crime, and I haven't arrested anyone yet tonight. How about we take a walk upstairs?"

The men broke into another mournful tune and helped each other up the stairs to the jail level. They looked around and straightened, suddenly quite sober. TJ handed back Doug's badge. "I lied. I have the hotel manager in cell two, but he isn't going anyplace soon. Well?"

The one with the black eye spoke. "I'm Hawke, and this is Jax. The room at the west end of the building is not in use tonight. Daisy was put out by that. She claims there was a fight in there last night and Belle needs a new mattress. I left Daisy and accidentally walked the wrong way. One of the bouncers was on me like a coon dog. He tossed me out and said I was done for the night. Doug said you assume

Belle wants your girl for a specific purpose. Since there's no talk of an auction, you could be right."

"When you came in for your rounds, three men reached for their guns. With the bouncer who tossed Hawke out, I count that Belle has four hired men keeping guard. I don't think I've seen more than two in a place the size of the Bull's-Eye."

"She usually has two."

"Who are more interested in you than the card shark at the second table," said Hawke.

TJ paced the space under the never-used gallows. "Assuming she is in there, any ideas on how to get Miss Wilson out?"

"I haven't tried going upstairs. I am assuming the room has a window…" Jax laid out his plan.

"That's relying on too many ifs and coincidences. At the opposite end of the hall there is a door. Doc says it looks to be a closet but actually goes into the theater. If we can get it open, we could access the second floor."

"How do I get into the theater?" asked Granger.

TJ looked at his timepiece. "There is a show still going. Pay the two bits for a ticket and stay close to Dr. Palmer. He found the door. We'll have to wake him up. Good thing he is used to it."

After outlining the plan, TJ led the men back to the main level. Hawke left for Dr. Palmer's house. Jax left through the back door.

Jerome returned from his rounds. "I think I found the cart. Someone tried pushing it over the cliffside into the river. It's lodged in a tree about fifteen feet down. We can get a better look in the morning."

Since Jerome wasn't going to be an active part of the rescue attempt, TJ didn't bother filling him in.

A half hour after midnight. TJ walked around the square to Second Street. Only a dozen men remained inside the Bull's-Eye, playing cards. Cline and Bart were no place to be seen. As he crossed to the bottom of the stairway, a large man stopped him. "Sheriff, you have no business here."

Two gunshots reverberated throughout the building. Right on schedule.

The man looked upstairs, and TJ pushed him aside. "Those shots make it my business to be here."

Two more shots rang out, and women started screaming. TJ took the stairs two at a time. Most of the working women were smart enough to keep their clients and themselves in their rooms. The Rangers had counted on that. Jax had his gun trained on Bart and Belle. Hawke kicked open the last door, and Aidan ducked inside. TJ held his gun on the two men blocking their exit at the bottom of the stairs.

Aidan exited the room with open arms. "It's empty!"

Belle cackled.

For the first time in months, Emily shivered because of the cold. A lantern hanging overhead illuminated the room they'd moved her to. As she lay on a thin mattress on the floor, snatches of memory floated around her. Cline stripping off her skirt, bustle, and jabot top, leaving her in only her corset, chemise, light petticoat, and drawers. Cline's laughter as he bound her wrists and ankles together, his hands lingering too long with every task. The entire time he'd talked and talked of things a gentleman would never discuss. After he'd rendered her immovable, he'd held her mouth open while Belle spooned in her poison.

The numbness in her wrists and feet attested to his creative roping abilities. She raised her hands, and her feet followed. Bringing her wrists to her mouth caused her to roll up and fall onto her side. Her teeth were no match for the knots.

Something scraped along the ceiling. A patch of square light appeared, then was blocked out as someone descended a ladder she hadn't noticed.

Nellie set a bundle on a shelf and straightened her skirt. "I brought your breakfast. But I have to feed it to you. Belle says I can't untie you." Nellie knelt on the floor and half lifted, half rolled Emily into a sitting position.

"Have the bread first." Nellie held a slice of warm bread to Emily's lips.

"They tried to rescue you last night. So romantic. Just like one of my books, only they were too late. You were already here. He will not be happy you're cold, but Belle will dress you up so he doesn't know Cline saw you in your drawers first. Cline's sweet on Belle, but she knows which brother keeps her in business. Best you don't tell him Cline saw you or anything else. He'll take his anger out on you too."

Emily swallowed. "He is the judge, right?"

"How do you know that? Did I give it away? He'll thrash me, you know. Doesn't matter my mother was his favorite. If I cross him, he'll kill me too. Ain't no proof I am his daughter, anyway. Other than he won't set me to working upstairs like the girls he is done with. Says he wouldn't even if I weren't as ugly as a dead hog. That's as far as his fatherly concern goes."

"Cline told me." Emily took another bite of the bread.

Nellie's shoulders lowered and she hung her head. "My uncle has him a death wish. Been itchin' for a fight for weeks now, ever since the judge shot their pa on account of him going after Rose. But he got his father in the end, didn't he? The Rangers will never find him. Who will go after the judge?"

Cecilia Rose's diary came back to her. The sentences with no meaning now fell into place. "Just a moment. Cole Pike is Cline *and* Judge Granger's father?"

"Yup. Lucky me. I got the devil for a father and a demon for a grandpappy. Guess I deserved to have my face this way. No one will ever mistake me as an angel child. I'm trying not to turn bad too fast, like Cline did. Maybe there is still a place for people like me." Nellie walked around the ladder.

"I don't think you're bad, and Rose didn't either."

Nellie spun round to face her. "How do you know about Rose? She run off and got herself killed for her troubles before you came."

"Who killed her?"

Nellie shrugged. "Not sure which one. Bart and Cline followed his orders. He was done with her anyhow."

"You know this for sure?"

"Sure as I'm sitting here. He told them he never wanted to see her again. They was talking in my kitchen after she run off. He said he didn't need her now that he ordered a replacement from Boston. When they realized I heard they told me to tell people that Indians got her. Which is stupid since the government moved them. But I know my place so I'll lie if it doesn't get anyone killed."

"I'm the replacement."

Nellie nodded. "Time for the eggs. Then you can sleep again."

"Please don't make me eat them."

"Sorry, miss, I really am, but I gotta. I'll tell Cline he needs to loosen your ropes, though. Your hands don't look right. It isn't like you'll find your way out of the cave." Nellie held out the spoon.

Cave? Emily studied the walls. In places, she could see where a pickax or a shovel had smoothed out the sides, but most of the walls were rough and curved.

Nellie pressed the spoon to Emily's lips. "Please eat, or I'll have to tell Belle."

Emily took a bite. If she could win Nellie over…She took another bite. Was it better to eat fast to get more food in?

"My cat, Hector, is down here somewhere. I put him here last night to keep the rats away. Cline thought the light would be enough, but I'd rather be safe."

Rats! Emily investigated the recesses of the cavern but saw nothing. The edges of her vision blurred as she took one more bite.

———◇———

There was no consolation in the fact that they'd all left the Bull's-Eye with their lives last night. Aidan had found Emily's torn skirt in the empty room, and they'd spent an hour speculating on where she could be. Assuming she'd been upstairs, they could have moved her out of the building, but where? The theater and Harold's bar were the closest. Every corner of the theater had been checked. The animosity between Harold and Belle was so great that Harold would have turned Emily over immediately. TJ traced his finger over the map. They'd missed something.

"Where are you?" The empty jail house didn't answer him. TJ hit the wall with his fist. The limestone bricks didn't budge. He shook his hand to relieve the pain.

Sleep eluded him. TJ had spent most of the night rereading Rose's journal for clues. One thing he knew for certain—he wouldn't stop trying to rescue Emily, even if it took months. And he'd never be like Roger. If Emily would have him, he'd marry her and take her anyplace she wanted to live, because he could no longer live in a town that allowed this to happen, nor could he work with a judge who permitted and promoted it.

Saturday morning brought no answers. Doug stopped by on his way out of town, offering his support. Hawke and Jax returned to Abigail's house. As TJ walked Doug and Sherman to the depot, the telegrapher ran out of the office and handed a telegram to TJ and another to Doug.

Slim dead. No leads. Hug Ma.

GW wouldn't be coming soon and warned there was still danger. TJ folded the paper and put it in his pocket. "I hope your news was better than mine."

Doug showed his wire to Jax, then tore it into tiny pieces. "We don't have to report until Tuesday as our prisoner died. If you want us to stay around, we can. I'd like to verify your hunch about Cole's son. Find the caves he hid out in. I don't like leaving loose ends."

"I'll be glad for any help I can get. I doubt we can get back into Belle's again."

"Not likely, but the skirt should be enough evidence to get you a warrant from the other judge. Let's go see if he is willing," said Sherman.

⟫◆⟪

"Emily!" TJ's voice woke her. The lantern flickered above. Someone had covered her with a scratchy wool blanket, her shivers replaced with itching.

Another dream. Emily closed her eyes, hoping to return to the place she'd dreamed of him.

"Emily!" The sound echoed in the cavern.

"I—"

A hand clamped over her mouth, and Cline's sour breath wafted over her face. "Keep quiet, and I'll untie your hands. Scream and your man dies. I'll gun him down myself."

Emily shut her mouth to avoid the taste of his hand.

"Good girl." He didn't remove his hand. "Do you think if he found you he would want you back? You've spent the night in a bordello dressed in nothing but your unmentionables. You can tell him you aren't ruined, but only a fool would believe that. The last woman we had here kept telling us her fiancé would save her. The judge told her hero where to find her, but instead of rescuing her, he spit on her and went across the hall to Daisy. Rose pined for him something awful. The boy got robbed on his way back home and was shot in the chest. The same place I intend to shoot your sheriff."

Emily closed her eyes to keep the tears at bay.

"Don't cry yet. You'll need those tears later. My brother likes crying women."

Heavy footfalls sounded above them.

"Looks like he's given up. We'll stay like this until Belle gives the all clear."

Someone was playing the piano again. Emily couldn't place the tune. Cline removed his hand.

"Let me see your hands. Nellie's pitching a fit saying I tied you up too tight." The long knife Cline held could easily cut more than rope.

Emily remained still as he cut her bindings. Pain like falling on a box of needles spread through her hands.

Cline swore as he rubbed her wrists. "Looks like Nellie was right. He'll have a fit if he sees this." Cline held the knife up to her face. "I'll free your ankles too. You can't make it up the ladder before I reach you, so don't try."

Emily nodded. The pain shooting through her feet was so intense that even if she wanted to run, she couldn't.

"Stand up."

The room spun and her feet wobbled. Emily fell back on the pallet.

"None of your games." Cline yanked her to her feet and into his chest. Emily tried to push back, but Cline held her firm.

"Let me go." She tried saying it with force but in her weakened state it came out in a hoarse whisper.

Cline laughed and held her tighter before stepping away and holding her by the shoulders. "Stand still while I tie this rope around you. If you're good, I'll give you enough rope that you can walk around and even get to the slop bucket."

Emily held still, but only because she wanted her stomach to stop clenching and the cavern to stop spinning. The rope around her middle was tight but not worse than a corset under a formal dress. She could breathe. Cline tied the other end to a support beam. "Eight feet. Enough to reach the bucket and to lie down. If we hear a sound out of you, I'll half that to four. Understand?"

Emily nodded.

"Good. Nellie will be down with your supper soon. In the meantime, don't think too much about the rats."

As soon as he left, Emily sagged against the support beam. If TJ couldn't rescue her, she needed to escape. If only her pounding head and sour stomach would cooperate.

The organ sat silent in church, a stark contrast to the wagging tongues speculating about Miss Wilson's disappearance. Becky glared at TJ and the other lawmen sitting at the back of the church. Donny sat with his mother and sisters, swiping at the tears that started when he looked at the empty organ bench. TJ found no solace in the minister's words. Nothing could erase the fact that he failed. His prayers for Emily's safety had failed.

Mrs. Long hobbled up to the organ and played an unrecognizable hymn.

Would it be wrong to pray that Emily die quickly and not have to live as Rose did?

TJ exited the church as the congregation sang an off-key rendition of "Jesus, Savior Pilot Me."

Amazing Grace, How sweet the sound
That saved a wretch like me...

Emily awoke humming the tune playing on the piano above her. She paused. It couldn't be. Hymns, here? Someone was singing along. Emily pulled the shawl Nellie had given her tight around her shoulders and stood to hear the words better. The hatch above her opened.

Belle descended. "I brought your breakfast." The hymn changed to a soulful, slow melody. Belle cast a disparaging look at the trapdoor above her. "Nellie insists on pretending she's worthy to attend church. I allow her a little fantasy as long as it doesn't interfere with work and she was obedient during the week." She set a basket on the table. "Don't worry, your food doesn't have any of my potion in it. I need you awake this morning so I can decide what you'll wear tomorrow and we can chat. I'll give you your dose before I return upstairs."

Belle sat down on a crate. The wrapper she wore gaped open, showing the lace trim on her undergarments. "He should arrive on the Monday afternoon train. It would be easier to take you upstairs, but the rest of the girls don't know you're here, and I can't risk them saying anything yet. They had a warrant yesterday. They found the other cellar, but not this one. Cline says you behaved well. For that, I brought you salve for your wrists and ankles."

Emily took the glass jar just like the one she bought from Donny. They would have brought her something anyway. From what she understood, the judge wouldn't be happy about the rope burns. The contents smelled of lavender and felt cool against her skin.

Belle's nose wrinkled. "You need a bath. A bucket and a cloth will have to do. Nellie will see to it in the morning." Belle pulled the small glass bottle out of her pocket. "Before I give you this, I'll need to fill you in on a few facts I believe you didn't learn at that hoity-toity school of yours."

Above them, Nellie played the introduction to Emily's favorite hymn. Singing the lyrics loudly in her head, she blocked out Belle's vile words.

Come, Thou Fount of every blessing
Tune my heart to sing Thy grace...

<hr>

Mrs. Reese, Thelma, and Becky looked up as one when TJ approached the screened-in porch. They motioned for him to enter.

"I see you've brought no good news. Sit down anyway." Mrs. Reese used her cane to point to the empty chair.

TJ sighed. "I can't figure out where they're keeping her. We searched every place we could with the warrant." They'd found the entrance to the secret room. From the cobwebs, they determined it wasn't in use and closed it before Belle and her men learned of the discovery. Surprisingly, it had stairs leading upward. Doug surmised it occupied a portion of the third floor of the theater.

"Did you check the cellar?" asked Thelma.

"Nothing but canned goods and flour."

"No, the other ones."

"There are more?"

Thelma set her knitting on the table. "There are three. One for the food, one for the liquor, and one to enter unseen. I never went down there myself. Back when Old Eddy built the place, they dug the first cellar into the side of a cave. I heard it was full of bats."

"How did I miss the entrances?"

"The liquor one has a trapdoor in the bottom of one of the cupboards in the bar, and there's another trapdoor in the food cellar. The shelf swings out. Eddy used to keep a barrel in front of the shelves to hide the marks on the floor. That way they could have the drink delivered with everything else but keep the girls out of it. The shelf is too heavy for one person to move." Thelma tapped her chin. "I don't think they'd keep her in there."

"Why not?

"It would look suspicious if they had to get to her during working hours. Can't have people disappearing behind the bar."

"So where is the other one?"

"That I don't know exactly. When I worked for Eddy, he only ever said it was in his rooms. He kept a private parlor, a gaming room, and a couple of bedrooms on the main floor. I'd see men come out of those rooms—men who hadn't come through the front door."

"Those must be the rooms Belle uses now." They'd been through those rooms, but had they looked for trapdoors? TJ pictured the sitting rooms and bedrooms. Sherman had pulled up the rugs in both. "Belle only has two rooms."

"Eddy had four rooms. I heard Belle made one into a proper bathroom with a large tub, and Nellie has the other room."

"Thelma, would you be willing to talk to the judge tomorrow? I need a new warrant."

Thelma's face drained of color. "Judge Granger? Not on your life!"

"He is out of town. I mean Judge Canadel. But why not Judge Granger?"

Thelma shook her head. "There are things I can't say without waking up dead. I've said too much already. If you'll excuse me." She retreated into the house.

"Becky, go keep Thelma company." Mrs. Reese shook her head when Becky opened her mouth to protest.

Nodding at them both, Becky left the same way Thelma did.

"I've never heard Thelma say that much at once about the year she spent working for old Eddy."

"Do you know anything about her and Judge Granger?"

Mrs. Reese used her cane to propel her chair into a gentle rock. "I have my suspicions. Thelma worked with Nellie's ma. She was the first to hear the little girl's screams after her ma poured lye and who knows what all on her face. Two weeks later, Thelma was nearly beaten to death by a customer. That is how she ended up with me. She won't leave town on account of Nellie. Anyone who saw the little girl before she was burned would have seen her mother's hair and her father's nose and eyes." She pointed at TJ with her cane. "Look close. Nellie has the judge's eyes."

TJ pushed his chair back. "Why didn't you tell me this before?"

"I didn't know you needed to know. If I told you all the secrets I know about this town, it would take years."

"There are only two secrets I need to know. One, who is Cole Pike's son, and two, where is Emily?"

"Cole Pike probably has dozens of children. He's been terrorizing the area since before I received my land grant from the Republic of Texas. He had a wife who died back in '46, I believe. I think her family took in their son, back in Georgia or Virginia. I always thought it was a blessing that child got away from his pa. He was about the age of my boy, maybe seven or eight, at the time."

"So, he'd be about forty-one or forty-two now?"

"Probably. If he survived the war." Unlike Mrs. Reese's son whose portrait sat above the mantel piece.

"What about other children?"

"Cole Pike had a couple women who ran with the gang. Never heard of any children. There was a widow who ran a small establishment over in Fort Worth who claimed the Pike gang used her services. Sorry, but the possibilities are endless."

"Pretty much the same conclusion I've come to. There aren't many women who would write Cole's name in the family Bible as the father of their child." TJ stared at the fireflies dancing around the bushes. There had to be some link.

Mrs. Reese gasped and dropped her cane. "Cole Pike's wife's maiden name was Granger."

TJ leapt to his feet. "And Judge Granger is in Waco. Excuse me, Mrs. Reese, I need to go find the Rangers." If the judge killed Slim and the lawmen can keep him in Waco…

ast night's food hadn't contained any sleeping potion. So Emily had listened to the rats fighting with Nellie's cat from the relative safety of the top of the table, which wasn't big enough to curl up on and sleep, which meant no nightmares or weird dreams. She yawned.

The trapdoor opened, and a bucket on a rope was lowered down. Light filtered through the hole. It must be morning. When Nellie brought last night's dinner, the light had been dimmer. Nellie descended carrying a basket. "I brought you a bath. The water is warm. There is also a hairbrush. Belle has clothes for you, but she says it is too dirty down here, so you will change later. The dress is right pretty and not so revealing as Daisy's dresses."

The thought was not as joyful as Nellie made it sound.

Nellie brought the bucket over to the table. "I'll go back up so you can have some privacy. There is a towel in the basket and some fresh bread. Make sure you wash behind your ears and everything. Belle is a stickler for cleanliness."

The trapdoor slammed shut after Nellie had left her alone again.

Doug and TJ left Judge Canadel's home empty-handed. He'd refused a second warrant. Even if they'd produced a witness to the cellars, they'd missed the entrance in their first search.

TJ suppressed the desire to hit something. "What we need to do is find the other end of the secret entrance, if one exists."

"You can eliminate the theater, as it has its own direct entrance. What buildings were here ten or fifteen years ago?" asked Doug.

TJ pictured the square as it had been when he was still in grammar school. "The church, hotel, and mercantile. And the bank. There was a fire five or so years ago that destroyed a saloon and the barbershop on the south side of the square. The new barber is on the east side. The old wood courthouse burned down too."

"Let's go walk around the square."

They untied their horses from the judge's hitching post.

Coming from the other direction, Ranger Sherman raced past them on his horse, then doubled back. "I got an answer to the telegram we sent yesterday from Glen Crossing in case your telegraph operator isn't discrete. Guess who was the last man to see Slim alive?"

"The judge?" guessed TJ.

"Yup. Unfortunately, he's left Waco." Sherman calmed his horse.

"At least we know where he will show up," said Doug.

"We found the son. One miracle down. Now for another one." TJ had been praying for that one since Friday afternoon.

Finding Cline's knot-tying skills more creative than effective, Emily slid the rope out of the last knot. Free!

The trapdoor flew open, the bang echoing throughout the cavern. Emily grabbed the rope and wound the end around her body. *Please don't be Cline!*

A woman stuck her head in. "I knew it." She climbed down the ladder. The short red-and-black dress she wore revealed more than it hid. "He ain't gonna replace me again." The woman jumped off the bottom rung and pulled a knife from her garter. "You can't have him!"

Emily took a step back. "I don't want him."

"You are just pretending. He likes his woman afeered. Belle done told you to cower and scream, didn't she?" The woman pointed the knife at Emily's throat.

"No." Emily backed up until she hit the cave wall.

"Liar!" The woman waved the knife in Emily's face. "No one lies to Daisy. Crazy Daisy. But I ain't that crazy. I know if'n I kills ya, he will kill me. Not with his own hands, though. He'll send baby brother and Bart, only Bart is in love with me so he'll try to kill baby brother. And that would ruin all my plans. Plus, I never murdered no one." Daisy slapped the flat of the knife against her palm. "I have a better idea. I let you go. Maybe you find your way out of these caves, maybe not. If you find your way out, you'll leave town, right?"

Emily gulped and nodded keeping one eye on the knife.

"If you don't find a way out, well, I didn't kill you. It's barely past noon, so you have an hour or two before Belle discovers you're missing. Bart says these caves are a maze. They may find you before you get out, but they may not. If Bart finds you first, he'll make sure the judge doesn't want you later." Daisy clapped her hands. "Won't this be fun?"

Only if you are insane.

"Turn around, and I'll cut the rope off you. I'm using Nellie's knife. Won't that drive Belle mad?"

Emily dropped the rope she held in place. "You don't need to cut it. I was about to take the lantern and find my way out."

Daisy's face fell. "You already had it figured out? You really don't want him, do you? That takes most of the fun out of it." Daisy walked around the ladder muttering. She turned to Emily, a crazed smile growing on her face. "I'll still make sure you have an hour. It won't be any fun if they can find you before the afternoon train gets here. Lump the blanket up by the wall and tie the rope to it. If they do look in, they'll think you're sleeping."

Emily followed Daisy's surprisingly sensible directions. "Good enough?" She reached for the lantern.

"Don't take the lamp if it is dark down here. They'll come to investigate. See the candles over there on the ledge? Use those. That's how they used to do it when they came this way before Belle became the ma-dame." Daisy pronounced the last word in a singsong voice.

Three candles should be enough. There was also a box of matches. Emily lit a candle and stuck the matches and extra candles down the front of her corset.

"Run, girl, run!" Daisy chuckled.

Emily slid around the crevice in the wall and out of Daisy's sight. Behind her, the trapdoor banged shut, cutting off Daisy's laughter. Emily turned back to check that Daisy wasn't following her. The storeroom was empty.

A narrow white line ran along the wall of the new cavern. Emily traced the painted line with her fingers, following it into the darkness. Rocks bit at her bare feet. A trail of blood would be easy to follow. Sitting on an outcropping of rock, Emily checked to make sure her feet weren't cut. Wax dripped from the candle. Emily growled in frustration. No matter what she did, she would leave a trail. The faster she got out of here, the better.

Following the line and watching for rocks, Emily made her way along the tunnel. A smaller tunnel broke off to the right. A large rat paused in his errand and sniffed the air before running off in the dark. Her candle flickered. Hector appeared around the corner and rubbed against her leg, then took off after the rat.

One hundred steps farther, a wall of rubble, cinder, and burned wood blocked her path. A rat chattered at her from a ceiling beam before disappearing into a hole smaller than the size of her fist and turning back to stare at her. She held her candle high to examine the wall of rock and debris. Two charred beams crossed the way. Someone had deliberately filled in the tunnel, which explained why it was no longer used.

A second rat climbed up the beam.

"You don't know another way out do you?"

The rat squeaked and disappeared.

Emily retraced her steps to the smaller tunnel. Wax or blood, they wouldn't need either to track her when there was only one option. Her candle flickered again.

Moving air! It must mean a way out!

⋙◆⋘

Doug examined the new buildings on the south side of Hiramsville square. "Do you know who built these newer buildings?"

"Nope, but some of the men working on the courthouse may." TJ ran across the street to the construction site.

Several of the workers stood in the north wall's shade, drinking from the water bucket. They nodded at him.

"Did any of you work on the reconstruction of the south buildings after the fire?"

Three of the men raised their hands.

"May I talk with you for a moment?"

The foreman stepped forward. "As long as they are back in five minutes."

"They will be." Five minutes was far too long, it meant five more minutes that Emily was missing. TJ walked around the courthouse, followed by the three workers, until they had a clear view of the buildings on the south. "Do any of these buildings have a cellar or tunnel under them?"

The oldest man spoke. "When the buildings collapsed, the barbershop fell into its cellar. It was easier to fill it in than dig everything out. There was a tunnel going off one side, but we blocked it. I think it was part of the caves. The architect out of Austin worried it might not be smart to build over the cave if we didn't fill it in, give it some stability from beneath. So we hauled in rocks and made it solid."

"I helped build the cellar under the café. We didn't find a cave there," answered another.

"When we dug the cellar for that building," the man pointed to the second from the corner, "we broke into a tunnel or cave. The owner didn't want the rats in his cellar. So we bricked it up real well. Used the same limestones we used for the jail."

TJ shook the men's hands. "Thanks, gentlemen. That helps."

Doug, Hawke, and Sherman waited under the café's awning. TJ explained what he'd learned.

"Not very helpful. Short of demolishing a building, we can't get into the caves from this side," said Hawke.

Sherman rubbed his jaw. "I'd like to get a look at the brickwork in the second building. Doug, you're the handsomest one. Go sweet-talk those women in the millinery shop."

Doug returned a few minutes later, smiling. "We need our own lantern, and I received an invitation to dinner."

ebbles skidded under Emily's knees as she crawled the last several feet of the final offshoot, her fears of Cline or Bart finding her lessening the farther she got. If she barely fit through the last tunnel, they never would. The tunnel grew wider, and Emily pushed the candle forward. The flickering light revealed a cavern with a pond filling most of the floor. The cavern was also lit from above where light flooded in through a large crack in the ceiling.

Water seeped from the far wall, feeding the pond. Emily circled the vast cavern twice, finding only two new exits—the tunnel the water took, and the crack ten feet or more above the center of the pond, the source of the breeze moving the air and a tiny patch of sunlight. Only a bird or a fish could escape.

Emily blew out her candle and sat at the bank of the pond.

Crying won't help.

Don't cry.

Think!

Her body betrayed her. Salty tears rolled down her cheeks.

At first she wiped them away, but realizing not a living creature was watching her, Emily indulged herself as random images floated through her mind—laughing in her dorm room with Amanda, Dr. Palmer's kind smile, Donny trying to escort her, and her first kiss on the banks of the Brazos. Then echoes of Aunt Melba's predictions of failure, Cline's leering face, and TJ's rebuke when he'd caught her walking alone replaced the happy images.

If only she'd waited for Donny as she'd promised, she wouldn't have been alone in the alley. TJ searched for her because it was his job. He'd begged her to trust him, and she hadn't followed his instructions. If Cline or Bart killed TJ as Cline had threatened, it would be on her head. There was no way to warn him unless she could get out and the only way out was back through Belle's.

Emily lay her head on her knees and bawled. Unless she thought of something soon, she would need to return to Belle's to save his life.

A dog barked from somewhere above her, rousing Emily from her tears and exhaustion-induced nightmare. Sunlight still danced on the pond. She cupped some water from the pond in her hands and rinsed her face. The water was cool and sweet. She drank her fill.

Tears gone, Emily resolved on two things—not to be the cause of TJ's death and to live long enough to apologize. Would he even accept it? He'd told her dozens of times not to be alone. Not to mention she'd been in a brothel since Friday. Absolutely no one would believe that she hadn't been ruined. Especially dressed, or not, dressed as she was. There wasn't a man on earth who wanted a ruined woman. Just like Cecilia's fiancé.

Mrs. Manning had said it was better to have loved for a little while than not at all. Three days was a very little while. Three weeks, counting their first meeting. It was enough.

Following through on her resolutions would be harder.

Another bark echoed from the opening. What if she screamed? Would someone hear her? She'd need to make the words clear so no one would mistake her for a cougar, but there was no telling who would find her. Screaming could wait. Emily pondered what facts she could.

1. I have water and light. I could stay here for a while.

2. Cline and Bart can't come in the way I did.

3. It is cold, but not as bad as a Massachusetts winter.

4. I don't see bats or rats. Snakes?

Emily closed her eyes. She'd never read about snakes in caves, but if one fell through the ceiling hole…She shuddered.

Swimming out? If she had the rope, she could tie it to… nothing.

If she stayed in here a day or two, they might give up. They might think she'd made it out or got caught in one of the other small tunnels. She'd lived on porridge and water for a week after she broke Aunt Melba's vase.

5. I can go a day or two without food.

Daisy came through the trapdoor with no one noticing. Emily might be able to exit undetected. But if she got caught...

Emily turned each fact over in her mind again and again. She could either die here or leave and quite possibly wish she had remained.

"To be or not to be." Hamlet had had an easier choice. How long before the judge would take out his wrath on TJ?

⋘⊷◆⊶⋙

A rat ran across the milliner's cellar floor.

"Maybe they didn't brick it up as well as the workman claimed." TJ set the lantern on top of a stack of crates and turned up the flame.

Sherman pushed on one of the pale stone square blocks stacked in the corner. "Didn't even use mortar. Give me a hand, and let's see if we can move this top one. Doug, you too."

Using a discarded board as a lever, the men removed the forty-pound block from the top of the stack. Sherman gave a low whistle. "We found us a tunnel."

The second block came off quicker. TJ held his finger to his lips and nodded at the lamp. Hawke turned down the flame and lowered the lamp to the floor on the far side of the crates, plunging them into darkness.

"I hear something."

Two male voices echoed through the opening.

The first voice was Bart's. "Maybe she's trying to dig her way out. Shame they filled it in after the fire. This tunnel was really useful."

"You shouldn't have burned the place down after you killed him."

TJ recognized the second voice as Cline's. Bart had killed the old barber with no one the wiser. Murder and arson.

Bart grunted. "At least I wasn't dumb enough to scalp a girl. Even the idiot sheriff knows there ain't any Indians 'round here no more."

Cline had killed Rose. TJ clenched his jaw and prayed they'd get the evidence they needed.

"She took the side tunnel. It was her only choice," said Cline

"This filly'd better be worth every penny your brother paid for her. I want double my pay for finding her."

Cline's laughter filled the tunnel. "You'll be lucky if he doesn't put a bullet between your eyes."

"I didn't let her go. It was Daisy."

"And if you hadn't grabbed Miss High and Mighty School-teacher early, she wouldn't have had time to get away. Belle's none too happy about the trouble she's caused. A search warrant. Judge isn't going to like that one bit."

"I didn't know he'd left town," Bart whined.

"Don't matter. He'll be on the 3:20 train, and if we don't have her back, he'll take her price out of us."

"This lamp is low on oil. I ain't wandering around down here in the dark. Let's go get a different one and some rope."

"We've got plenty. Aren't nearly as many places to go as when I was a kid. People keep filling them in or turning them into cellars. I'm not wasting time when the judge is on his way."

"Look at that flame. I'm getting another lamp"

The retreating bouncer's footsteps echoed in the tunnel.

A second later another set followed.

After a few moments, Hawke turned the lantern up enough to see outlines of the crates and stairway. TJ grabbed the third stone and pulled it out of the corner, widening the entrance. It wasn't enough. He grabbed another.

Doug stopped him with a hand on the shoulder. "Plan." He pointed to the ceiling, then ascended the stairs, the others following. TJ grabbed the lamp as he was last. Doug had two minutes. No more.

TJ led them across the ally and into the jail. "We need to get back down to the caves now."

Doug put a hand on TJ's shoulder. "We have just over an hour before the train arrives. Arresting Judge Granger is my priority."

"My priority is finding Emily."

"You also can't go back without a light and rope. Where are they?" asked Sherman.

TJ took an old miners' lantern off the shelf. "I need to go back *now*, before Cline and Bart find her."

"I say we split up. With what we heard, the two in the tunnels are as dirty as the judge, and saving Miss Wilson should be a priority. And one of the men after her is the judge's brother," said Sherman.

TJ leaned against the doorpost, ready to bolt. "That was Cline. I recognized his voice. The other one is Bart. They'll be back down there anytime. I want to get them before they get to Emily."

"Let's split up. Doug, you'd recognize the judge, so you watch the station with the deputy. Sherman, TJ, and I can take care of those two in the tunnel. We should have them before the train comes. And I can join you at the station," said Hawke.

Doug stood. "On my way to the station, I'll alert Dr. Palmer."

"Why?" asked TJ.

"That girl of yours is bound to be hurt." Doug gave an apologetic shrug.

No. Not hurt. Please not hurt. TJ nodded. "Let's go find Emily."

⊰◈⊱

Two male voices called her name. Emily scrambled closer to the tunnel connecting the cavern back to the Bull's Eye.

"Emily!"

"Miss Wilson?"

"Come out, girl! We won't hurt you!"

The second voice was Cline's. After the last three days, Emily doubted she'd ever forget it.

Liar.

Emily pressed against the side of the cave. What if they made it in? She looked around for a weapon and found a large rock.

"Look, more wax."

Grunt. "I can't fit through that tiny hole."

"Let's go get Nellie."

"Hear that? There ain't no way out but back through here. I know. I explored this cave when I was a kid. All the good tunnels I remember are blocked off now. Does the cavern still have water? You can't stay there forever." Malice laced Cline's voice.

Emily flinched and rubbed her hands on her arms.

"You could save us all some trouble and come out right now. You don't want to see how angry the judge can get."

"We're wasting time. Let's go get Nellie," said Cline.

Emily explored the walls again. If she was a spider, she might be able to climb to the shaft where the light came through. Rounding the pond, she studied the outlet. There was a little space above the water in the tunnel, but then rock met water. How far would she have to swim? It could be miles, or it might empty into the Brazos in a few feet. Emily bit her lip. If there was no other choice...It wasn't like Nellie could force her out of the cave, anyway. Unless she dragged her out through the tunnel.

Emily picked up a fist-sized rock, then dropped it. She'd swim into the unknown before she would use it on Nellie. But what of TJ? If she never came out, would they kill him?

The passage they entered from the shop's cellar was taller than TJ expected. Sherman carried the lantern turned as low as possible, ready to drop the cover at a moment's notice. They moved silently along the passage, searching for a side tunnel. Hawke raised his hand for them to stop. TJ moved to the opposite side, where Hawke pointed at a side tunnel.

Voices carried.

Hawke gave the signal to shutter the lantern as the voices drew closer.

"We should send Daisy in, not Nellie. Nellie don't have the guts to force that blasted woman out."

"Daisy is just as likely to kill her. Can't—Ouch! Hold the lamp up so I can see where I'm going."

"What about the new girl? She ain't nothing but skin and bones. She could get in easy."

Light seeped in from the tunnel, and TJ pressed his back against the wall. If only they could get both men out of the side tunnel before they were noticed. He heard Hawke step back as the conversation continued.

"That one is likely to try to run away."

"Nah, her family needs the money. Give her a twenty dollar gold coin and tell her she doesn't have to work for four days and she'll do it."

Cline stepped into the large tunnel. His head was turned toward Bart, who carried the lantern arguing. As Cline turned forward, TJ waited only a heartbeat before he punched the bouncer in the jaw. A second punch dropped the man to the floor.

Hawke hit Bart, who dropped instantly, his lantern rolling across the ground.

Sherman raised the shutters on his.

TJ flipped Cline over and put the handcuffs on him. Hawke did the same to Bart.

Cline groaned. "What?"

"Cline and Bart, you are under arrest for kidnapping and murder. I'm sure there will be more charges, but that is good enough for now." TJ pushed Cline in the direction of the milliner's cellar, following Hawke and Bart.

Sherman scooped up the extra lantern and held out the one the lawman had brought down for TJ. "Take this and go find your girl. We'll take these two to the jail."

TJ took the lantern from Sherman and dove into the side tunnel, which quickly narrowed. Every so often a drop of wax glistened in the lamplight. Determined to follow every branch clockwise, TJ took the first tunnel to his left. It ended in a crevice too small to stick his arm into, and he backed out. As the top of the side tunnel lowered, TJ crouched down to continue.

Another few feet and he was forced to crawl. "Emily?"

Only his voice echoed back.

A faint voice answered his second call. "TJ?"

"It's me, Emily! Where are you?"

"You can't fit through here." Her voice grew stronger. "I'm coming!"

A faint, flickering light filled the tunnel in front of him accompanied by a shuffling sound. TJ backed up a few feet until he could sit.

The light disappeared. "TJ, are you still there?"

"Yes, darling." *Where are you?*

"Where are Cline and Bart? They were here just before you."

TJ scratched his head. "They're being taken to the jail."

"This is going to sound stupid. Tell me something only you know. I need to know this isn't another of those dreams. Or Cline trying to trick me. And it can't be our first kiss. Belle knows about that."

"Why don't you come out, then you can see me?"

"Please just tell me something." Emily's voice was higher pitched than normal.

"As soon as I have you safely out of here, I'm going to propose."

"What?" Her voice squeaked.

"I haven't slept for the past three nights for worry. And I decided the first thing I was going to do was propose."

A shuffling in the tunnel came toward him. Emily's voice wobbled as it came out of the dark. "But I've been at Belle's for three days."

"I don't care if you've been at Belle's for three months. I will still propose. And I'll keep proposing until you agree."

"Why? I've caused you so much trouble." She took a choking breath.

"Emily please come out."

"The judge will kill you on account of me. Your life is in danger!" The sound of rustling cloth came from just beyond the circle of light extending from his lantern. "He killed Cecilia Rose's fiancé. Did you know that? Cline and Bart are coming back. You've got to leave. I don't want you to die." There was no mistaking the sound of crying in her voice.

TJ took a deep breath to answer everything at once. "Remember, I said I arrested Bart and Cline. Doug is going after the judge now."

"He's a judge. You aren't safe. No one will prosecute him, they all say that."

"Emily come out and we can leave together."

"No. I can't."

"I am not leaving without you."

"I don't want you killed."

"I'm not going to get killed. We are going to get married."

A sob echoed in the darkness. "Why? You know where I've been."

"And I am proposing because you are the stubbornest, smartest woman I know. I've missed your smile every minute of this week. My scar doesn't scare you. You might not want to stay in Hiramsville, but I'll move. I'll even learn how to walk in snow if you'll have me."

He moved the lamp, hoping to catch her in the light. Emily's giggle came from just outside the reach of his light. "Walk in snow?"

"If that is what it takes. I thought I would die when I had to pretend to end our relationship. The look on your face—I hurt you so bad. The Rangers advised it for your safety, but when Donny told me you were gone, I felt like I'd been wrenched in two."

"You'd really want to marry me, even if the very worst thing happened at Belle's?"

TJ didn't hesitate. "Yes."

Emily wanted to close the distance and leap into his arms. She'd moved as close as she dared, her lack of clothing keeping her in the shadows. From her vantage point, she could see the expressions of his face. She wiped her eyes. This was real. "What if I want to stay here and help you get rid of the brothels?"

"We can live here. Since we've arrested Cline and Bart and the Rangers should have arrested the judge, we are already partway to shutting them down. We can also arrest Belle for your kidnapping."

"The judge is Cole Pike's son, and so is Cline, and Nellie is the judge's daughter. Judge Granger gave the order to kill Cecilia Rose."

"I know, darling. Are you going to come closer?"

Emily ran her hand down her corset, the only piece of clothing on her body still in one piece. "I'm not exactly fit to be seen."

"I'm pretty filthy myself." He dusted off his shirt.

"They took my clothes. I am only in my underthings. I don't want you to see me."

"You must be freezing." He took off his vest and tossed it in her direction. "Sorry I don't have my jacket. July heat. Follow me out."

The vest only partially covered her. "You promise you won't look?"

"As little as possible." He turned his back to her.

Emily followed him. "If we were back in Boston, my uncle would force you to marry me if you looked."

TJ smiled. "Good thing I already proposed."

"I never heard a question."

"Well, I was going to ask later, when we weren't in a freezing cave."

"It is better than melting in the sun."

TJ's rich laughter filled the cavern. "True, but I want to look into your eyes when I ask you to be my wife. Let's get out of here."

Emily followed TJ through a side tunnel and into the main tunnel. Light poured out of an opening that hadn't been there when she explored it earlier.

"That's the milliner's cellar. Wait here. I'll find something to cover you." True to his word, he hadn't looked at her.

Emily waited against the wall, her legs shaking. Everything was shaking. The cold nipped at her toes.

TJ appeared a moment later holding a blanket between them. "Step into it. I'm not looking."

"I can't move." Emily spoke through chattering teeth.

TJ wrapped the blanket around her and picked her up. "Let's get you out of here."

Safe in his arms, Emily allowed her eyes to close and oblivion to take over.

Emily rinsed her hair again. Becky tapped on the door. "Mrs. Reese says you need to hurry or we won't have time to put your hair up before the wedding. I think it's bad luck for the bride to have wet hair."

"It will be dry." Emily pulled the plug on the drain, the scented water gurgled its way out of the tub. All the bruises and cuts from her ordeal four weeks ago had healed. After the initial questioning from the Rangers, no one asked her about what happened. She'd told Mrs. Reese late one night when a nightmare woke her up, then TJ during a long walk along the river. And he still wanted to marry her. A fact he made very clear with a kiss and a proper proposal in the heat of the Texas evening.

Emily sighed and stepped out of the tub.

Becky tapped again. "Mrs. Morgan is here, and your cousin is coming in an hour."

"Becky, go help Thelma. You'll see her dress soon enough." Mrs. Reese's rescuing voice came through the door. "Emily, I hope you have your dressing gown on. I'm coming in, in ten seconds."

"Give me thirty."

"Thirty, then." Mrs. Reese's voice rang with laughter

It was closer to a minute when Emily opened the door.

"Your things are laid out in my room." Mrs. Reese followed her down the hall. "Sit, and I'll work on your hair."

Emily sat at the handsome dressing table.

Mrs. Reese parted Emily's hair and paused, meeting Emily's eyes in the mirror. "Whatever Belle told you about relations, you need to forget. TJ loves you. A man who loves you and shares your bed is very different from one who only wants your services." The reflection in the mirror showed the pain in Mrs. Reese's expression.

"How—"

Mrs. Reese leaned on her cane. "There was a dark desperate time after my son was born, before my land grant. A man offered to pay for all my needs. In exchange, my door was to always be open to him. I told him I would think on it. That night I prayed harder than I ever have for a miracle. The next day, I received the news about my grant. I left our mortgaged farm that day. Although he did no more than kiss me, I knew what he'd offered wasn't even close to love. It's because God saved me that I work so hard to rescue the Beckys and Thelmas of the world. God gave me a chance some women don't even know to ask for. Becky is already on her way to being an excellent seamstress. As soon as the state court finishes with the trials, I intend to purchase the Bull's-Eye and turn it into a school for women with few choices in life. I'd like you to be one of the teachers."

Emily turned in her seat. "Wonderful. What are you going to call it?"

"I thought of Rose's Rescue."

Emily blinked back the tears. "What about Nellie?"

"No tears. Not today. I'll keep her on as the cook if she

wants to stay. The chance to go to school again should entice her."

Someone tapped on the door. "Emily?"

Mrs. Reese patted Emily's shoulder. "Come in, Becky."

Becky bounced into the room. "Are you ready to get dressed? I can't wait to see the dress on you!"

Emily rolled her eyes. "I've tried it on five times for fittings."

"But this is my first dress. I mean, you helped and all, but still my first I've made over with a sewing machine."

Emily slipped behind the changing screen. The dress she pulled over her head looked completely different than the graduation dress. "Wait a moment, and you can help me button up all these tiny buttons."

"Thelma says not to cinch yourself up too much. She doesn't want you swooning at your own wedding. Bad enough you're getting married in August."

"We would have done it sooner, but I wanted to wait for my cousin to come."

Percy brought Uncle Carl's present and just over $8000 that should have been hers from her father's third of the business. There was also an apology note from Uncle Harlan. He didn't exactly say what happened other than his wife's accounts were in error. Percy had rolled his eyes at that explanation and declared it was a "funny way to write embezzled."

Her Uncle's note was accompanied with an order slip for a set of china "purchased from his own funds."

"Are you really going to live in the jail? Newlyweds shouldn't live in jails."

Emily pulled up her stockings. "I'm not living in the jail, just in the accommodations below it until TJ finishes building the house on his property. Then the new deputies will move in."

"Do you think your cousin will stay? He is so very handsome."

Emily came out from behind the screen. "I'm not sure. I heard him discussing the need for a furniture-and-cabinetry shop in town."

"Oh, I forgot! Your friend and her new husband arrived from Austin. Thelma put them in the parlor."

"Amanda is here! Please go get her, Becky. We have so much to talk about and so little time. Then I will put on the dress."

⬤◆⬤

The organ music didn't sound as good without Emily playing, but a bride could hardly play at her own wedding. Mrs. Long announced that after today she was retiring, although she would be available if Emily needed to miss a Sunday or two around a year from now. The pews overflowed with well-wishers. After the Bull's-Eye was closed down, Mr. Tarr and his group couldn't stop singing Emily's praises.

All the windows of the church were open, and the women waved their fans double time. TJ shifted his weight from one foot to the other, wishing he could feel the breeze at the front of the church.

"Stop looking so nervous," GW hissed in his ear. "I saw the carriage pull up. Look, there go Percy and Donny." Emily's cousin and the boy exited the church. The reverend nodded to the organist, and she switched to a softer song.

Donny entered first, followed by Becky. And TJ's heart stopped beating and restarted in double time at the sight of his bride on Percy's arm. Emily smiled serenely as she walked far too slowly toward him. GW tapped his arm, reminding him to breathe and be patient. Then she was there, and the minister spoke.

And spoke…

And "Thomas Jefferson Morgan…"

He must have said the correct words as the next thing that registered was the notation he could and should kiss his bride. Which he did, though not as thoroughly as he wanted to. They still had to cross the street and have their wedding photo taken at the new photographer's and then all the food and the people. Hannah had made five of her peach pies plus one just for them. Then he could take her to the jail. TJ laughed against her lips.

"What is so funny, husband?"

He leaned close so only she could hear. "I was thinking of taking you off to the jail."

"Am I being arrested?" Emily's eyes twinkled.

"I could. You are a thief."

Emily's eyes widened.

"You've stolen my heart."

"No, I rescued it." Emily leaned in for another kiss.

End Notes

The Republic of Texas was rich in one resource, land. They used this land to reward many citizens including the wives of those who died at the Alamo. On February 2, 1856, Mrs. Elizabeth Crockett was awarded a league, 4,428.4 acres, of land near what is now Acton, Texas. In the Acton Cemetery stands her statue forever scanning the horizon waiting for her husband David to return. Even today area locals take great pride in the smallest Texas State park being in their cemetery. (The Acton State Historic Site is no longer part of the State Park system, but locals remain proud.) Such is the legacy of the Alamo.

Mrs. Reese is a figment of my imagination. I wanted to honor the memory of widows like Mrs. Crockett who died in 1860, nineteen years before my story begins. Long live the spirit of Texas.

Founded in 1803 as a Co-educational academy, Bradford College operated for nearly two centuries before closing its doors. In 1836, the academy, equivalent to our modern-day high schools, graduated to a women's junior college. Many of the early graduates became Christian missionaries while others became educators. Some like Esther Louise Forbes became authors. In 1971 the school became co-educational again, admitting men and expanding the curriculum. Facing financial difficulties, the school closed in 2000. The buildings still stand today in Haverhill, Massachusetts as part of a private Christian College. The motto, Surgo Ut Prosim (I Rise to Serve) appears on the school logo.

Acknowledgments

For more than two years this book has been sitting in my computer waiting for the right time to be published. It has been read, and reread by my friends as they encouraged me to return to historical fiction.

As always, thanks to Tammy, Nanette, Julie, and Cami who are so willing to help make all my projects better and to read for all my mistakes. I would never make it through a day without Mara, Nichole and Cindy whose advice keeps me going. Thank you wonderful ladies.

Big thanks to Michele for the excellent edits. And to my excellent proofreaders who are not to be blamed for any remaining errors. Thank you all!

My family, for sharing their home with the fictional characters who often get fed better than they did. And my husband who encourages me every crazy step of the way and puts up with all my messy spreadsheets.

And to my Father in Heaven for putting these wonderful people, and any I may have forgotten to mention, in my life. I am grateful for every experience and blessing I have been granted.

About the Author

orin Grace was born in Colorado and has been moving around the country ever since, living in eight states and several imaginary worlds. She holds a degree in graphic design which comes in handy with creating book covers. Currently, she lives with her husband, and a dog who is insanely jealous of her laptop.

When not writing, Lorin enjoys creating graphics, visiting historical sites, museums, painting furniture, and reading. Three of her books, her debut novel, *Waking Lucy* (2017), *Mending Fences* (2018), and *Not the Bodyguard's Baby* (2020) have won Recommend Read awards in the League of Utah Writers Published book contest.